The
PIECE
THAT
BREAKS

N.J. GRAY

For anyone burdened by the pain of their past.
Keep going. It's worth it.

Trigger Warning

Scenes and topics depicted in this book might be sensitive to some readers. Topics include substance abuse, depression, sexual assault, and mentions of suicide. Please read with caution and care.

1

Danny

Falling wasn't so scary when you'd reached the bottom before and survived. It was a powerful and freeing feeling, surviving something you shouldn't have.

Right now, I was plummeting to my death and loving every second of it. Arms stretched wide, wind blanketing my chest, detaching from gravity's pull. The sensation was that of being onstage during one of our band's shows. There was a high that came from playing guitar in front of ten thousand screaming fans while being perfectly in sync with my three other bandmates—Lexie, Liam, and Tic. I craved it like an addiction.

I wasn't sure where the ledge was that I had jumped from or how long I had been falling, but I wasn't wondering when my final moment would come. I was simply enjoying the sense of freedom that came from losing control and the high of adrenaline surging through my veins.

"Danny!" I heard a voice shout my name, and my consciousness grew clearer. "Danny, wake up!"

My eyes jolted open when a pillow slammed into my naked back.

"Jesus! You were shaking in your sleep and scaring the shit out of me."

I looked up and saw Hannah standing next to the bed with her coat and purse, like she was ready to sneak out—her usual routine after she spent the night. I usually had to fight girls to leave my bed, but not Hannah. She woke up in my arms as if she wasn't sure how she had gotten there.

Rubbing my eyes, I turned over onto my back, and the gray sheet slipped down to my hips.

"Glad to see you're not having a seizure or whatever." She tossed the pillow at the end of the bed and rolled her eyes. "Look, last night was fun, but I can't keep doing this, okay?"

I shifted my hand behind my head with a raised brow. "We're back here again, are we?" I asked, my voice still raspy from sleep.

"This time isn't like the others. I'm serious, Danny."

"Mmhmm."

She aggressively pulled her hair back into a ponytail, shaking her head. "I can't be this girl for you."

I'd never been a one-girl-type of guy, nor had I ever had any expectations of Hannah when we started this … well, whatever this was. Ever. She'd kept me from wandering too far into the darkness that usually accompanied loneliness too many times to count, and all I asked of her was to stay. She never did—but she always came back … eventually. That had to count for something, didn't it? My bandmates had all tried to talk me out of getting back with Hannah time after time, but she was the closest thing I'd felt to love in my life. Sure, I'd have a few fans spend a night with me here and there, but that was just to forget the fact that I never had someone waiting for me when the stage, the microphone, and the lights were gone.

"What kind of girl is that?" I asked, quirking my eyebrow.

"A girl who can choose one person for the rest of her life. That's a stupid fantasy. That kind of relationship doesn't exist, Danny. Not for the long haul." Hannah shook her head.

"This is about me not wanting you to sleep with other guys when you're with me." I scoffed. "Is that seriously too much to ask?"

She dragged her lip through her teeth while tapping her foot. "Maybe it is. Maybe I don't want to be tied down with all these rules. You know I hate being told what I can and cannot do."

"That I do."

"Every time we start this, you say it's just for fun, and then you get all serious. That's not me. That's not what I want."

Anger worked its way up my spine. "Ah, I get it. What you want is to sleep around, but as soon as your favorite guitar-playing fuckboy tries to move on with *anyone* else, you stand in his way."

"What the hell is that supposed to mean?"

I rose up onto my forearms, narrowing my eyes. "You're fucking kidding, right? Don't you see the double standard? The hypocrisy? Every time you see me with another girl after a concert or when you invite yourself over to one of our parties, you're on me with your claws out."

She shrugged. "Some men find that endearing."

3

I ground my teeth together. "You can't have me whenever it's convenient for *you*."

"All this time together … the on and off … it's taught me that I can have you whenever I want." She took a step closer to the bed and leaned over me, meeting my gaze with a petty smile. "You're so in love with me that you can't stand the idea that I don't love you back. And you're willing to take anything that you can from me—any touch, any kiss—just to try and change that fact. But I'm never going to be that girl for you, Danny. I'm never going to love you. What I do love is watching your pathetic attempts at trying to convince me otherwise."

I swallowed back my anger, searching for numbness. But it didn't come, and I still felt everything.

Alone.

Unwanted.

Unloved.

I needed a drink—or three—and my guitar.

The muscles in my forearms danced as I fisted the sheets. "You've never wanted me to be happy, have you? You just want me to be miserable without you, so I keep coming back."

She let out a maniacal laugh, like she'd won whatever fucked-up battle she'd created in her head.

"I'm fucking sick of it."

"Oh, Danny. Give it a week or two, and you'll be back, telling me how much you've missed me."

"Get the fuck out. Now," I said through gritted teeth.

Hannah crossed her arms, pursing her faded red lips with pride.

"I said, get the fuck out, Hannah!" I erupted, throwing my arms up and pointing at the door. "GET THE FUCK OUT!"

I heard Liam's door open across the hall as Hannah's face fell. I'd never screamed at her like that, but if she didn't leave in the next three seconds, I was going to do it again.

Luckily, Hannah quickly masked her hurt with rage and stormed out of my room, my door ricocheting off the wall in her wake.

Liam stood in his doorway, rubbing the back of his head as he watched Hannah flee. "You good, Danny boy?"

I nodded once. "I really don't want to hear it today, Liam."

He held his hands up in surrender. "I'll go start on breakfast then."

Liam's footsteps disappeared down the hallway, and I was surprised not to see my sister, Avery, following behind him. It'd been over a year since she had moved out of the spare bedroom downstairs, but I saw her more now than I ever had then. I was close to asking Liam to just move out already so they could get a place together, but that felt like crossing a line. That felt too close to breaking up the band. We had all lived under the same roof since we could afford to leave home. It'd be a bad omen to change that now.

I let out a breath as silence filled my room—finally.

Unfortunately, two knocks sounded on my open door not a second later, stealing my brief serenity.

I looked up and saw Lexie peeking her head in.

"She's fucking crazy, that one. I told you." She shook her head, making her pink hair shake with it.

"Get outta here, Lex!" I threw my pillow at my bassist, and she ducked just in time to miss it.

"Jeesh! You're always so crabby when you get dumped."

"Lexie!" I growled, my nose flaring.

"All right, all right. I'm going." She rolled her eyes as she stepped away from my room.

Sometimes, it was nice to have all of us living together. We didn't have to go anywhere to rehearse or to record our music. But privacy here was nearly nonexistent. I couldn't take a shower without one of them barging in to brush their teeth or use the mirror. Hell, I couldn't buy myself food without expecting to share with three other people. Four, if our manager, Nikko, was around. It was like we were married to each other in the sense of *what's mine is always theirs*.

That included Hannah. She'd been with each of us at one time or another. First with Liam, back when we had first started touring a couple of years back. Liam had been with a lot of girls that never meant anything before he ended up with my sister. Then, Hannah had a drunken one-night stand with Tic. He was so confused the next morning that it was actually kind of funny. After that, Hannah wanted to experiment with her sexuality and spent the night in Lexie's bed. She claimed she was still straight, but that hadn't stopped her from staying the night with Lexie a half-dozen times more. I wasn't positive if she'd been with Nikko yet, but I wouldn't put it past either one of them. They'd both been with ... well, let's just say, there weren't too many in our crowd that they hadn't been with.

For a while, though, I was the only one Hannah spent her nights with. Sure, we fought and went our separate ways more times than I could count, but we always found our way back together again. I used to think that was the cut-and-dry definition of fate, but I was beginning to realize that repeating the same toxic cycle over and over again wasn't fate at all. It was torture. And like my many other toxic habits, I needed to break this one too. I needed to end it with Hannah for good.

I let my shoulders fall back onto the mattress and released an exasperated sigh. I could hear Nikko now, telling me to go write some music while I was still feeling like shit. I always hated when he got on us, but he was usually right; rage and heartache made for the best music, and we needed to finish our new album.

When the smell of bacon hit my nose, I rolled out of bed, slid on a pair of briefs and jeans, and then threaded my arms through my nearest button-down flannel. I could feel Lexie's and Liam's eyes on me as I wandered downstairs into the kitchen to fetch a couple of pieces of bacon from the plate next to the frying pan Liam was tending to. Lexie was cracking some eggs into a bowl, but Liam tore it out of her hands when she was done. We all knew better than to let Lexie cook for us, even with something as simple as scrambled eggs. She couldn't even microwave popcorn without burning it.

"Lex, there are shells in here!" Liam scolded her as he picked through the bowl, and I chuckled.

She huffed as she plopped herself down at the kitchen table. "I think you mean, *Thank you for helping me prepare breakfast, Lexie. That's so nice of you.* I don't see these two apes stepping in to help." She gestured to Tic and me as he made his way into the kitchen behind me, propping himself against the fridge with his shoulder.

"I saw Hannah rushing out of here, almost in tears. I didn't think that girl knew how to cry. What were you two yelling about?" Tic asked.

I took a bite of bacon and chewed. "Don't worry about it."

The room went silent for a moment, but I could feel the pressure building—the curiosity and the need to know that every goddamn thing was going to be all right.

"I'll be outside," I said before anyone could ask if I needed a fucking hug or a shoulder to cry on.

They were used to Hannah coming and going, the arguing and the breakups. But they'd never heard me shout at a woman like that, other than my sister—but that was Avery, and she usually shouted first.

I grabbed my guitar resting at the end of the couch just outside the kitchen and walked out the front door onto the porch. Nights ended late for us, so mornings usually started around ten o'clock when the sun was already sitting brightly in the sky. My eyes squinted as I adjusted to the light, but once they did, I took my usual seat on the cushioned wicker chair next to the table, still holding my empty notebook from yesterday.

I shook my head at the blank pages. Lyrics hadn't been coming to me lately, so I was focusing more of my time on the ballads. Something would come to me sooner or later; otherwise, Liam had been killing it with the last few songs he wrote. I used to think he was stealing some ideas from Avery's school projects, but I knew Liam well enough to know he wouldn't put something on our record without giving proper credit. And so far, the only song he claimed she'd helped with was "Hollow Again" on our last album. Liam had come clean about that after the song was already playing on all of our local radio stations and some throughout the States, so it wasn't like I could take it off our last album. Though the thought still crossed my mind.

I loved my sister, but I hated the idea that she had any claim to our success. Sure, her relationship with Liam had impacted his songwriting capabilities, but those were still his words. His lyrics. I didn't want her anywhere near the actual artistry side of things even if her new fancy music school was turning her into quite the little lyrical poet. Avery was talented, but she needed to figure out what to do with that talent on her own.

I vacantly stared out at the quiet suburban street while I worked my callous fingers through the strings of my guitar to the same melody as yesterday. I hummed along to where I thought lyrics would fit, and when I made it through to the end, I immediately started all over again. On my seventh run-through, the bang of what sounded like clanging metal broke me from my concentration.

I frowned and leaned forward in my seat, searching for the source of the noise, but I didn't have to look far.

Three houses down across the street, a girl in an oversize shirt and jeans jumped on the ramp of a moving truck with her arms in the air, trying to get the roll-up door to stay open. It was a valiant effort on her part, but she was just too short. Her T-shirt lifted as she stretched her arms up, and her ponytail bounced as she tried again and again.

It looked tiresome and oh-so entertaining.

I grinned, finding it difficult not to laugh. I wondered how long I could watch her struggle before someone would come to her rescue and help her. As soon as I stood and put my guitar down, the truck's door miraculously retracted all the way up and stayed there. The girl thrust her hands up, and she shook her hips in victory before slumping over with exhaustion.

9

I chuckled and stayed standing, conflicted on whether I should still go over anyway and ask if she needed a hand. The neighborly thing to do would be to introduce myself to my cute new neighbor, right?

It didn't take much to convince myself as I took my first step off the porch. What stopped me from taking a second was the six-foot-something guy who appeared at the end of my new neighbor's driveway. He rushed to grab the top of the stack of boxes blocking her vision as she made her way down the ramp. I could see her smile at whatever he had said to her, even from here. The faint sound of an angelic laugh made my heart dance in a way it wasn't used to, and my grin fell.

I retreated back to my seat as the two of them disappeared through the open front door.

"Looks like we got some new neighbors!" Lexie's voice behind me sent a brief shiver of panic up my spine.

"Jesus, Lex. You're like a fucking jack-in-the-box from hell. Can you try and make your footsteps a little less ninja-like?" I scowled as I fell back into my chair.

"What if I like sneaking up on you?" she replied, giggling. "Were you about to go introduce yourself?"

"Nope," I lied, peering over again as the two made another trip back to get more boxes.

"I think you should. I doubt we're loud enough to reach them down that far, but it's still nice to warn them about what we do in case our music bothers them."

She made a good point. We were lucky none of our neighbors had made a noise complaint yet, but we had spared no expense when we decided to install a recording studio in our basement. The walls and ceiling had soundproofing panels and foam, but we still played loud enough to break through that barrier—and we partied even louder.

I nodded. "Yeah, maybe."

Lexie paused in thought and then lit up with an idea. "Why don't I make some muffins and bring them by later?"

My face twisted. "You want to poison them?"

She scowled back at me. "Ha-ha."

"I just don't think that'll leave the best first impression—" I stopped myself when I realized I was alone again. I shook my head once and picked my guitar back up.

After a few strums, I peeked over the railing blocking my view of her, and my grin quickly returned.

My melody must've been loud enough to reach her ears because she was standing alone at the entrance of the truck, looking over her shoulder in my direction.

I played louder, hoping that if she liked it enough or was curious enough, I could lure her over here instead.

A smile stretched across her face again before something back inside the house pulled her attention away from me, and it was like a spark lit up in my chest because I knew in that brief moment that *smile* belonged to me.

2

Logan

"Will you have sex with me?"

Horror quickly filled my best friend's features as he looked up from his phone—the same horror I felt now, having heard myself actually say that out loud. It sounded so much worse than it had in my head.

That was a lie. It'd sounded terrible in there too.

"Wh-what?" Andre stuttered, his big brown eyes widening.

I shrugged the blanket we were sharing up over my shoulders and tucked it beneath my chin, wishing I could crawl underneath it and never be seen again. It had taken me thirty minutes to muster up the courage to ask the first time. I wasn't sure I had it in me to ask again.

"Logan?"

"Forget it." I shrank myself down, darting my eyes back to the television he'd just help me set up.

"Oh-ho. No, you don't." Andre pivoted his whole body on the couch cushion next to me, making me shift from his weight. "Logan, look at me."

I swallowed the giant lump in my throat and peered over at him. A deep crease had formed between his brows, like a crack in a glacier. I was sure my baffling question was going to make the rest of his face split in two if I didn't explain myself quickly.

His brows rose as he waited.

I threw my head back and let out an exasperated sigh that sounded like I was either choking or heaving out my very last breath. Believe me; I wished it were the latter.

"It's been over a year," I finally said.

"Since?"

"Since …" I made a motion with my hands, hoping he would finish that thought silently.

The tension on his face slowly melted into realization. "Ah. Since your kitten was touched?"

My cheeks had to look like two giant tomatoes with how deeply they burned. "Oh, my God! That's a horrifying way to put it. Can you never say that again?"

Andre snickered.

I rolled my eyes and forced myself to continue, "I haven't been … intimate with anyone"—embarrassment made me light up like a matchstick—"since I've been clean. Really clean."

His face slowly fell. "Oh."

"Yeah. Oh."

"And you want to break that streak with me?"

"Can you not look so disgusted?" I shrieked.

14

"That's not—" His shoulders fell. "I'm not. I'm just a little lost here, L. Why me?"

It was more than a fair question.

Andre and I had been the best of friends since freshman year of high school. When Nick Turner—the captain of the football team—began putting unwarranted hands on me when he passed me in the halls, Andre started walking me to my classes. His little sister had had the same problem with him the year prior, so Andre couldn't help but feel protective of anyone Nick thought he had the right to just because he was some hotshot quarterback.

I still didn't know why, but Andre had stayed by my side—even after I started dating Nick sophomore year and then a year later, when I dated the town bad boy, Brayden, after said quarterback cheated on me and broke my heart.

Brayden came into my life when I was at my lowest and took the pain away. It was as easy as swallowing a pill, like an aspirin for the heart. I thought the reason why I'd fallen so hard for him was because I believed he could fix me. My broken parts didn't feel so broken when I was with him—or when he was filling my pockets with painkillers. But in reality, he had single-handedly ruined the next six years of my life.

Let's just say, I'd never had the best taste in boys. But apparently, I'd done a decent job at finding the best of guy friends. Andre might've saved my life on more than one occasion, and he didn't even know it.

"Do you have any idea how terrifying it is to have sex for the first time … sober? It's so much more personal when you're not high out of your mind."

Andre knew everything about me, including my screwups. Talking about my addiction with him was normal. Safe. He was the one person who never judged me about that part of my life. But for some reason, talking about sex with him made me fidget with unease.

"You're right. It is personal, Logan. That's why we can't." He began to look around the room in thought. "I mean, we've known each other forever."

I groaned, burying my face in my hands. "I know! It would be so weird. Forget I said anything."

"Logan …"

"No, no, no. It would ruin everything. I don't know why I thought it would be a good idea."

His hand encased mine and squeezed with reassurance. "Because you want it to be with someone you trust. Someone you know won't hurt you."

I peeked up at him.

"You know I'd do anything for you, right?"

I nodded. "Just not this. I get it."

A smile pulled at the corner of his mouth. "I'm honored, Logan. Really. But, damn, you weren't even going to offer to take me on a date first?"

"What, you don't think today was fun?" I asked, gesturing around to all the moving boxes covering almost every square inch of the living room.

"If this is your idea of a date, then it's no wonder you're struggling in the dating pool."

We both laughed, releasing some of the awkward tension.

His hand fell to my knee, warming it. "We'll find someone for you. Don't worry."

"I don't know. I'm scared of being rejected."

He grimaced. "You seemed to handle me rejecting you just fine."

"That's different. You're not rejecting me because you don't like me. You're rejecting me because you love me too much."

"Don't be dumb, Logan. No man would turn you down if you wanted their attention. Look at you."

"Did you just call me dumb?"

"Well, yeah. But I also insinuated you are good-looking." He winked.

I narrowed my eyes at him.

"What? You are dumb if you think being modest is going to win anyone over. Strut your shit. Stop covering everything up with these oversize shirts and baggy pants." He picked at my clothing.

"Excuse me, but these are jeans," I argued.

Andre rolled his eyes. "That you borrowed from your mom because you'd accidentally packed all your clothes away before changing out of your pajamas this morning."

I giggled at my mistake. "Whatever. I like my clothes. They're comfortable."

Andre pursed his lips. "And safe. That's what you really mean, right?"

I tugged at the hem of my shirt. He wasn't just referring to my clothes. I was practically a hermit now. My social life was nonexistent—unless you counted movie nights with Andre. My solitary job of photography was enjoyable, but I sometimes wished there were more than just me in the field. I never went out anywhere unless I was running errands or if my daughter,

Violet, wanted to go somewhere. Keeping things close to home and alone made my routine that much simpler.

"Being safe keeps everything predictable. That's what I need right now."

"Is that what you think you need or what Violet needs?"

I looked behind the couch and down the hall at the door decorated with pink and yellow paper flowers. She had wanted to make sure she added her own touch to it as soon as she got here so everyone knew which room was hers.

"What's the difference? Her life is my life now. You know that," I said, turning back to Andre.

"You don't have to protect her from your past. You got help, you put in the work, and you're clean now. It's over, L. What are you so worried about?"

"That I'll do something to lose her again." My eyes burned at the thought. "I finally have my little girl. I can't—"

"You won't." Andre met my gaze. "She's not going anywhere, okay? You two are finally home. Together. Logan and Violet against the world."

I liked the sound of that.

I looked around at the stacks of cardboard boxes surrounding us in the house left to me in my late aunt's will. Violet and I would still be living with my parents if cancer hadn't taken her from us two months ago. Aunt Gigi hadn't had much to her name other than this place. And with no other nieces or nephews and no children, she had left everything to the only family member she actually liked—*me*.

It was a beautiful home—only one level and a small basement, but a lot of open space in the main area for Violet to play. The walls were brightly painted in colors that matched the photographs my aunt had kept up on the walls from her time spent in Italy. I kept them up to remind me of all the places I wanted to go someday and added a few canvas prints of my own beside hers. My parents had wanted me to sell the house, use the money to get something smaller, and put the rest aside for Violet. But I hadn't wanted her starting her new life with me in a small, shitty apartment. I wanted her to be in a place we both felt safe. A place for her to move and grow and to create memories in. I hated that I'd had to lose my loving aunt to gain all of this. It was a gift I'd never be able to repay. But maybe bringing life back into her home was the best way I could show her my gratitude, even if she wasn't here to see it.

A light knock sounded from the front door—I barely heard it. "Was that the—"

Another louder knock answered my unfinished question and made me spring to my feet. It was nearly eight o'clock, and I was afraid if I didn't answer fast enough, the next knock would wake up Violet.

"Maybe your parents got back from their weekend at the lake early?" Andre suggested.

That was doubtful. My mom and dad had conveniently taken a trip to their cabin the day before I moved into my late aunt's home, which they hadn't wanted me to have in the first place. They were probably enjoying margaritas and cozied up in front of a bonfire right now.

I looked through the peephole and saw a girl with bright pink hair standing with a small box in her hands. Her little knuckles closed into a fist as she prepared to knock again, but I quickly threw the door open before she could make contact.

Her eyes popped open wider when she saw me and smiled. "Hi!"

"Hi?" I greeted back, but it sounded more like a question.

"I'm sorry to bug you. I saw the moving truck in your driveway earlier, and I wanted to bring you a little welcome gift." She held out the box in her hands, and I took it. "They're muffins."

"Oh, wow. That's perfect, actually. Now, I don't have to make breakfast tomorrow morning." I chuckled.

Her bright eyes warmed at my response. "I'm Lexie, by the way. I live across the street in the white house with all the cars in the driveway." She twisted and pointed over a few houses at the one I'd heard music coming from earlier.

"I'm Logan. It's so nice to meet you." I held out my hand.

She shook it absentmindedly, distracted by something behind me.

I peered over my shoulder, seeing Andre standing beside the couch and folding the blanket we had shared.

"Is that your husband?" Lexie asked.

The laugh that escaped me made my new neighbor jump with alarm. "Sorry, no. That's my friend. He was just helping me out today. Maybe if I share these with him"—I jiggled the box of muffins—"he'll forgive me for the sore back in the morning."

"Unlikely!" I heard him call out.

She bounced a little as she shouted back, "They're chocolate chip!"

"Oh, well, in that case …" Andre chuckled.

She gave him another long look of approval before tucking her hands in her back pockets. "Listen, I just want to give you a little heads-up. I don't live alone. My band and I live together, and we have a studio in our basement with all the bells and whistles, but you still might hear us practicing every now and then. None of the other neighbors have complained about it, and we do take precautions, but I just thought I'd warn you."

"Well, if it was anything like what I heard earlier, you won't get any complaints from me." I smiled.

Lexie's mouth twitched with intrigue. "You must've heard Danny. He plays outside on our porch most mornings. If it ever bothers you, just come and let me know. I love putting my boys in their place."

"*Your* boys?" I pried, wishing I hadn't. It was none of my business who they were to her.

Her head tilted before she realized what I was asking. "Oh! We're like family. It's not like that at all."

I shook my head, feeling my cheeks warm. "I'm sorry. That's absolutely none of my business. It's been a very long day, and my mouth just seems to have a mind of its own."

I heard Andre scoff from the living room, and I ground my teeth together in an effort to keep from spitting something sarcastic back at him.

"Thanks for stopping by and for the muffins. My daughter will be so excited tomorrow morning," I lied because it was the polite thing to do. Violet was lactose intolerant, so I was very careful with what I let her eat, especially when I wasn't sure what was in it. "We'll have to repay the favor sometime and come meet the rest of your band."

Lexie sprang for a hug I didn't see coming. She wrapped her arms around my middle and then pulled away before I could decide what to do with my arms. "They'd love to meet you. Come by anytime."

I waved at her as she retreated down my driveway and toward her house and then closed the door slowly, feeling slightly off-kilter from our interaction.

"She seemed friendly," Andre teased, eyeing the box in my hands as I walked them to the kitchen.

"Very." I chuckled. "Go ahead. Violet probably can't eat them anyway."

Andre flipped the box open, snatching a muffin out with his mitt of a hand. I was grateful he was standing near the sink because as soon as he took a bite, he quickly spat it back out. "Oh, my God."

I frowned. "Are they that bad?"

His face contorted with disgust. "I think she swapped the sugar with salt."

"Oh no." A smile pinched my cheeks as I fought away a bubble of laughter.

"What do you think is so funny, huh? Here." Andre tried shoving the muffin into my face, but I swatted him away, giggling.

"I guess Violet and I will have to run to the grocery store straightaway tomorrow morning." I'd thought I'd have enough time to pick up a few things after unloading the truck, but the day had gotten away from me.

Andre reached into the pantry and pulled out a box of Violet's favorite cereal as if he just opened the door to Narnia.

My mouth practically hung open. "How?"

He just shrugged and opened the fridge, revealing a carton of oat milk and a basket of blueberries.

"Andre—" His name got caught in my throat.

"I know. I'm the best." He gave me a smug grin. When he saw the tears welling up in my eyes, he set the box of fruity puffs down and pulled me into his arms. "It's just a little breakfast, L."

"I know, but it's also *everything.*" I buried my face into his T-shirt, making my next words inaudible. "You're so wonderful."

A deep laugh rumbled from his chest.

"What did I do to deserve you?"

"I'm not sure, but I think a certain green-eyed three-year-old with a weird obsession with porcupines might have something to do with it."

I smiled and sniffled. "She is kind of amazing, isn't she?"

Andre pulled away and looked at me. "Where do you think she gets it from?"

I shook my head. I couldn't help but wonder if the amazing parts of my daughter had come from *him* rather than me. But that wasn't something I'd ever know the answer to.

3

Danny

"Where's the bridge going to come in again?" Tic asked as he twirled his drumsticks through his fingers.

I kicked one of my boots up on the wicker table in front of me and brought my guitar closer to my bare chest. It was in the eighties today—an unusually hot August day in Northern California—which warranted minimal clothing. Even Tic had on next to nothing with his ripped shorts and a T-shirt that looked like it'd been used as a rag to clean up oil spills in a bike shop; the thing was nearly sheer and had holes and stains all over it. Come to think of it; I was pretty sure I'd seen him use it to clean off his motorcycle. He treated that thing better than any girl I'd ever seen him with, and that was saying something.

I sighed. "Between my and Lexie's harmony and your drum solo. Here, listen." I played the proper chords, singing and humming some of the lyrics, and then gave him a nod when the lifeless bridge came in.

Tic tapped his fingers to the beat in his head as he counted it out and then began beating his drumsticks against the side of the table when his solo started.

"Still struggling with that hook?" Liam asked, stepping out onto the porch. "Think fast," he said, tossing apples at my and Tic's faces.

I caught it with one hand and took a bite. "Wanna grab your guitar and help?" I suggested, my mouth full.

He ran his hand through his dark hair. "Maybe when I get back?"

"Back from where?" Tic asked, tossing his apple up and down.

Liam looked at me and then back at Tic, and I felt like I was missing something, but I didn't press. What he did with my sister was his own business.

"I've just got an errand to run for Avery. I'll be back in a couple of hours, and we can play as much as you want."

"Yeah, whatever," I commented with another mouthful.

Liam held out his hands. "Drop the attitude, man. I said I'll be back to help, and I mean it."

I nodded. "Fine. But pick up some food on your way home. I'm starving."

"I just fed you two!"

I patted my hard stomach. "I'm a growing boy."

"Me too." Tic flashed a bright smile, flexing his bicep.

Liam flared his nostrils with a side-eye. "Burgers or wings?"

"Both," Tic and I answered in unison.

"Where's Lex at?" Tic frowned.

"She's … preoccupied." Liam gave a knowing lift of his brows as he pulled his truck keys out of his pocket.

I shook my head. "That girl never tires. Seriously, is there anyone in a forty-mile radius she hasn't slept with?"

Tic scratched his head. "Us?"

The three of us chuckled.

"I'll see you guys later." Liam threw up his hand as he left.

"All right, play it again, Danny boy." Tic's command only made my irritation snake further up my spine as I watched Liam back out of the driveway.

An errand to run for Avery.

What could she possibly need help with that she couldn't do on her own?

My sister had become Miss Independent since she'd moved out. Paying her way through a new school and paying her own bills. Well, half. She and her friend Nina had an apartment together on the other side of town, and I couldn't help but wonder if this errand Liam was running had something to do with finding their own place to live together. Nina didn't need the help paying rent, and if I were in a relationship like theirs, I'd want the privacy of my own home. Hell, I wanted that *now*. Maybe it was all in my head, but Liam was gone more than he used to be, and something about that didn't sit right with me.

"Hello? Earth to Danny!" Tic waved his drumsticks in front of my face.

"Sorry."

He leaned his elbows onto his knees. "You good?"

I snatched a cigarette from the box on the table and put it between my lips. "Peachy."

Tic swiveled his head at something while I dug through my pockets for a lighter. "Hey, is that the new neighbor you and Lexie were talking about?"

I snapped my head up, searching through Lexie's railing planters filled with daisies and fucking petunias.

And then I saw her. *Logan.*

Lexie had teased me with minimal details on her visit earlier in the week, but I'd finally gotten my hot new neighbor's name from her after holding her favorite red wig hostage and threatening to cut bangs into it with a pair of dull scissors. Evil, I know. But drastic times called for drastic measures.

Logan's long black hair came into my view, and then the rest of her. The cigarette dropped from my mouth in disbelief as I took her in with each step she took toward our house.

I'd spent every morning this week out on the porch, waiting to catch a glimpse of her again, but I wasn't prepared to see her walking up my driveway.

What was she doing here?

The oversize university sweatshirt hanging off her petite frame covered what I was sure was a well-sculpted ass. I didn't know how she wasn't burning up wearing that with a pair of tight black leggings, but I'd be more than happy to help remove either one.

She gripped the handles of a reusable bag in one hand and a little girl's hand in the other as she ascended the porch stairs.

I froze. I didn't know why, but my instinct reaction was to wait and listen, to watch, which was why she probably didn't notice us when she rang our doorbell. It wasn't until the little girl standing beside her peered around her hip and pointed at me that she finally saw us.

Logan's golden eyes landed on me, melting my frozen stature, and I sprang to life again.

I lifted my chin with a flirty smirk. "Looking for someone?"

"Um, yes." She fidgeted, looking between me and Tic. Her eyes lingered on me when they returned. "Is Lexie around?"

"She's a bit tied up at the moment, but I can grab her if it's urgent?" I sat up.

My thumb lightly brushed the strings of my guitar as I moved it to rest beside my chair, and the little girl's eyes lit up.

"Awe yew in a band?" the little girl asked, already halfway across the porch.

Her arms stretched out for my guitar when Logan yelled after her, "Violet!"

The girl halted just shy of my strings and dropped her shoulders with the saddest frown I'd ever seen.

"I *am* in a band." I glanced up at Logan with a smile and saw her cheeks warm with the perfect shade of pink. "I don't mind. I'm sure her little hands won't do any harm. Besides"— I tilted my head down toward Violet, leaned over the armrest, and strummed the five strings as encouragement— "instruments are meant to be played. Don't you think, sweetheart?"

Violet's face lit back up as she nodded. She mirrored my actions to the best of her ability and dragged her fingers across the strings, releasing a burst of giggles when the guitar responded with an uneven tune.

Something inside my chest danced at the angelic sound.

Easily distracted, she looked at my arm resting beside the neck of my guitar, and she reached up, trailing the tattoo sticking out of the rolled-up cuff of my sleeve.

"What's dat?" she asked, her wide green eyes finding mine.

Logan set her bag down and took three giant steps forward, swiftly wrapping soft hands around Violet. "Vi, you can't go around touching strangers."

Oh, how I wanted to be acquainted with Logan long enough to touch *her*.

Logan chuckled and looked up at me. "I'm sorry …" She waited for me to respond.

"Danny," I answered.

"Danny," she repeated.

I swallowed when I was hit with the sweet sound of my name coming from her soft lips.

"I'm—"

"Logan," I answered for her. "Yeah, I know."

The subtle tilt of her head and the smile she gave me made my breath catch in my throat before her eyes shifted to Tic.

Being the gentleman that he was, he held out his hand. "Hi, Logan. I'm Tic."

She reached her left hand out toward his, and I noted the absence of a wedding band sitting on her ring finger. "Nice to meet you, Tic."

"Tic?" Violet squealed. "Like a bug?"

Tic chuckled and pulled his drumsticks out of his pockets. "No, because I have this nervous tic and tap these on everything I see!" He banged them all the way across the table and then reached up, pretending to play them on Violet's head while he made a drumming sound with his mouth.

Violet and Logan giggled with delight, and I resisted the urge to give Tic a warning look for being more charming than me.

She was standing close enough that I could really take in her features now. Her strikingly *beautiful* features. My eyes danced across her face, trying to find my favorite one, but I couldn't choose. The golden flecks shining in her hazel stare, lined with thick lashes. The subtle dusting of freckles across the tops of her cheeks and nose. The loose black curls she'd tucked behind her ears. Or the crease in the center of her bottom lip that made it look downright edible. My mouth watered just looking at them. At *her*. So much so that I rolled my bottom lip through my teeth as our gazes crossed again.

"And I'm Viowet!" Violet chimed in, and the hint of tension between me and Logan broke as fast as it had appeared.

Another smile pinched my cheeks. "And what a pretty name that is!"

"He's not a swanger *now*, Mommy," Violet said, looking up at her mom through long lashes.

The more I looked between the two of them, the more I could see their similarities. Violet had all her mother's elegant features, down to the freckles on her cheeks. But her eyes were greener than the golden hue of Logan's hazel irises. Not to mention their style choices; Logan kept her attire more casual and comfortable, whereas Violet let her personality shine with a purple dress covered in glitter that sparkled in the sun.

Logan righted herself. "That still doesn't mean you should touch him."

Violet frowned. "Why not?"

"What if he doesn't want to be touched?"

31

"It's okay if you want to see my tattoo. I've got a lot. Here." I pushed my sleeve up, revealing the full tattoo she'd been interested in, and a few others stamped randomly across my forearm. "This is a drawing of the guitar my father used to play. Tic designed it. I have the real thing inside, but I keep it safe in a case so it doesn't get damaged."

"But I thought they wew meant to be pwayed?" Violet inquired, and, oh, how I loved her little brain.

"You're right; they should be. Just not this one." My smile faltered, and so did Logan's once she noticed.

Tic cleared his throat, breaking the awkward pause in conversation. "Did you guys bring something by for Lex?" He nodded at the bag Logan had set down by the front door.

Logan tore her gaze away from mine and blinked.

A light bulb lit up above Violet's head as she sprinted over to the bag and pulled out a covered baking pan. "My cupcakes!"

She ran back over and slid the pan of frosted cupcakes onto the table.

"Did you make those yourself?" I asked, watching her round cheeks pinch.

Violet nodded with pride.

The frosting wasn't smeared haphazardly or falling off the sides. It had been piped with care. A little shaky, but the sprinkles helped cover up the imperfections. There were a few neater than the others, no doubt the work of Logan's steadier hands.

"Very impressive, Violet."

"She loves to bake and wanted to return the favor and bring you guys a little treat too. You know, after Lexie was kind enough to bring us those muffins." Logan's voice was so light and airy. I wasn't sure if I enjoyed listening to her or Violet more.

"I'm gwad I'm wactose intowewent because Uncle Andwe says those muffins tasted awfow!" Violet scrunched up her face.

Tic and I burst into laughter as Logan lurched forward, shushing her.

Violet peered up at Logan with a scowl as she covered her mouth.

Logan smiled at us, clearly trying to hide her mortification. "Three-year-olds apparently don't have a filter. I'm so sorry."

Violet pushed her mom's hand away and held up her finger. "I'm almost fow!" she corrected matter-of-factly.

"Oh!" My eyebrows leaped up my forehead. "Well then, that filter must be coming soon then, huh?"

Logan winced with another apology.

I reached for a sprinkled cupcake and shifted back in my seat. My shirt fell open wider at my movements, and Logan's gaze drifted to my naked chest for a half-second. I waited for her to meet my eyes again before I ran my tongue along the edge of the frosting, humming as I coated the tip with the fluffy sweetness.

Logan dragged her bottom lip through her teeth as she watched, her cheeks flushing again.

"We should actually be apologizing to you," Tic added, reaching for his own cupcake. "Lexie can't cook for shit."

Violet drew in a shocked breath and then held the tips of her fingers tightly over her mouth.

I snapped my head at my bandmate. "*Language*, man."

Tic shuddered in his chair. "I am so sorry, Violet."

I looked back at Logan, but she just smiled and shrugged. "Don't worry about it, guys. She's heard worse slip out of me every now and then."

Violet giggled and lowered her hands. "Yeah, but Uncle Andwe is *so* bad at it."

My mind recalled the man helping her move. Lexie, being the prying little thing she was, had discovered that he was only a friend, but I wanted to confirm it for myself and that there hopefully wasn't anyone else in the picture either. I still hadn't seen another car in her driveway in the three days she'd been in her new house. Not that I was paying close attention …

"You've got siblings, too, huh?" It wasn't smooth.

It was an awkward time to ask personal questions, and Tic let me know that with a slight tilt of his head.

Thanks, man.

Logan's lashes flickered. "Oh. No. I'm an only child. Andre is a friend of mine. She's just always called him that. He's practically family."

"I get that," I said. "We don't always get to choose who our family is, but sometimes, our family chooses us."

She smiled at my words.

"Want to join us for a quick drink?" Tic offered. "It's a scorcher today."

"Thank you, but I'll have to pass today. I promised this little one a date at the park down the road."

"I want to go fwy!" Violet pointed up at the sky.

Logan smiled and smoothed her daughter's dark hair. "Yes, you can go on the swings as much as you want."

Panic crawled up my throat as she backed away a step, preparing to leave. "We're having some friends over on Saturday if you want to stop by."

I caught Tic's quizzical look out of the corner of my eye. We didn't actually have plans, but I was desperate to see her again.

"Oh, um—"

I could see the excuses playing out in her head.

"Super casual. Just some drinks, maybe a little music." I was a second away from begging on my knees, but I kept my composure long enough to see her considering it. "I'd love to see you again."

She rewarded me with the sweetest of smiles. "I'll try and stop by."

Hope blossomed in my chest.

"It was nice meeting you guys. Please thank Lexie for the muffins for me." She paused. "And maybe leave out the part about what Violet said?"

"Sure thing." Tic chuckled.

"Thanks for the treat." I lifted the cupcake as Violet waved goodbye.

Logan hesitated before she retreated down the front steps with her daughter, and that brief moment that her eyes bored into mine, I felt that spark that I had gotten the day she heard me playing.

"No." Tic's stern voice broke me from my thoughts as soon as they were out of earshot.

"What?" I shrugged.

"You can't sleep with our neighbor."

I barked out a laugh. "Since when is that one of our rules?"

Muscles worked in his jaw. "I just made it one."

"You can't just make up rules, Tic." I shook my head. "Besides, I just want to get to know her a little better."

"Yeah. Naked," he deadpanned.

I took a bite of my cupcake, trying to fight the grin on my face. Once I finished, I picked my guitar back up, ignoring his warning, and began working on where we had left off. This time, a bit more inspired.

4

Logan

"You like him." Andre sported the smuggest of grins.

I nearly choked on my bite of pizza. "What? No!"

"That was entirely too defensive. Try again."

I rolled my eyes and finished chewing. "Why are you like this?"

"Like what? *Right?*"

"I don't like anyone. How could I? I don't even know them. I was just saying that they were nice."

His brow rose. "You said more than that. You haven't stopped talking about that guy with the guitar since yesterday."

"His name is Danny." You'd think, for how much he had claimed I was talking about him, he could at least remember his name.

His grin grew wider as if what I had just said only furthered his point.

I narrowed my eyes at him and pinched my lips together to fight the grin threatening to ruin my poker face. "I hate you."

"You do not."

"You're impossible to talk to." I shrugged.

He leaned forward onto his elbows. "Why is it so hard for you to admit you like him? Or at the very least, that you're attracted to him?"

"Fine. He's good-looking. Whatever."

That didn't even begin to cover it. Anyone with two working eyes and a libido would grow weak in the knees, staring too long into Danny's bright blue eyes. The way he had sat in that chair with his shirt open, naked chest, black and gray tattoos everywhere, holding his guitar made him look like he was posing on the front cover of rock star *GQ* magazine—if that were such a thing. Ugh, and that charming smile of his. I felt off-kilter just being around him for the short time I was there. He didn't seem real. But that's all my attraction to him was. Fiction. A fantasy. It ended there. He was the kind of man women chased after during the rebellious stage of their lives. The perfect bad boy who fucked you senseless in the back of his car and then broke your heart. I'd finally outrun that "stage" of my life years ago, and I wasn't turning back now.

"You said he was good with Violet," Andre added.

I glanced over at the couch where Violet was fast asleep, curled up in a fuzzy blanket with her favorite stuffed animal. I wanted to move her into her bedroom, but she looked too peaceful to wake.

"Everyone likes Vi," I argued.

"But Vi doesn't like everyone, and she liked him. You said so yourself. She's like a dog."

My brows shot up. "Excuse me?"

"What? Dogs have a good sense of character. So does Vi."

"Huh. My daughter has a sixth sense that I didn't know about. Thank you for enlightening me."

He smiled. "You're welcome."

"That girl would run into an unmarked van if the driver said there were Popsicles and porcupines inside!" I shouted in a hushed tone.

His face soured. "That sounds so sticky and sharp."

I stood up and crumpled my napkin on top of my empty plate, pinning him with a scowl.

"All I'm saying is, your daughter liked him. Clearly, *you* liked him. Why are you getting so worked up?"

"Because you're accusing me of falling for my neighbor."

"Falling?" His eyes sparkled.

He was enjoying pressing my buttons.

"You know what I mean, Andre."

"Whatever you say, L." He stopped teasing me and started helping me clean up the kitchen.

As grateful as I was for the conversation to be over, I couldn't help adding one last detail. "They invited me over to their house tomorrow night."

I'd been trying to talk myself out of it ever since Danny had asked, but maybe I wanted someone to talk me *into* it. Andre would be the only person to do it.

"You should go."

For Christ's sake, those three words were convincing enough to excite me at the idea. The possibilities. I was too easily persuaded. Danny wanted to see me again, and *I* wanted to see *him*. So, would there be any harm in simply entertaining the idea for the sake of getting to know my neighbors better?

And now, I was convincing myself. Not even a full week on my own, and I was already contemplating hanging out with rock stars.

Andre put away the leftovers in the fridge. "I'm free tomorrow. I can watch Vi."

I shook my head, glancing over at Violet again. "I don't think that's necessary. I looked them up after I left their house yesterday and saw everything I needed to see. A rock star on the rise is the last thing I need messing up my life."

Andre gaped at me in shock. "Since when are you Miss Judgmental? You know nothing about him."

"Now, look who's defending him," I smirked. "Are you falling for Mr. GQ?"

Andre snorted. "Mr. GQ?"

I shrugged. "I already admitted to being attracted to him."

"Maybe you can go over to their place tomorrow night and admit that to his face." He bumped my shoulder with his as he piled the dirty dishes into the sink. "Maybe scratch that itch you were talking about the other day?"

His wink was what really sent me over the edge. I wet the rag I pulled from a drawer, squeezed out the excess water, and wound it up, getting ready to snap it at his backside.

He saw me preparing my weapon and bolted for the living room, using a sleeping Violet as his shield before my wrist could even warm up.

I narrowed my eyes at him from the kitchen. "Coward," I whispered.

Andre held his hands to his chest, mouthing, "*Me?*"

I chewed on that for a moment as my cheeks returned to their normal shade of pale pink. Maybe I was a coward. Maybe I was scared. I never used to be this way. I used to face the thrill of the unknown, the high of an adventure, and swoony bad boys with my head held high and a smile on my face.

When my mother got annoyed at my reckless behavior, she'd ask me that cliché question, "If your friends jumped off a bridge, would you do it too?"

I could honestly answer that I was the one to jump first. Bridges, cliffs … if there was water below and a chance of surviving, I didn't weigh the odds not being in my favor.

What had happened to that girl? Sure, I didn't miss the drugs or the time lost when I was out of my head, but I missed the confidence to live life like there was no tomorrow. Even when, some days, I wasn't sure there was going to be one. I missed seizing the day and all that poetic shit. I even had the tattoo to prove it—not that I needed the reminder of when I had gotten it.

"Logan?" Andre whispered.

My eyes were fixed on the thin black script etched into my wrist that read *Carpe Diem*. Sixteen-year-old Logan thought it had made her both a badass and a free-spirited inspiration. Now, it just kind of made me sad.

"Logan?" Andre repeated, and I dragged my eyes up to meet his. He smoothed a hand over Violet's forehead. "Stop being so afraid of living your life now that you have the very best it has to offer. She will learn to do the same. Do you really want that for her?"

Tears pricked in my eyes, blurring my vision.

41

I wasn't sure what I wanted for Violet, but Andre was right; it wasn't this version of myself. And it most certainly wasn't the person I used to be. It was somewhere in between. I just wasn't sure how to get there without risking losing the one thing that mattered most.

Her.

5

Danny

I curled my fingers around my beer bottle and brought it to my lips, staring at the front door. "She's not coming."

Liam slapped a hand on my shoulder. "Maybe she had something come up."

I nodded, but I had seen the indecision in Logan's eyes when I asked her to be here tonight. She might've wanted to, but something about me had scared her off enough to convince her otherwise.

"You said she had a little girl?" Liam asked.

I nodded again, giving a quick survey of the room to make sure I hadn't missed her. It would be nearly impossible, as I'd been looking at the door every ten seconds for the last two hours, but there was still a chance.

"Maybe she couldn't find anyone to babysit? She did just move here."

"Sure, Liam," I agreed because I didn't want to hear another excuse.

Disappointment knotted in my stomach as I glanced around the room for the hundredth time. It was never hard to fill our house up with strangers, even on short notice, but it wasn't as big of a crowd as we usually had. I thought a smaller group would be less intimidating to someone like Logan, who didn't look like the kind of girl to be tipped upside down on a keg.

Of course, Hannah couldn't miss one of our parties and showed up with a few friends I'd never seen before. She shifted her gaze from her position on the couch toward me right as the guy beside her started kissing her neck.

"Hey, Danny!" My sister appeared at my best friend's side with a warm smile, rescuing me from the torturous self-loathing snaking up my spine.

I gave her a nod and tossed back what was left of my beer.

A part of Liam visibly relaxed as he kissed the top of Avery's brunette hair and pulled her tighter into him. She fit perfectly at his side, and I couldn't help the pang of jealousy that hit my chest whenever I saw the two of them together.

Avery was the golden child, and as much as I'd been working on letting the fault of that stay with my parents, I still found it difficult not to hate her a little for it too.

Okay, *hate* was a strong word. I loved Avery more than I often admitted. But there was a lot that Avery had had, growing up, that I wished I'd had too.

But this—what she had with Liam—I wanted it more than any of the attention or extra love she'd gotten from our parents. Unfortunately, the only type of girls I seemed to attract were the ones who enjoyed breaking me more than putting me back together—girls who took what they wanted from me and then moved on.

As if on cue, Hannah let out a soft moan to gain my attention back as the man sitting beside her devoured her clavicle. Her eyes locked on to me with a devilish grin.

"This is lame. I'll be out back," I said, disappearing through the sliding glass door before I could break my fist open on the guy's eye socket. I didn't want to give her the satisfaction.

"Danny!" Nikko shouted from the hot tub when he saw me. "Hey, can you grab me another beer?"

"Sure thing. Nina, you want anything?" I asked, but she shook her head, making her short blonde hair dance across her shoulders.

I was surprised to see her here with Nikko. Being Avery's roommate, she often tagged along with my sister to these things. She and Nikko were constantly on and off again, like me and Hannah, but Nina was pretty easygoing about it. I'd just thought this was one of the times that they were *off*. Nikko had never been into dating one girl at a time, but this was the closest he'd ever gotten. I wasn't sure who was really using who in this relationship—if it was just sex or an honest, open relationship—but they both seemed to be okay with it.

I grabbed an IPA from the giant cooler beside the pool and walked it over.

"Man, why is Hannah here?" I asked Nikko as I handed him the drink.

He was the one in charge of fetching a crowd at the last minute, which meant he was the one who had invited Hannah and her friends.

"What do you mean? She's always here," he said, cracking the can open.

"Yeah, I'd like that to change."

He scoffed. "You guys aren't screwing at the moment or what?"

My jaw worked. "No. We're done. *I'm* done."

"Sure, okay." Nikko rolled his eyes as if he'd heard that before.

He had. They all had.

"Nah, I'm serious. She's history to me. History I'm sick of repeating."

He settled his back against the tub wall, resting his arms across the top edge. "What the fuck do you want me to do about it?"

"Stop inviting her. I don't want her around here anymore," I said firmly.

"Look, Danny. I manage you and the rest of the band. That includes your expenses, your schedules, travel, and PR." He listed them out on his fingers. "What I don't manage is the amount of pussy you get and who gives it to you."

Nina snapped her head up at him, disgusted at his words.

"Fuck you, Nikko!" I spat.

He took a sip of his beer and glared at me. "Danny boy, go find a drink and some other girl to suck your cock for the night. It shouldn't be that hard."

"What the hell, Nikko?" Nina splashed his chest and climbed out of the hot tub.

He held his hands out. "I'm not fucking wrong, am I?"

My hands clenched into fists at my sides. "Watch it, Nikko. Just because we're friends doesn't mean I can't fire you."

"Fire me?" He choked out a laugh. "Over an ex-fuck who showed up at your house? Dude, get over it! Hannah will always be Hannah. You know that."

"Hey, what's going on?" Tic appeared between us.

"Tic, get this man a blunt or a fucking Xanax and tell him to chill the fuck out."

Before Nikko could get all his words out, I leaped toward him, but Tic snaked a solid arm in front of my chest and held me back.

"Ooh. What are you going to do? Hit me?" Nikko joked. "Go ahead, tough guy."

Tic managed to step in front of me and push me back a bit. "Hey, hey, hey! That's Nikko, man. What're you doing?"

Out of the corner of my eye, I saw Nikko's friends stand. Wes, Carlton, and Stephen watched me carefully as they prepared themselves for a fight.

I wasn't sure I could win with that many people against me. Tic and Liam might have my back, no matter what, but I wasn't so sure they'd back me when it came to Nikko. He might not be a band member, but he was one of us.

Defeated, outnumbered, and scared I might do something I'd regret, I jerked my shoulder out of Tic's grasp and went back inside, snatching an open bottle of whiskey from an end table on my way upstairs. I took a long pull when I reached my room and wiped my mouth with the back of my hand. I paced back and forth, waiting for the anger bubbling inside me to settle and numb itself.

Reasonably, I knew Nikko wasn't the one who deserved that rage. I wasn't sure anyone did but myself. Avery had told me to be careful—that turning to alcohol only fueled that flame once I was mad enough—but it was the only sure way to fix this. Fix *me*.

Fisting the neck of the bottle, I took another long pull as I sank down onto the end of my bed. My shoulders fell forward with the disappointment I felt in letting Hannah get the better of me again.

From the outside, looking in, I had it all. I had the privilege of playing music for a living, and not only was I damn good at it, but I also loved it more than anything. I had the kind of friends who would walk through fire for me. Who would come running if I asked them to, no matter what. I woke up every day knowing I didn't have to worry about how I was going to pay for rent or food or gas. I didn't have to wonder how I was going to come up with the money for recording time in a studio or the up-front cost of a time slot at small venues just to try and get noticed. Because it hadn't been that long ago when those things were a struggle for us.

Now, we had a record label and a studio in our own home. We sold out nearly every venue we played at across the country and had a loyal fan base that kept on growing. If I wanted to, I'd never have to go to bed alone. I was loved by so many people I had never met. Some even ventured so far as to call me their idol. A god even.

The irony of being surrounded by people who loved me and who wanted to be me and still coming up short didn't evade me. Maybe after all the years I'd been cold to the ones who cared the most, the universe had decided my fate was to always be a little bit empty.

The burn of the whiskey lessened with each shot I took from the bottle, and my body began to fill with the comforting warmth I was looking for.

It wasn't until I went to reach for my phone charging besides the bed that I felt my center of balance turn on its axis. I fell to my side, catching a glimpse of the streetlight outside my window, illuminating the houses across from it.

Logan's blue one-story with the white shutters was just barely visible from where I sat, and soft light shone from one of her windows.

A smile spread across my face as I lazily picked myself up, determined to make it to her front door before I lost the ability to walk straight.

No one even noticed as I stumbled through the house and out the front door. I was sure Liam and Avery had already left for her place or gone to bed upstairs. Lexie was stuffing her face full of nachos in the kitchen with some friends. And Tic was probably still out back with Nikko or down in his room in the basement. I didn't even look for Hannah as I passed the couch, but something told me she was still floating around the place somewhere. She didn't typically leave parties until morning, so I was bound to see her when the sun came up. *Joy.*

Logan's house was a lot farther away than I remembered it being. Only a few houses down, it felt like I'd walked a mile by the time I was standing in front of her porch. I didn't remember who had lived here before Logan and Violet moved in. The house had seemed empty for as long as I could remember, but whoever it was had made sure to keep the exterior in good shape in their absence. From what I could see in the dark and the minimal glow of the porch light, the rose

49

bushes on either side of the stairs had been trimmed into a perfect shape, unlike our next-door neighbor's, who must've forgotten about theirs. Those overgrown, thorny fuckers cut the hell out of me every time I mowed up to their fence line.

I was lucky there were only two steps because I tripped on the first and caught myself on the second, just in time to come eye-level with a purple chalk drawing—*er, unicorn?*—on the white boards in front of her doormat.

Violet's questionable art made me laugh as I righted myself and prepared to knock, but just as I lifted my knuckles to the door, I stopped.

Violet.

I couldn't wake up Violet.

The realization was fuzzy but there. The light in one of the bedrooms was still on, but that could very well be Violet's. And what would that matter anyway? It was still the middle of the night, and I was standing in front of a girl's house I had only just met.

"What are you doing here?" I asked myself under my breath, backing away.

As I sank down to sit on the front step, I heard that question repeated. Only it wasn't me asking it.

It was Logan.

6

Logan

"What the hell am I supposed to do with him?" I asked, holding my phone tightly to my ear, staring over the back of my couch at a lifeless Danny.

Andre's laugh did nothing to ease my concern. "Go back to bed and hope he leaves by the time you wake back up?" he suggested.

"That was my plan! But it's seven in the morning, and he's still here!" I whispered aggressively into the phone. "Oh my God, why did I open the door last night?"

Andre was silent for a moment and then asked, "Do I really need to tell you that, or do you know the answer?"

I narrowed my eyes and lowered my voice. "It's not because I like him! I just panicked! What would you have done if you had gotten a notification from your security camera and saw that your neighbor was standing outside your door?"

"Well, first, I'd probably scream because no one should be outside my door at two in the motherfucking morning. And then I would probably not answer the door. I'd wait until they left and ask them about it when it was daylight outside!"

"Well, excuse me for being curious!" I retorted.

"Why are you yelling in lowercase? Are you standing next to him?" Andre asked.

"Maybe."

He laughed.

"He looks so … peaceful. I don't want to wake him, but I need him to leave before Violet gets up. Which will be any minute. Is there any chance you could—"

"Nope," he said, popping the P. "I'm already running late for work, and this is your mess. You deal with him."

My shoulders fell. "Ugh! I only let him in for a glass of water and some ibuprofen. He was wasted! How was I supposed to know he was going to pass out on the couch before I could even get back from the kitchen?"

"This is all very entertaining for me; I hope you know that." I could hear the giant grin in his voice.

Danny's head shifted on one of my throw pillows, and I released a small yipe.

"What?" Andre pressed.

I waited, frozen like a statue, until I knew the coast was clear. "He moved."

"Is that all? Logan, the man, passed out only a few hours ago, drunk as a skunk. He's not waking up anytime soon. If you want him to leave, you're going to have to wake him yourself. Throw some water on him or get a blowhorn.

Whatever it is, let me know how it goes. I'm just getting in my car. I'll call you later, okay?"

"Wait! Andre!" I pleaded.

"Good luck!"

The phone call ended, and I was back to the anxiety-filled silence of my living room.

I snuck another peek over the couch at Danny. His brown hair was tousled over his forehead in a messy way from sleep, and the simple black V-neck shirt he wore allowed me to really see all his forearm tattoos.

There wasn't a trace of color anywhere. The black and gray artwork seemed random in both placement and style. There was his father's guitar tattoo on his forearm that he had shown Violet, done in more of a realism style. Then, there was a faded tribal tattoo further up on his inner left arm and a neo-traditional lion sticking out from his sleeve on his other arm.

I leaned in closer, trying to make out some of the fine-line tattoos that he seemed to have a lot more of. A small black rose on his wrist. An angel that looked like it was dropping from the heavens. A shattered compass was painted across his bicep. And ... the Deathly Hallows triangle?

He's a Harry Potter fan? No wonder I like him.

My eyes wandered over his arms, marveling at the immense detail that went into each tattoo and the strong bands of muscle beneath them.

Some small lettering tattooed just below his elbow caught my eye, but it was covered with the throw blanket I'd placed over him last night. Checking his face for any sign of consciousness, I reached over him and carefully lifted the corner of the chenille blanket to try and read it, but it was upside down and … possibly in another language?

I rose up onto my toes, my entire torso hovering above Danny as I frowned and squinted at the words. I pushed myself further, closer until my toes were barely touching the wood floor.

Vivamus, moriendum est, I mouthed the phrase silently.

"Let us live since we must die."

Danny's raspy words sent a jolt of terror through me as my socks lost any traction they'd once had on the ground beneath me.

I squeaked—or squawked—as I fell onto him, but I was too distracted by the way the arms I had just been admiring wrapped around me to notice. My legs were still hanging over the back of the couch while he cradled me.

"You and your daughter are very curious women." Danny's voice vibrated in his chest beneath me, and my eyes opened to meet his.

Somewhere along my embarrassing tip over my hot neighbor, I had squeezed my eyes shut to try and wake up from this nightmarish mistake. But now that I opened them again, it felt more like a dream.

His arms were warm and comforting, the scent of his cologne still lingering in the fabric of his shirt I was fisting.

Fisting?

And those two gorgeous blue eyes were boring into mine.

"Logan?" He drew his brows together the longer I stared at him, silently making an alarm go off in my head.

Say something, idiot.

"Good morning."

Nice.

"Mornin'." His lips twitched. "Can you tell me where I am and how I got here?"

"Oh, um …" I tried to wiggle myself free, but I wasn't in the easiest position to make a graceful getaway. "You're on my couch and …" I paused as I tried to push away from him again.

Danny noticed my struggle and lent me a hand. Threading his arm under my legs and cradling my torso with the other, he sat up and swiveled me over his lap so I could sit beside him. That quick of a motion seemed to do some damage to his head.

He moaned and held a hand to his head. "Never mind. I think I know how I got here."

I winced with him, knowing all too well the pain of a hangover.

He looked up at the coffee table, still holding the glass of water and medicine I'd left for him, and then peered over at me with an apology written on his face. "Was I an asshole? Please tell me I wasn't an asshole."

The smile I gave him eased the tension on his face. "No. You were quite the drunken gentleman. But I'm not sure I can call you saintly for showing up on my doorstep at two in the morning."

"Shit." He closed his eyes and shook his head. "I'm so sorry, Logan. I didn't wake Violet, did I?"

"No, but she'll be up soon." I nodded over my shoulder at the hallway leading to her room.

"Of course. I should go." He went to stand, but I caught his arm and led him back down.

"Take this first," I said, handing him the water.

He gave me a look I couldn't quite make out. He was either annoyed I was pushing it on him or surprised I cared enough to offer it.

His eyes softened as he searched my face. "Thank you."

I took a long inhale and let it out slowly while he tossed the entire glass back with the medicine in a few short seconds. I wiggled in my seat, preparing to ask him some questions, but as soon as I opened my mouth, he began to ask his own.

"What were you doing?" His voice was so deep that it made my lips part.

"What?"

"A second ago, when you were bending over the couch."

Heat rose to my cheeks. "I, uh, thought I saw a bug on you."

Danny chuckled deeply. "A bug, huh?"

"Yep," I lied. "I didn't want to kill it until I knew for sure."

"Is that why you seem so squirmy, or is it because I make you nervous?"

My heart did a little flip. "Nervous? Why would you make me nervous?"

He smiled. "You tell me."

I scoffed. "If you made me nervous, I wouldn't have let you in last night. You wouldn't have spent the night on my couch."

"That's because I make you feel the good kind of nervous. The kind that makes your skin heat and your hair stand on end. The kind that makes your heart beat faster as the rush of adrenaline sucks the air out of your lungs." He lifted a hand to the side of my neck and placed it there softly. "You see? Just like this."

I wasn't sure why I was letting him touch me, but I'd made no effort to stop him.

His thumb glided over the small knob on my throat, and I swallowed, feeling all of the things he'd just listed off and more. The skin on my arms was alive with chills, like I had just been hit with subzero temperatures, only my body felt like it was burning from the inside out. My breathing had kicked up too. But my pulse … ugh, it was beating out of my chest, and he could feel every single pathetic pitter-patter, giving me away.

"Okay, maybe you're right," I started. "You do make me nervous."

Danny's gaze heated at my admission, and he dropped his hand.

"But"—I shifted, putting some distance between us—"there is no *good kind of nervous* from my perspective. I know your type, Danny. I've shed a lot of tears over guys like you, and all they've taught me is that I'm damn good at picking myself up on my own. I don't want the butterflies and the rush of adrenaline. Those are all giant red flags for me. I want to feel safe and secure."

"That doesn't sound like much fun."

I shrugged, rolling my lips between my teeth.

"So, you've already got me all figured out then, huh?" He frowned.

"I know I didn't have one innocent reason to open that door last night, but I did anyway. And that's enough of a warning sign for me."

"You can't trust yourself to make good decisions?" The corner of his mouth slid up into a mischievous grin. "Or great ones?"

I shook my head. "If you knew who I used to be, you'd know the answer to that question."

His brow twitched at that. "I suppose showing up drunk on your doorstep didn't win me any points."

I scrunched my nose. "Not really."

"Sorry again."

"Why did you?"

"Come here? Oh, fuck if I know. But if I had to guess, I'm sure it wasn't far off from your reasons why you let me in."

The red-flagged goosebumps returned.

"Mommy?" Violet's small voice echoed from down the hall.

I swiftly pushed Danny over and covered him with the blanket, trying to hide him. "Hi, sweetie! You want some breakfast?" I asked, looking over the back of the couch.

She squeezed her stuffed porcupine to her side and nodded, wiping away the sleep in her eyes.

I could feel Danny silently laughing beneath my grip, and I had to stifle a laugh myself.

"What are you hungry for, baby?" I managed.

"Pancakes?" she asked, shuffling toward me.

I smiled, hoping to hide the panic on my face. "Okay. Want to go get the mixing bowl out for me? I'll be right there."

"Okay," she said.

As she walked into the kitchen, I pulled the blanket off Danny and began ushering him off the couch. His face was in tears from laughing.

"Hurry up before she sees you!" I urged.

He stumbled a few steps before he got his footing and then paused, holding his head again. "Ohh," he moaned.

I shushed him and kept pushing him toward the door.

"I'm going!" he whispered back.

We made it to the door when I heard Violet's giggle from the edge of the kitchen.

"What awe yew doing?"

Shit. We'd been discovered.

Danny pivoted and waved at Violet, but I was still facing the door, cursing under my breath.

"Danny!" Violet called, and then I heard her footsteps padding across the floor.

Danny knelt to get on her level. "Good morning, sweetheart."

"Mowning!" She rushed over, stopping just before she crashed into him.

My heart somersaulted on itself when I saw the grin on her face.

"Whatcha got here?" Danny asked her as he pinched her stuffed animal's nose.

She held the stuffed porcupine in his face. "Dis is Quiwiam. He's a pokeepine."

"Quilliam, huh? That's a clever name." He chuckled.

"She named it after her favorite one at the zoo. Isn't that right?" I smoothed the hair on the top of her head.

Violet nodded and hugged Quilliam to her chest tightly. "Where's yow guitaw?" she asked Danny.

He ran his fingers through his hair. "Believe it or not, I don't take it with me everywhere. I'm sorry, sweetheart."

She jutted her lip out in disappointment.

"I can bring it by next time and play for you and your mom. How's that sound?"

Next time?

Oh, I see what he's doing.

"Pwomise?" Violet fiddled with Quilliam.

Danny lifted his mischievous eyes to mine and then looked back down at Vi. "Anything for you."

"What awe yew doing hewe then? Did yew come to have bweakfast with us?"

His brows rose at the opportunity.

"Not today, Vi," I said.

Danny flinched at the firmness in my tone. "Yeah. You know, I came by to return that muffin pan of yours, but I completely forgot it at my house."

"Yew foegot it?" Her mouth dropped open like his lie was the most absurd mistake she'd ever heard.

He shrugged. "I'll just have to stop by another day, right?"

"You don't have to do that," I said. "We have plenty of pans."

We did have a lot, but I really wanted that one back. It was practically brand-new. But I could tell Danny was looking for any opportunity to come over again, and I wasn't about to hand them out to him if I could help it.

"Nonsense. How about tomorrow?" he asked.

"No," I answered too quickly, which piqued his interest. "I just mean, we have plans tomorrow."

"No, we don't." Violet frowned at me.

"Grandma and Papa are coming to visit, remember?"

She wouldn't remember because I'd never told her that.

Her face lit up. "They awe?"

I nodded.

"And you're not ready for me to meet the 'rents yet?" Danny quirked a brow and grinned at me. "I get it."

I narrowed my eyes at him. He was so frustratingly confident, and I wasn't sure if that was more of a flaw or a strength.

He stood, giving Violet's messy bed hair a shake to say goodbye before she headed back into the kitchen.

My hand reached for the doorknob, but Danny stepped closer and placed his hand on mine.

"What will it take?" he asked.

I shook my head, confused. "Wh-what?"

His eyes pierced into me. "To convince you to go out with me sometime?"

He was standing so close that his warmth covered me like a blanket, and I had the oddest desire to wrap myself up in it. Being near him gave me a thrilling rush and a sense of comfort all at once, and I wasn't sure what to do with it other than call it another red flag. Anything foreign to me right now couldn't be trusted, especially when it had me opening the door for strangers after dark. Even more so when that stranger was the bad-boy rock-star type I was extremely attracted to.

"You don't even know me."

My eyes fell to the ground, but he caught my chin and lifted my gaze to his.

"But I want to," he said.

I sighed. "Danny …"

"I want to know your favorite color and the way you take your coffee. I want to know what your laugh sounds like when you think something is really funny. I want to know what kind of music makes you want to dance and the kind of dessert you save room for at a restaurant." His cheek barely brushed mine as he leaned next to my ear. "I want to know what parts of your skin I can kiss to turn you on …"

My breath hitched as I waited for him to continue.

"And the breathless ways you can say my name when I tease you with my tongue."

"Danny …" I said his name again, but it came out ragged.

He pulled back enough for me to meet his gaze again. "Yeah, I'd imagine it sounds something like that."

I took a steady inhale to try and clear my head. "It's not going to happen, okay?"

"It could if you wanted it to."

"Mommy! I can't weach the fwowah!" Violet yelled from the kitchen, giving me a much-needed dose of reality.

"I'll be right there, baby!" I called back, tightening my grip on the door handle and sucking in some air.

Danny stepped aside so I could open the door.

"I'm just not interested, okay?"

He suppressed a smile. "You keep telling yourself that, beautiful."

I gritted my teeth and was about to argue with him when he finally took his leave.

Before I closed the door, he threw over his shoulder, "I'll be sure to bring that pan back, *neighbor*."

And when I knew he couldn't see me anymore, I smiled.

7

Logan

Two honks sounded from the driveway, signaling the arrival of my parents. Violet was on the couch, coloring, too absorbed in the cartoons on the television to notice.

"Vi, baby?" I called from the kitchen as I pulled a casserole dish from the oven. "Guess who's here!"

"Gwandma and Papa?" She perked up.

"Yep!"

I heard crayons scatter onto the floor as she took off, running for the front door. She flung the door open right as my mom was walking up. "Gwandma!"

"Hey, sweetie! Oh, how I've missed you!" My mother hugged Violet at her side with her free hand while the other supported a large glass salad bowl.

She'd taught me everything I knew about cooking during my pregnancy. Anything and everything I had a craving for, she insisted on teaching me to make on my own. It had made the time being "locked up" at home easier, and I was grateful to have a little knowledge in the kitchen, for Violet's sake. Not that Vi wasn't accustomed to pizza nights and frozen dinosaur nuggets on occasion. My mother had also taught me how important it was never to arrive empty-handed when someone invited you into their home. So, I wasn't surprised when she walked into the kitchen with her famous roasted pear salad, even after I told her not to bring anything.

"Perfect timing, Mom," I said, kissing her on the cheek. "I'm just warming the dinner rolls."

The small creases by her eyes deepened with her smile when she saw the Tuscan chicken casserole I'd prepared. "That looks wonderful, honey."

"Thanks. Where's Dad?" I asked.

"He's coming," she said. "He's just letting Moose stretch his legs in the front yard for a minute."

Violet jumped up and down. "Moose is hewe?"

My mother nodded down at her and avoided my questioning gaze.

With a giddy smile, Violet took off outside to meet them both. I could see a clear shot of Moose licking Violet's face over and over from the kitchen.

"Mom?"

She busied herself by becoming acquainted with my kitchen. "Yes, honey?"

"Why did Dad bring Moose along?"

It wasn't that I didn't like my parents' dog or wasn't okay with them bringing him over. The thing was, Moose was also my dad's old work partner—a retired police dog. He was the reason I had gotten caught so much when I was younger. It had been impossible to sneak anything illegal into my house without Moose alerting my dad. Which was why I spent so much of my time away from home.

My mother still hadn't met my gaze, which only grew my suspicions. "Oh, he just didn't want to leave him all cooped up at home. We weren't sure how long we would be gone."

I frowned. "You guys live twenty minutes away. I'm sure he would have been fine. Unless you guys were planning on spending the night? Which, if that's the case, I'll have to check with Vi to see if she's willing to give up her bed for you two."

She sighed at my sarcasm, tucking a piece of her short black hair behind her ear. "Logan …"

"Come on, Papa! I want to show you my woom!" Violet dragged my dad through the front door by the hem of his shirt.

He just laughed at her and followed her lead, waving at me as he rounded the corner of the hallway.

Moose came running in behind them, but when he crossed the threshold, his nose hit the ground, and he went to work.

"What is he doing?" I clenched my teeth.

My mom feigned ignorance while peering over my shoulder. "What do you mean?"

I crossed my arms at her. "Moose. He's sniffing every square inch of this place."

"It's just a perimeter check. He can't help it, dear. He was trained for this."

"And what exactly are you expecting him to find?"

"Nothing. Don't be ridiculous." She waved me off, but I couldn't help but watch Moose's determination with unease.

Of course, there would never be anything here for him to find, but that didn't mean it didn't hurt to see him looking, even if it was just out of habit.

My shoulders slumped as I dragged my bottom lip through my teeth. "Did you guys bring him here because you don't trust me?"

"Of course not, honey!" She rushed to my side but didn't deny it any more than that.

My mom was a terrible liar. She and I had that in common. Her tell had always been the squeakiness of her voice, and she knew it, so she usually tried to keep her words short.

"It was Dad's idea, wasn't it?"

She shook her head. "I told you, he—"

"What's for dinner, Lo?" Dad patted his stomach as he sauntered into the kitchen with a sticker of a bumblebee on the collar of his shirt. Violet loved her stickers. "I'm starvin'."

My gaze followed Moose until he disappeared down the hallway toward the bedrooms. I forced a smile up at my dad so he wouldn't see the hurt still lingering in my eyes. It must've worked because he didn't detect a hint of disappointment from me, though the man wasn't very empathetically aware most of the time.

My dad was the analytical type—a problem solver. Emotions were too unpredictable and complicated to ever try to figure them out. I thought that was why he had always wanted a boy. First with me and then when I'd had Violet. Not that he didn't love us both. I just often wondered if he would've gone through half the shit I'd put him through if he'd gotten the Logan he really wanted instead of me. His life would've been far less complicated—that was for sure.

"I made your favorite, Daddy," I told him.

His eyes lit up as he thanked me with a lukewarm pat on the shoulder, and then he found a seat at the head of the kitchen table.

Mom lingered by me for a moment until Violet skipped into the kitchen with Quilliam.

"I want to sit next to Gwandma!" Violet stated.

"Okay, okay. Go show Grandma to her chair, and I'll bring everything out."

My mom followed Violet to the table, and then I quickly set everything up to be served.

The sound of our silverware hitting our plates filled the room for the first few long minutes. Violet quickly broke up the monotony when she started humming a song between bites and dancing in her seat.

"After we finish, I can show you guys around the house if you want," I offered. I would've done a tour when they arrived, but I didn't want the food to get cold.

"What for, dear? We know our way around," Mom said dismissively.

Dad chuckled. "This was her sister's place, Lo."

"I know that. I just thought you'd like to see how I've decorated and what I have planned. I was going to turn the basement into—"

"I saw everything when I came in," he said, shoveling in another mouthful of casserole.

I stabbed a pear with my fork and sank further down into my seat.

My mom tilted her head toward Violet. "How do you like your new home, sweetie?"

"I wove it! My woom is so big! And theow's a pawk down the stweet Mommy took me to that has the best swings! I got up so high!"

Mom gave her a wide grin. "You did?"

Violet nodded with enthusiasm. "Oh! And we made cupcakes fow the neighbows. They have so many tattoos."

My pulse kicked up.

Violet looked over at me and then up at my mom, whispering, "Danny was hewe yestewday to bwing the pan back, but he fowgot it."

Mom giggled with a frown. "Why are you whispering, sweetie?"

"Because it's a seekwet, and you have to be quiet when you tell seekwets," Violet answered, cupping her hands around her mouth to better direct her whisper toward them.

I wanted to bury my head in my hands. I had told Violet to keep Danny's visit our little secret to avoid being grilled by my parents about why a boy was leaving our house so early in the morning. Apparently, Violet was still grasping the concept of what a secret was ... and I was slowly realizing I shouldn't rely on a three-year-old to keep mine.

"Care to explain what she's talking about, Logan?" My dad's somber expression sent a familiar chill down my spine.

I picked at my plate, fighting the urge to roll my eyes. "Our neighbor came by to say hello after we dropped off some cupcakes at their house. That's all."

"You're making friends, honey? Oh, that's wonderful," Mom added.

"And he has a guitaw! He's going to come ovah and pway fow me and Mommy!" Violet added.

Great.

A piece of chicken fell off my dad's fork as he paused mid-bite. His eyes narrowed. "How old is this neighbor of yours?"

"Oh, he's older." I nodded, trying to reassure my dad.

To be fair, I was almost certain Danny was older than me. At least he looked a bit older. Maybe only a couple of years, but still *older.* I didn't feel the need to elaborate that we were closer in age than I let on. It would be better if my dad thought there was a sixty-something-year-old who wanted to pay me and Violet a visit and play old blues songs instead of the gorgeous, tattooed guitarist who practiced on his porch, nearly naked, every morning.

My eyes remained fixed on my plate even though I could feel them both staring holes into my head.

"Anything I should be worried about, Lo?" Dad asked after a moment.

I shook my head and finally met his gaze. "He's harmless, Daddy." Luckily, the laugh that left my throat softened the crease between my dad's brows.

Moose cut the remaining tension in the room with a small whimper from under the table, and Violet snuck a piece of food down to him.

My dad tried to scold her but ended up cracking a smile instead. She knew she wasn't supposed to give Moose scraps, but it was so hard to deny him when he gave that puppy face look. I was much stealthier than Violet when I snuck a piece to him later after clearing off the table.

We talked and played a game of Uno before my mom volunteered to put Violet down for bed, which left me alone in the living room with my dad and a sleeping Moose.

"Did you have fun at the cabin?" I fiddled with my thumbs.

He nodded. "We did. Actually, your mom and I were thinking it would be fun to take Violet there before it gets too cold. What do ya think?"

I noticed he hadn't extended the invitation to me, but I wasn't surprised.

The last time I had been at the cabin was just after my high school graduation. Twelve of my not-so-close friends and I snuck up there to celebrate, and while I was passed out on a hammock by the lake, half of the cabin caught fire. Fortunately, everyone made it out unscathed. The firefighters said some outdated wiring had been the cause, but my father was always convinced I was to blame.

It took over a year, but my parents finally got the place restored and renovated. They talked and talked about how happy they were with the renovations, almost like the fire had done them a favor, but they didn't go up there the first couple of years after it was finished because they didn't trust me enough to leave me on my own. And then I got pregnant. It seemed ironic that they had this shiny new thing to dangle in my face—something I wasn't allowed to have because I'd screwed up—but they also didn't get to enjoy it themselves because of me.

No wonder they hated me so much back then.

"I figured it would help give you some time to get some work done," my dad added.

I shrugged. "I sold a couple of large prints at the gallery before we moved. I'm doing okay."

"That's great 'n' all, but you don't have a car, Lo. How do you expect to get anything done without a car?"

"Andre doesn't mind helping me out when I need it. And I'm saving up. I'm really close," I told him. And I was.

Some of my photographs sold for three to four thousand at a time, depending on the size of the print. That was huge for me compared to when I'd first started selling pieces for two to three hundred just a couple years ago. I sold some of my work online. But Jennifer, the owner of the Simonet Gallery downtown, had sold a few of my pieces over the last year, which had gotten me a lot of exposure. She wanted to see a full collection from me to possibly feature in my own show. I just hadn't decided yet what kind of collection I wanted to present to her. She had a lot of great artists, and I hadn't liked anything I'd come up with so far.

Dad shook his head. "Logan, come on."

"What?"

"I just want you to be realistic. Not every person with a camera and a good eye can make it out there. It wouldn't be such a bad idea to find another job, even if it's only for a little while." He tilted his head and hesitated before saying, "It's also not too late … I know you said you don't want to, but you can still put this place on the market. I know it would fetch a good price. You and Violet could use that money."

Anger rose in my throat. As I fought back the rude comments I desperately wanted to lay on him, my eyes began to burn with tears instead. "I don't need another job, and I'm not selling this house, Dad." My voice was shaky, but the tears stayed at bay. "I'm going to make this work, no matter what. I talked to Jennifer, and she said it's only a matter of time before I get my work exhibited at the gallery. I can do this, trust me."

I regretted it as soon as the words left my mouth. Those two little words were too much to ask of my father.

Trust me.

I hadn't just lost his trust long ago; I'd strung it up to the ceiling and beaten it with a baseball bat. There was nothing left of it, and I knew I'd never get it back. Ugh! I just wanted him to hear me. I wanted him to let me figure this out on my own. But most of all, I wanted him to stop worrying so much about me. He'd spent too much of his life doing it, and he had far too much gray hair for his age that I was responsible for.

"Okay, she's down for the count," my mom whispered from the hallway as she gently closed Violet's bedroom door. "Though she could be faking it because she fell asleep in the middle of my Kermit the Frog impression, and I wasn't doing a very good job."

Dad's gaze stayed on me for another moment before he smiled at his wife. "You want to get going, Char? It's getting late."

"Sure, honey. Did you ask her about taking Violet to the cabin?" Mom's eyes shifted between the two of us.

I hated the idea of being away from Violet for more than even a couple of hours, but in a weird way, they were offering to help me find some time to work. It wasn't all that easy to find a good spot to shoot with Violet running around. I usually just ended up taking pictures of her instead because she could be quite the character. I also knew that my parents missed having her around.

"Maybe just a weekend?" I finally said.

Dad's lips stretched into a small grin. "We'll take whatever you give us."

It was strange having the power over the relationship they had with my daughter after going so long without it. I hoped they didn't think they couldn't still be as much a part of Violet's life just because we had moved away.

"You know you guys can see Vi whenever you want, right?"

There was a hint of relief that washed over my mom's face when I said that. "Maybe we can try doing this dinner thing once a week too? I'm not used to going so long without seeing my girls."

"Sure, Mom."

Dad rubbed his hands on his knees and stood. "Thanks for dinner, Lo. I'll check with work and get back to you on a weekend that'll work best to go to the cabin."

"We can just talk about it next week over dinner. How's that sound?" my mom asked, grabbing her things.

I nodded in agreement and gave them both hugs on their way out. Moose kissed me on the cheek and followed them into the cool night air. My sweatshirt kept me warm enough from the breeze as I waited for them to back out of my driveway.

As I waved them off, my eyes landed on the light illuminating Danny's front porch across the street.

Butterflies came alive in my stomach when I heard the faint sound of a guitar as my parents' engine faded away in the distance, and the neighborhood became quiet again.

I couldn't see *him* from here, which probably meant he couldn't see me either. So, I closed my eyes and sat there, listening to the soothing melody for a while.

8

Danny

It was two months until the tour, and I was chomping at the bit to get onstage again. I missed the chaos and the adrenaline of walking out from behind the curtain and hearing our names being chanted. I missed playing music that we had spent hours, days, and even months writing and getting to hear the fans screaming every lyric back at us. I'd never felt more at home than being onstage with my three bandmates and my guitar in my hands. It was the best feeling on earth. It was what I lived for.

When I was younger, I had seen my dad play every instrument under the sun. But when he picked up his guitar, he couldn't get me to leave his side until, one day; he surprised me with my very first lesson. Avery was taught piano, and I was taught how to play guitar. My mother hated how loud the house was all the time, but my dad always encouraged it. When he died during my sophomore year of high school, our house had never sounded so quiet. So empty. Avery had stopped playing back then, but me? You couldn't tear my guitar out of my arms.

I wished he were still here to see how far I'd made it. I'd give anything to look out into the crowd of fans one day and see my dad standing front and center with his hands in the air and that smile of his plastered across his face.

My eyes landed on the old guitar case propped in the back of the room. I took it out to look at it sometimes, but holding my dad's guitar felt like holding a rare diamond over the edge of a cliff. It was beautiful, but I was scared I'd do something to it that would change how he'd left it.

"Where'd you go, Danny boy?" Liam snapped his fingers at me from behind the soundboard.

I shook my head and grabbed the pick I'd been holding between my teeth and strummed a few chords. "My bad, guys. I'm ready to go again."

Adjusting the guitar in my hands, I waited in the empty booth and listened through the headphones for my cue.

Lexie, Liam, and Tic listened with me, bobbing their heads to Tic's drumbeats in the background.

Liam's recorded vocals broke off at the end of the chorus, and my fingers curled around the neck of my Fender Stratocaster guitar. It was a short solo I had to play for this track, but I made it count and shredded the electric chords until Liam's vocals came back in for the next verse.

"Yeah, I like the sound of that a lot better. The tone is a bit darker than the Gibson," I said as they cut the playback. I glanced over at the guitar stand holding my two other electric guitars I had tested out on my first couple of run-throughs. "What do you guys think?"

Tic stuck his tongue out and beat his sticks on the back of Lexie's chair with excitement.

Liam just grinned and shook his head. "Fuck, man. I don't think we need to run that again. You nailed it."

Lexie nodded in agreement.

"Don't I fuckin' know it." I smirked. "Let's do one more from the top for good measure though."

Liam nodded and hit some buttons on the panel to cue up the start of the song. He and I were the perfectionists of the group, so it was no surprise to anyone whenever I demanded another run-through.

"You okay hitting some vocals right after? I think we can wrap this one up today." Liam looked at me through the glass.

"Yeah. Let me have a smoke real quick, and then I can knock that out," I said, getting my fingers ready again.

When I finished recording, I switched places with Liam so he could tweak one of the high notes at the end he wasn't happy with while I found my way outside on the porch.

I cupped my hand over the lighter to combat the wind as I lit the end of my cigarette and sat on the front step. The overcast made the midafternoon sky dreary and gray, and the dry ground begged for the drink of rain that was coming.

I peered over at Logan's house. It was out of habit at this point. I hadn't seen her come or go the last few days, apart from the older couple I had seen leaving the night before last.

My cigarette was halfway through when a delivery truck pulled up at the end of Logan's driveway. The man inside loaded up a dolly full of various-sized boxes, wheeled them up, and stacked them by her door. As soon as he drove off, the front door of her house swung open, and Logan walked out, picking up a box that was much heavier than it was for the deliveryman.

Her stance wavered, but she managed to carry it inside, leaving the door cracked open. There were over a half-dozen more, and I wasn't about to watch her struggle with the rest.

The sky finally opened up, painting the pavement leading to her house in dark-colored spots. The tops of my shoulders were already soaked, strands of hair matted to my face when I reached her front steps. I tested each box sitting in front of her door, searching for the heaviest. When I found it, Logan stood in the doorway and greeted me with a quizzical brow.

"Danny. Hi." Her velvety tone sent a shiver down my spine. "What are you doing here?"

"I saw a tower of boxes and figured you could use a hand." I flashed a wide grin.

Her hair was pulled back into a clip, making it easier to take in the soft edges of her face.

A pink flush covered her cheeks as she looked at me.

"May I?" I nodded at her position that was blocking the entry.

After a second, she moved aside.

"Where do you want it?" I asked, glancing back at her for direction.

She carried a lighter box in her hands. "Basement, please."

"Danny!" Violet popped up from the couch.

I threw her a wink. "Hey, sweetheart! How are you?"

"Good," she answered. "Still no guitaw?"

"I haven't forgotten," I said.

Violet crossed her arms at me.

I chuckled. "You name the time and place."

"Wight now!" she protested, and my heart squeezed a little.

Logan shook her head at her. "Vi, that's not how we ask for things. Remember?"

"Sowwy, Danny."

"Danny is just helping Mommy today. Okay?"

She whined and disappeared into the couch cushions.

"I'm sorry," Logan said. "It's this door here."

I rounded the corner and followed her down the staircase to the basement. She pulled on a string hanging from the ceiling, illuminating the small concrete room.

"Cozy," I said, raising a brow at the blacked-out windows and tarp on the floor. "Didn't know we had a serial killer in the neighborhood."

She followed my gaze around the room and giggled. And, *fuck*, did I love the sound. It was light. Sweet.

Logan ran a hand over her face as if she was trying to wipe away the smile I'd just put there. "Not a serial killer."

"It's cool. I'll keep my doors unlocked either way." My mouth quirked up, and I winked.

"It's a darkroom," she said, stating the obvious.

"Yeah, I got that."

"No." She laughed again. "Like, for photography. I can't have any light in here when I'm processing film."

I tilted my head. "You're a photographer?"

"Sometimes." Her prideful smile contradicted the shy words she muttered.

"That's amazing, Logan. Can I see some of your work?"

"Help me bring down the rest of the boxes?" she offered as a trade.

"Of course."

When all the boxes were stacked in two piles at the bottom of the stairs, she walked to the table pushed against one of the walls, and rummaged through some things. "Thanks for the extra set of hands, by the way. You didn't have to do that."

"Just helping out a neighbor," I said playfully.

She threw me a look that hinted at flirtatiousness.

I dragged my gaze from her legs to the sliver of skin between her leggings and T-shirt that showed while she stretched up to reach the shelf above.

"Sorry, this place is a mess. I'm still trying to organize everything—ah! Here's some." She lowered back down onto her bare heels and waved me over.

"You really need to stop apologizing for everything." My boots thudded across the floor until I reached her side, taking the printed photographs from her hands.

The way her eyes lit up as she told me about each one was mesmerizing. Where she had been when she took it. What lens she had used. Something about the exposure and other shit I couldn't understand. But I didn't dare interrupt her with questions with the way she was glowing.

She was so caught up in telling me about her photographs that I didn't think she realized how she had pressed the side of her body into mine.

I clung to her warmth. Scared that if she noticed, she'd pull away and I'd never feel it again.

She peered up at me through thick lashes with a waiting look.

Shit. She'd asked a question.

I blinked. "I'm sorry, what?"

Her gaze dropped to my mouth and then flicked back up to my eyes with a smile. "What do you think?"

What do I think?

My immediate thoughts were about her lips and how badly I wanted to know if they felt as soft as they looked. Or what they'd feel like while running between my teeth. I quickly found my sanity and looked back at the photos she'd laid out. They really were incredible. So much emotion in such simplistic places and things we walked past every day.

"You really have an eye for this, Logan. Like, wow."

"Thanks." She smiled softly. "I have an analog camera and a digital so I can shoot and print however I see fit, but I like using the analog so I can develop the pictures myself down here. It's sort of therapeutic for me, being more hands-on."

I reached in front of her and picked up an image of a man sitting in a park alone with a bouquet of wilted flowers. "This one's interesting. It should be sad, but he's smiling. Why do you think he's smiling?"

She shrugged. "I'm not sure, but I like to make up theories in my head whenever I start to wonder."

"And what do you think this guy's story is?"

Logan tilted her head up at me and searched my face. "I'd like to know what you see."

It was hard to tear my eyes from her when she looked at me the way she was, but I eventually looked back at the photograph. "I don't know. I don't think I'll be very good at it." I shook my head, staring down at the black-and-white photo in my hand.

"That's okay. It's not going in a book or anything. Use your musician brain." She bumped my shoulder as encouragement. "Don't songs tell stories? If this image had lyrics, how would you write them?"

She made me nervous. I wasn't sure the last time a girl had made me nervous. It was just a fucking question about a picture, for Christ's sake. But I liked that she understood how the creative mind worked. When she described it like writing a song, it was easier for me to envision his story, even if it wasn't real.

"Well, I'm not about to write a song on the spot. Sometimes, it comes to me that easily, but not lately." I shook my head.

She lightly touched my arm with her hand, sending fucking shivers up to my shoulder. My confidence around her grew shaky, and I pinched my eyes shut to try and gain it back.

"All right. Maybe he bought the love of his life her favorite flowers like he did every Sunday or Monday or any day of the week, I guess."

"Okay …" Logan listened intently, waiting for me to continue.

"Only he went home that day, looked her in the eyes, and didn't see the person he had fallen in love with all those years ago. He saw the love had faded and was replaced by snarky words, resentment, and a longing for happiness. She had stopped appreciating the little things he did for her to show his affection and just started expecting them. Never returning the love he selflessly gave to her every day." I paused, taking in her smile. "Maybe he took the flowers for himself and left. He walked for hours with them in his hand, feeling the weight of the world lift off his shoulders and a sense of freedom finally opening his lungs enough to breathe. Until he found a bench in a park that he stopped at to rest his tired legs." I looked down at her with a smile. "And this beautiful girl with a camera in her hands walked by at that moment and took his picture."

Logan dug her teeth into the pad of her thumb as her smile grew.

"What? Is that stupid?" I asked.

"Not at all!" she quickly reassured me. "I think that was brilliant, actually. I wasn't expecting such detail, but I don't know why—I'm not surprised either. This is why I love photographs. I could look at them all day and see different things."

I breathed out a laugh and set the picture down. "For the record, I don't have a wife that fell out of love with me or anything."

She laughed, and my chest felt lighter.

"I don't have anyone, really," I added.

Her soft gaze found mine again, and her smile faded.

Our bodies were still gently pressed against one another, and her body heat only seemed to get hotter as the seconds passed.

I turned ever so slightly into her, my knuckles grazing hers. She didn't pull away.

"What are your favorite flowers?" I asked, inching closer.

"I don't know if I should tell you. For all I know, you might start showing up at my door every day with a bouquet in your hands," she teased.

"Not *every* day." I cocked my head. "Seriously, what are they?"

Her fingers barely threaded through mine as she glanced up at the ceiling and then back at me with a soft grin. "Violets."

I smiled back. Of course they were.

As if the thought of her could make her appear, Violet's tiny footsteps shuffled down the wooden steps.

"Mommy?"

Logan swiftly pulled away, her cheeks flushed. Running her fingers through the ends of her raven-black hair, she swallowed and greeted Violet, "Yeah, baby?"

My hand flexed at my side, missing her warmth.

Violet hopped into the room. "I'm hungwy!" she complained, carrying out the *Y*.

"Did you already eat the plate of snacks I'd set out for you?" Logan asked as if she already knew the answer.

She batted her lashes innocently. "No."

Logan folded her hands in front of her.

While they argued over food, my phone dinged in my pocket with an incoming text.

> *Liam: Dude, this is the longest smoke break in the history of smoke breaks.*

Shit, I'd forgotten about the song we were finishing up. Another text came through.

> *Tic: Where you at, man?*

I sighed and quickly typed out a response to them both. Violet headed back upstairs as I shoved my phone into my pocket. "I've got some work to finish up in the studio, but I'm really glad I got to see some of your photos."

She bit her lip and started walking toward the stairs. "Oh, yeah. Thank you again for your help in bringing everything down."

I was following her up when I got an idea. "Hey, do you and Violet want to come hang out with us while we do some recording?"

She paused at the top steps.

"Lexie and Tic are there," I continued. "And I don't think you've met Liam yet. It'll be fun."

"I don't know if that's a good idea. I mean, do you really want a three-year-old in your studio?"

"I already work with toddlers." I chuckled. "I think she'd love it."

I saw the conflict in her eyes, and I wished I knew her better so I would know why it was there. There had to be a way to gain her trust.

"Thank you," she finally said. "But not today."

I nodded, trying not to seem too disappointed. "Okay. Well, I'll try and bring that pan by later. Oh, and my guitar. Don't want to let Violet down, ya know?" I smirked, rounding the corner of the hallway.

"Bye, Danny." Logan emphasized her words, ushering me out.

I laughed and waved at Violet as I took my leave.

Heading back across the street, I was glad the rain had let up. Tiny droplets sprinkled onto my face, cooling my heated skin. There was something about being around Logan that lit me on fire. She was like the sun, covering me in an addictive warmth, even from a distance, and her smile cast light on my shadows. I just feared that maybe I was her moon and we weren't destined to meet at all.

I was nearing my driveway when I heard my name being called. I twisted my head and saw Logan holding Violet's hand on her front porch. My frown softened as she glanced down at her daughter and then back up at me with a shrug.

There was a look of defeat on her face as they both scurried out into the rain to catch up with me, and I felt that warmth growing in my chest again the closer she got.

Maybe I was gaining her trust after all.

9

Logan

"Took you long enough!" I heard a deep voice say when Danny reached the bottom of the stairs before us.

The room was organized chaos. Instruments and equipment were scattered around the room, carpeted in red and black rugs overlaying each other. A giant board with a million buttons sat in the very center, in front of a windowed booth encasing a microphone hanging from the ceiling.

My heart started to pound as three pairs of eyes landed on me and Violet as we came into view.

"I brought some friends," Danny told the only pair of eyes I didn't recognize. They were dark brown, matching his tousled hair.

He was good-looking, just like the other three, and I suddenly felt very average in comparison.

Violet shyly hid her face in my hip.

"Logan! Hey!" Lexie got up from her chair and wrapped me in a quick hug like we'd known each other for years.

Violet's eyes lit up at her bright pink hair as she peeked around me. "Wow! I wike yow haow!"

"Thanks, cutie!" Lexie bent down to her level, letting her run her fingers through the silky strands.

Tic waved from a swiveling stool, giving Violet a smile.

She giggled and waved back, quickly gaining her confidence back. "Hi, Tic!"

I looked up at the tall one again and extended my hand. "You must be Liam? I'm your new neighbor. This is my daughter, Violet."

His face lit up with recognition, like he already knew me, and clasped his hand around mine. "Ah, yes. It's nice to put a face to the name finally." He dipped his chin down at Violet. "And you, Violet."

"Awe yew guys going to pway music fow us?" She looked up at him, hopeful.

Liam glanced sideways at Danny. "Well, we're working on some stuff for our new album that hasn't been released yet ..."

Danny rolled his eyes and shrugged out of his flannel shirt, giving me a nice view of his arms. "C'mon, Liam. Look at her face."

Liam flicked his eyes back down to Violet, and I could see him giving in to her doe-eyed plea.

I swallowed back some embarrassment. "We don't want to bother you guys. Danny just offered to play for her and—"

"It's no bother at all," Tic chimed. "Right, Liam?"

Violet held his stare.

His face slowly stretched into a smile. "Depends. Can you keep a secret, Violet?"

She nodded her head with enthusiasm, and a burst of laughter escaped me.

Liam raised his brow at me.

I cleared my throat and shrugged. "Well, one of us can."

He chuckled. "All right, Danny boy. Wanna pick up where we left off?"

Danny pulled up a couple of chairs for me and Violet and nodded at his bandmate. "That's fine. Maybe we can squeeze in some of the next track too."

"Look at you, being an overachiever," Liam said.

Lexie scoffed. "More like a show-off."

Danny walked into the booth opposite the control panel–looking thing and covered his ears with a pair of headphones.

"Everyone, watch your language around the little lady," Tic warned.

Violet stared widely at all the instruments surrounding us and then danced in her chair.

"Is this pretty exciting, baby?"

"Yeah!"

"Just remember not to touch anything without permission," I said.

"Okay, Mommy." Violet frowned at Danny standing in front of the microphone. "Doesn't he need his guitaw?"

Lexie peered over at us. "Not for this. He's recording some vocals."

"Wait. Danny sings too?" I didn't mean to sound so surprised.

You know how they call people triple threats when they can act, sing, and dance? Well, I was quickly discovering that Danny was *all* the threats. My God, the man was *dripping* with sex. I could wash my clothes on the vast hills and grooves of his abs that he had put on display the first day we met. He played guitar. He could apparently sing too. Not to mention the tattoos and the killer blue eyes that made me weak in the knees. His confidence, though, might be the most threateningly attractive thing about him. I craved to be around him long enough in hopes that it might wear off on me.

"Liam here is our singer, but Danny helps with backup on some of the tracks," Tic clarified.

"He's good too," Liam added as he pushed a button on the board.

The playback of drums, guitar, bass, and Liam's singing cut through the room.

Goosebumps covered my arms. It sounded incredible.

Violet squealed and bounced at my side, waiting for Danny as he stared at the sheet of music in front of him.

His blue eyes disappeared for a moment as he filled his lungs with air. And then he parted his lips and sang.

Faded jeans and twisted lies
I've become a passenger in those eyes
You take away all the air I breathe
And drive me wild with the way you tease

I was screwed.

So totally screwed.

His silky tenor invaded me and turned all my insides to complete and utter mush. I gripped the edge of my chair to keep steady as I listened to his breathy, strong voice. I thought I'd be okay until he flicked his eyes up to mine.

He smirked like he could see the effect he was having on me.

Was I that obvious?

Liam's piercing vocals came in for another verse over the recording. When they cut out again, Danny repeated the same lyrics as before, like a haunting echo I wanted to listen to repeatedly.

The music became more intense with heavier drums and guitar when the song was nearly finished. Danny squeezed his eyes shut and howled, distancing himself from the microphone as he did it. And then as the song faded out, he hummed and moaned these raspy and sexy lower notes that made my palms sweaty and mouth dry.

Danny ran his hands through his hair as he waited for the band to approve his take. I couldn't imagine it sounding better, but Liam and he decided to give it one more go, proving me wrong.

Lexie twisted in her chair when Danny finished. "What did you think?"

"I ... I loved it." I blinked, trying to find the words.

Danny grinned widely and pulled the headphones from his ears before leaving the booth.

"You look pleased with yourself." Tic nodded at him.

Danny's gaze met mine, and then he winked. "I'm not the only one pleased with my performance."

My skin ignited from his stare.

"Right, well, I think we got it," Liam said. "Well done, guys. I'll send this over to the label to get a final word, but I think this might be our first single off the album. What do you guys say?"

"Label?" I blinked. "So, you guys are, like, legit?"

All four band members turned their heads to me.

"Oh gosh. I-I don't mean that in a bad way. Of course, you guys are legit. But I didn't know you, uh …"

Lexie gave me a look as if she thought my ignorance was adorable.

"She doesn't know about the band?" Liam's brow arched.

Danny shrugged. "So what?"

"Don't tell me you're not a fan of rock music, Logan." Lexie jutted out her bottom lip.

"No, I am …"

"She woves wock music!" Violet nodded with enthusiasm.

Tic chuckled, clearly amused.

I frowned. "What's so funny?"

"Nothing. It's just … you're the first girl Danny's ever been with since we took off that hasn't known about his … career," Lexie clarified.

"Whoa, we're not—" I began to argue.

"Guys, can we not?" Danny's face twisted with annoyance.

My eyes shot to his, searching for an explanation.

Was it that absurd to not know who they were? Come to think of it, I'd never even asked *who* they were. I didn't know their faces. At least they weren't plastered on billboards or television. But the main question lingering on the tip of my tongue was why they'd made it seem like girls only got with Danny for his talent with a guitar. I'd only known him for a little while now, but I knew there was so much more to him than that. If anything, his career as a musician was what scared me the most about this attraction I kept trying to fight. And if they were really as famous as they were making themselves out to be, maybe that red flag was even bigger than I'd thought.

I decided to ask the simpler question. "What's your band name?"

Danny lifted the side of his mouth. "We're called A Quiet Peril."

A Quiet Peril. I'd heard that name before, but I couldn't put my finger on exactly where or how I knew it.

But then it hit me.

"You guys aren't the ones that had that song 'Hollow Again,' are you?"

Danny nodded modestly.

"So, you have heard of us?" Lexie smiled.

I shook my head, surprised. "I've heard that so many times on the radio. You must've hit charts with that, right?"

Danny nodded again.

"We've had other songs on the radio too." Liam lifted his shoulders.

"If you pway on the wadio, does that mean you guys awe famous?" Violet asked.

"Not really." Danny grinned down at her. "There are just some people who know who the four of us are."

That was the type of thing only famous people would say.

"Some? Try four hundred seventy thousand." Lexie scoffed. "That's just our online followers. Far more people listen to us than that."

My eyes rounded.

"Way to be modest, Lex," Liam murmured.

She rolled her eyes. "What's the point in that? We're amazing, and we worked damn hard to get here. We have fans all over the world, not just here. Spain, Denmark, Australia, Korea, Germany … I can't wait until we can do a world tour."

Tic tapped his drumsticks on the back of Liam's chair, nodding in agreement.

World tour?

My head swarmed with questions and curiosity, but the first thing I thought to ask wasn't even near the top of the list. "Why do you guys all choose to live … here?"

"It used to be Tic's mom's house until we saved up enough and bought it from her. This house is kind of the start of when we began to take off." Danny chuckled. "Where do you expect us to live? Hollywood Hills?"

"I don't know," I said. "The suburbs of Silicon Valley don't exactly scream rock-band territory. I just thought you guys would need to be closer to wherever your label is. Maybe have more security? Besides, don't you eventually want your own place? Or do you like being around each other twenty-four/seven?"

Danny picked up an electric guitar from a stand in the corner of the room. "It's worked so far. You know what they say—*don't mess with success.*"

Tic and Liam exchanged glances.

"Why don't you want them to wive by us, Mommy?" Violet peered up at me with a frown.

"Yeah, *Mommy?*" Lexie rolled her tongue over her bottom lip and then giggled.

Danny stepped in front of Lexie and flashed a wide smile at me. "I know why."

I narrowed my eyes at him.

"It's because I make her nervous," he said, threading himself through the strap of the guitar.

"What's that mean, Mommy?" Violet asked.

I tried not to smile as his blue irises taunted me. "Nothing, Vi."

His gaze finally dropped to Violet. "You ready to hear some guitar, sweetheart?"

She brought her hands to her face. "Wiwwy?"

"Really. A promise is a promise, and I always keep my word," he told her before giving me another cocky grin. He strolled into the booth again and slid his concentration face back on.

Violet stood and waited as the next song began, sans the vocals. I guessed that Liam hadn't had his turn in the booth for this one yet. It was exciting, getting to watch the process of making a song right in front of me.

Danny's hand choked the neck of his guitar while the other strummed through the tight strings in a leisurely rhythm. Tic's drums began, and Danny bobbed his head to the beat until his playing became faster and more intricate. Soon, he was completely consumed by what he was doing, closing his eyes and moving his hands like he was possessed by some sort of rock god. It was fascinating and sexy to watch.

There was something about the way his fingers worked and made the muscles in his corded forearm dance that caused my breath to catch in my throat. As his skilled fingers moved down the neck of the guitar and the high-pitched notes wailed through the speakers, I had to press my thighs together in my seat to fight off the throbbing between them. I'd never been turned on by a guitar before, but, *damn*, the sound was perfection.

I had known Danny was special since the moment I'd met him—hell, maybe I had known from the moment I heard him that day I moved in across the street—but I hadn't been prepared for this. For how special he truly was. It wasn't about how well he could play his guitar. It was the way he came alive when he did. I believed there was something out there for everyone. Something that was like a light switch in your soul that flicked on when you found it and made everything brighter. This was Danny's. It was undeniable.

My jaw ached with a smile as the song came to an end.

Danny dropped his shoulders and tilted his head back before giving me a crooked-smile look that, under other circumstances, could be perceived as postorgasmic bliss.

The dull throbbing returned.

Liam pushed down one of the headphones from his ear and spoke into the microphone. "Well, that was fu—" He paused before cursing, glancing over his shoulder at Violet. "That was great, Danny boy. We should invite your company more often. Want to run it again for good measure?"

Danny looked at his bandmates for a second before shifting his focus to me. His eyes trailed down my body and back up slowly, making me fidget in place. "Nah, I think I nailed it."

I bit my cheek hard to keep from smiling back at him.

"Cool. Can we pack it up for the day? I'm starving," Lexie complained. "Where's Nikko with the food?"

"He's on his way," Tic said, holding up his cell phone.

Liam lifted a chin over at me. "Would you and Violet like to join us? Our manager will be here soon with pizza and beer. There will be more than enough."

"Violet's lactose intolerant," Danny said, exiting the booth. "But we can give him a call, and he can pick something else up for her."

Violet clapped her hands over her head as Danny approached the two of us. His breathing was slightly heavier, and a bead of sweat trickled down his temple.

I swallowed the dry lump in my throat. "That's really nice of you to offer, but—"

"What's this?" Danny looked at Violet's arms stretching out for him. "Do I get a hug?"

I watched as Danny twisted the guitar backward behind him, and he wrapped my daughter up in his arms. Violet had only ever reached for two men in my life—my dad and Andre. Now, I had to add Danny to that short list, and my chest tightened as I did so.

When he let her go, he ruffled her hair, and she giggled. "Thanks for that, sweetheart. Did you like the song?"

Violet beamed up at him like he was her favorite person in the whole world. "Yes!"

Danny shifted a step closer toward me, meeting my stare. "What did you think, Logan?"

My heart hammered in my ribs, and I dropped my eyes to the floor, too intimidated to meet his gaze this close when my body was still buzzing.

Then, there was pressure under my chin, guiding my head back up.

Danny dropped his hand and asked me again, "Logan?"

"I really liked it," I answered, but it came out breathier than I'd wanted.

He lifted his lips. "Good."

As if he could sense that I was close to breaking, he stepped back a foot, giving me space to think straight.

"What do you say? Want to join us?" he asked.

I shook my head. "Not tonight. I've still got some work to do to get my darkroom up and running."

His smile grew, and he shook his head, like he'd expected me to decline his offer. "Okay, what are your plans for next Friday? We're having some friends over to celebrate our album release. It'll be fun. You're welcome to bring some of your friends if you want."

I wasn't sure if it was the chaos of the studio, the music, or Danny, but my senses were overwhelmed.

Even though I shouldn't have said the next words, I gave in. "I'll … think about it."

I knew it didn't seem like much, but I figured giving Danny even a glimpse of hope was the same as giving him a definite yes, anyway. But I wasn't quite ready to commit to going. The look in his eyes made me realize my theory was correct, and I suddenly felt a switch turn on somewhere inside me that I couldn't remember ever turning off.

10

Danny

We finished recording the last song of the album and quickly sent it off to the record label by the end of the week. They weren't happy with how late we had pushed our deadline, but they'd come to expect it from us at the same time. No matter how many times they begged us to fly in and record at their studio, we always refused. We liked having a sense of control over our music and the comfort and ease that came with being able to do it on our own time, in our own space. It was … simpler. And with how chaotic things got with touring, the industry, and our rising popularity, we wanted to hold on to the simple things for as long as we could. I knew it wouldn't last forever—nothing ever did—but that was a discussion for another time.

"Dude, when are you going to give her up?" Liam asked, catching me staring across the street at Logan's front door.

"What do you care?" I flicked the butt of my cigarette at him, and he flinched out of the way, giving me the middle finger before returning his hands to his guitar.

"At some point, it's just stalking," he said with a lift of his brow. "And she might not find it as hot as you did with that girl who broke into our house to watch you sleep last year."

My arms locked across my chest, and I snarled, "Shut the fuck up. I'm not stalking her."

I wasn't. Was I?

"I just … want to see what all this chemistry between us is about."

He paused from playing. "You really think something's there?"

"I do." I nodded my head. "She's just trying to find a reason not to trust me, and I'm not sure why."

"You're not sure why?" Liam breathed out a laugh. "You don't have a great track record of keeping a girlfriend, Danny boy."

"She doesn't know my history," I retorted.

"And you don't know hers," he countered. "Maybe it's not you. She could have a problem trusting anyone. If that's the case, you might have to wait until she decides to come to you."

My jaw worked.

"I know your impatient ass hates that idea."

I did. But he might've had a point. I didn't want to push her too far and scare her off. She liked me. I was sure of it. Well, the odds were in the high nineties, at least. I just had to convince her I was worth her time. Her trust.

I quickly stood and swiped my car keys off the table.

Liam held his hands out. "Where are you going?"

"Out," I said. "I'll be back in time to talk tour shit; don't worry."

My knee bounced as I stared at the floor, pretending to pay attention to Nikko's breakdown of the different venues we would be playing at in the coming months, schedules for sound check, and … some curfew bullshit?

Yeah. Not happening.

"Danny, you know this is for you, right?" Nikko's gaze fixed on me when he noticed a disgusted look on my face.

"I'm fucking twenty-seven years old," I stated as if that meant anything more to him than saying I was *ten* years old.

"And I had to talk the police out of arresting you for indecent exposure when you went skinny-dipping in Lake Minnetonka."

"That was two years ago!" I said.

His facial expression didn't change.

"Oh, come on. We played at First Avenue. I had to. It was an initiation," I defended.

Tic raised a beer at me. "It was pretty funny watching the three policemen trying to catch you while you covered your junk with one of their hats."

I grinned and gave Tic a nod.

"Yeah, how about that night in Dallas?" Nikko added. "I wasn't laughing when I had to pick you up at three a.m. outside of a strip club after you threw up on some girl's tits."

I winced, trying not to find that fuzzy memory amusing. We had learned a valuable lesson that day—don't put Lexie in charge of ordering drinks. I still couldn't look at vanilla vodka without gagging.

"You were laughing about it the next day—don't lie, man," Liam raised a brow at Nikko, coming to my defense.

"Memories," I sang out in a horrible key, trying to get Nikko to loosen up.

He slammed his tablet down and pinched the bridge of his nose. I wasn't sure why he was getting so worked up over this—it wasn't like him. Sure, touring was stressful, and I was glad I wasn't in charge of much more than myself, but it was also fun as hell. He had a lot to manage, but he still went out drinking with us on occasion and got laid whenever he wanted.

Lexie tossed her hair over her shoulder and shook her head at our manager. "C'mon, Nikko. It's not that serious."

He hit the heel of his fist on the table in front of us. "I'm not fucking dealing with it on this tour. I don't have the fucking time or the fucking patience. Curfew. All of you."

Lexie scoffed. "Okay, *Dad.*"

The four of us eyed each other, clearly in agreement that we weren't taking this curfew idea seriously. But we kept our mouths shut and listened to the rest of Nikko's lecture. It wasn't really a lecture, but it felt like one. It was all the same shit as our previous tours, only slightly larger venues and bigger crowds. I didn't need to concern myself with writing down what city I was going to be in one day versus the next. As long as I was on the tour bus the morning after a show, they could trust I'd be in the right place for the next one.

As we wrapped up our meeting and signed some albums for a few lucky fans who had entered a radio contest, I was itching to see if the flowers I'd left outside Logan's door were still there.

It felt so fucking lame, but whatever. I'd bought Logan flowers. It took three different shops to find a place that sold violets, but when I showed up at her house, she wasn't there. Not knowing the proper etiquette for what to do in that situation—because I had never bought a girl flowers before— I'd left them on her welcome mat.

That was three miserable hours ago.

I wasn't sure what I was expecting to happen when she got them. I didn't think I was expecting anything at all really. But when I looked out the window and saw the flowers were gone, I realized all I wanted was to have been able to see her face when she found them there. Had they made her smile? Did she know they were from me? Fuck. For all I knew, they could be sitting at the bottom of her trash bin.

Liam appeared at my side. "Maybe you should've gotten roses or lilies?"

I pinned him with a glare.

"I'm just joking, man. I'm sure she loved 'em." He patted my shoulder.

I nodded, appreciating his attempt at easing my thoughts. My gaze returned to her front door.

"Remember what I said, Danny. Let her come to you."

Before he could even finish, I found myself backing away from the window, my feet already carrying me to the front door.

Liam sighed, shaking his head. "Anyone ever tell you you're terrible at taking advice?"

I ran my bottom lip through my teeth and smiled. "I'll let you know when I need some."

11

Danny

"Uh, hi, sir. I'm Danny." I held my hand out to the man who had answered Logan's door instead of her.

He took it in a firm grasp. Almost too firm, like he was trying to make a point of his strength. He stood the same height as me, only a bit wider, and his shoulders were strong and built, but it didn't look like he went to the gym on a regular basis. Gray hair peppered the thick black hair atop his head, and his eyes had the same flecks of gold in them that Logan's were filled with. His stare wasn't as soft as hers though. Much more severe. Cautious even.

"Is Logan around?" I asked, looking over his shoulder.

He finally released his grip on me, trying to fill up more of the doorway. "You got a last name, boy?"

"Dad?" Logan's voice questioned from a distance. When she reached the small space between the door and his shoulder, she wiggled her way into the gap and stared up at me. "What are you doing here, Danny?"

"I wanted to make sure you got my flowers."

The crease between her brows softened as a smile touched her lips. "I put them in a vase already. Thank you."

"So, you're the new neighbor who's been bothering my daughter?"

"Daddy!" Logan shrieked, turning bright red. She looked at me with big, round eyes. "I did not say that."

I laughed.

"She didn't," a woman with similar black hair to Logan's appeared at the man's side. "He's just being overprotective and trying to scare you off. Knock it off, John."

"It's nice to meet you, John," I said. "And you?" I extended my hand to the woman.

"Charlene." She smiled. "Logan's mom."

"Chief Ellis is fine," John said.

Charlene swatted his shoulder. "Oh, John."

"Well, Chief Ellis, I'm afraid I don't scare so easily." I grinned down at his daughter. "I'm sorry to interrupt. I didn't know Logan and Violet had company."

"You should join us!" Charlene suggested, and her husband stiffened at her side. "Logan makes a mean pot roast."

I searched Logan's face for permission, and she gave a gentle nod.

John held his hand to my chest before I could step inside. "You still haven't given me a last name, boy."

"Dad. Stop," Logan scolded him, looking both embarrassed and annoyed. "Don't tell him that, Danny. He just wants to do a background check on you when he gets home to make sure you're not a serial killer or something."

"There's nothing wrong with that. I like to know what kind of person is hanging around my daughter and my granddaughter."

"I don't have anything to hide, Logan." I shrugged. "It's Fox. Danny Fox."

"Danny Fox?" he repeated with a quizzical brow. "You know, that sounds kind of familiar."

"Well, I play some music, sir," I replied.

He didn't look like he would enjoy the kind of music I made, but ya never know.

"Music, huh?" He pondered over that like he couldn't believe someone just did that for a living.

"He's in a band, Dad. He plays guitar," Logan added, and her proud tone did something to my chest.

The way her dad pressed his lips into a firm line made me think he didn't approve of my profession. It wasn't the first time I'd seen that look. My mother had perfected it from the time I was nine and took my father's razer and shaved my hair into a Mohawk. She hadn't approved of much that I did after that. The difference was, unlike with my mother, I felt this strange desire for his approval. His opinion of me mattered to Logan, I could tell, so it mattered to me.

"I'd be happy to play for you sometime, sir."

He grumbled something under his breath and then stepped aside so I could come in.

I couldn't help myself as I followed behind Logan, touching the ends of her silky hair floating down her back with my fingertips. I didn't think she would feel it, but her hand snaked up behind her back, interlocking her fingers with mine while we all filed into the kitchen. I didn't want to let go, but as her dad turned to face us, she released my hand faster than I could tighten my hold.

"You bought those?" he asked, gesturing to the flowers at the center of the kitchen table.

I straightened a fraction. "I did."

"What for?"

Charlene shook her head at her husband. "John. Seriously?"

"Do you need a reason to buy a beautiful woman flowers?" I shifted my gaze across the table to Logan, watching a small smile form on her lips.

Charlene let out a tiny sigh while John murmured something to himself. I wasn't winning him over yet, but from the looks of it, I was winning over Logan.

In the next moment, Violet came trotting into the kitchen, followed by a very large German shepherd. "Danny! Yow hewe!"

"So are you," I said, bending down to her waiting arms. I picked her up and hugged her to my chest while the dog thoroughly sniffed at my feet and ankles.

Violet leaned back, looking me in the eyes. "I missed you."

My fucking heart exploded. "I missed you too, sweetheart."

"Awe yew eating wif us?"

"If that's okay with you?" I poked her nose.

She nodded, and I set her down and pulled out her chair before sitting in mine.

John and Charlene watched me silently while Logan filled the center of the table with food.

"Smells incredible, Logan. Thank you so much for having me," I said, giving John a nod.

He looked away and started loading up his plate.

Logan brushed against my side as she set the last dish down. There was plenty of room between me and Violet, so I knew she had done it intentionally. I dropped my hand to my side and let my thumb graze her leg before she walked to her seat, hearing her breath catch in her throat.

"So, Danny," John started, "tell me about your music."

I finished helping Violet fill her plate with small portions and took a sip of my water. "What would you like to know?"

He finished swallowing his first bite. "What kind of music do you play?"

"My band is a mix of rock, punk rock, and alternative music."

"And they awe amazing!" Violet added, stabbing her fork around her plate.

I gave her a grateful nod. "Thanks, sweetheart."

Logan smiled across the table as she chewed.

"You've heard their music, Vi?" Charlene asked.

Logan turned to her mom. "They invited us to come watch them record a song for their new album. It was really ... interesting."

The side of my mouth turned up at the way she had searched for the word to describe it. *Interesting* was clearly not her first choice, and I suddenly remembered the way her breath had changed and her legs had pushed together when she watched me play. I wet my lip, thinking of what a live show could do to her.

John looked between the two of us and frowned. "So, your band has an album out and everything?"

"Four. Our fifth one releases this Friday."

Charlene looked at me with the same dumbfounded expression Logan had given me when she found out we weren't some band practicing in our garage for small-town bars. Not that there was anything wrong with that. That was where we had started. I kind of loved the fact that Logan hadn't really known who we were, apart from a song or two she had heard on the radio. It was hard to come across many these days who weren't already fans or in the industry.

"Does your band play anywhere around here?" Charlene asked.

My mouth was full, so Logan answered for me, "Not just here. He tours around the country, Mom."

Charlene and John stared at me with vastly different looks on their faces. One of shock and respect and the other of unsettled and perturbed.

"That must be fun! What's your favorite place you've been to so far?" Charlene asked with excitement in her eyes.

"Hmm …" I thought about it. "Probably New York. They've got some killer pizza out there. But I haven't found a place that I haven't liked yet. The fans are the best, no matter where I am."

John cleared his throat. "Do your parents agree with your choice of career?"

Logan slumped in her chair and shot her dad a look. "Really, Daddy?"

He lifted his shoulders. "What? I think it's a fair question. I'd be worried sick about you if you were traveling around the country, meeting strangers and whatnot."

Logan rolled her eyes, knowing that wasn't the intent of his question, but I didn't mind.

"To be honest, my mother isn't the biggest fan of my music. But she's not the biggest fan of *me*, so I don't know if it would matter to her if I did this or something else for the rest of my life."

He chewed on that for a second. "And what about your father?"

I swallowed. "He passed almost twelve years ago."

The table went silent.

I smiled and lifted my gaze to Logan's dad. "But he taught me everything I know about music. I'd like to think he'd be proud of me."

Logan nodded. "He would be."

"I'm sorry about your father," Charlene added. "You must've been, what? Fourteen? Fifteen years old?"

"Thank you. I was sixteen at the time."

"May I ask how?" John asked with a slightly softer tone.

"Um, it was an accident. My sister was with him, but she made it out all right." I looked around the room and frowned. "The details are not great dinner talk, I'm sorry."

"I apologize. I shouldn't have asked," John said, looking down at his plate.

The air in the room changed, and I hated it, but I guessed talking about your dead dad never livened up a conversation. Logan's golden gaze found mine, making the tension in my shoulders disappear.

"Did you finish your darkroom?" I asked her, taking another bite of my food.

"I did! Took me longer than I'd expected, but it's everything I wanted it to be." She grinned and glanced at her father to see his reaction.

To my surprise, he didn't have one.

Irritation prickled at my skin, but I brought my attention back to Logan so I wouldn't let it get to me any more than it already had.

"Now, I just have to find something to photograph so I can use it." She laughed, seemingly unfazed by her dad's lack of interest.

"Me! Take pictows of me!" Violet volunteered.

"Great idea, sweetie," Charlene cooed.

I asked Logan more questions about her work, trying to keep the focus on her rather than me. John still kept an eye on me the rest of the evening, but he stopped grilling me with questions.

After we finished eating, I made friends with Logan's parents' dog, Moose. That seemed to ease some of John's concerns about me.

Despite wanting some one-on-one time with Logan, I thought it was best for me to leave when Charlene went to put Violet down for the night. After I got a quick hug from Violet, Logan led me out onto the front porch. I could feel Logan's dad staring holes into my back until she closed the door behind us.

"This is not what I had planned when I came over here earlier, I promise," I said, making an X motion over my heart. "I did want to see you again, though."

She rubbed her hands together. "Yeah, I wanted to see you again too." Her delivery made it seem like it was hard for her to admit, but it sounded sincere.

"It was nice getting to meet your parents, even though your dad seems like a hard one to win over."

"He's always been that way," she said. "Don't take it personally."

"And what about you?"

"Me?"

"You're not that easy to win over either. Should I take that personally?"

The way the moonlight cast shadows across her face made it so I couldn't see the change in color on her cheeks, but I knew it was there.

"No," she nearly whispered, looking ashamed. "It's complicated. You haven't done anything wrong."

I stepped closer, tucking a strand of hair behind her ear. The gesture made her breath catch.

"Maybe I've already won you over, but you're too scared to realize it."

She pressed her lips together, fighting a smile. "Awfully confident, are we?"

I shook my head once, keeping my eyes on hers. "I've seen the way you look at me, Logan. There's no denying the fact that you're attracted to me. But there's more, isn't there? Tell me you don't feel that pull that I feel every time I'm near you."

The subtle way she moved her bottom lip through her teeth stole my attention, and I closed the gap left between us.

"It's addictive as hell."

I had my hand on her cheek for only a moment before she closed her eyes and slowly removed it. The hand she'd wrapped around my wrist though stayed there at our sides.

"You know, I should be annoyed with your persistence," she told me, shaking her head. "But I'm starting to think it's what makes you so charming."

"Charming, huh?" I curled my lips.

"Did I say charming? I meant really fucking annoying." She looked up at me with a sultry stare, sliding her hand into mine.

"I believe that's the first time I've heard you curse, Logan." I lowered my chin next to her face and whispered, "You have no idea all the vulgar things I can make that pretty mouth of yours sing if you let me."

Her smile faded as her heated gaze fell to my lips.

Fuck me. I wanted to kiss her so badly; it took everything in me to restrain myself. But it wasn't the right moment. I knew when I kissed her for the first time, it wasn't going to be some soft peck that was over before I could feel her tongue against mine. And it certainly wasn't going to happen with the likely chance of her father walking out here and ruining it.

Logan leaned in closer, waiting for me to end our torment.

Instead, I brushed my lips against her cheek with a soft kiss and swallowed back the growing desire to grip the back of her head and take what I wanted.

My breath was heavier as I moved away, fisting my hands at my sides.

She blinked up at me, confused. Like she thought I was rejecting her.

"I want to." I looked down at her pillow-like lips and back up at her. "Those lips will be mine someday, just not when your dad could be watching us through the curtains. I'm still trying to get on his good side."

My words wiped away any concern that had been there before, and she smiled.

"Will I see you on Friday?" I asked.

Her mouth twitched. "I'll do my best."

A bubble of excitement crept up my throat as I turned my back to her and headed home.

"Danny?"

I paused in her driveway, looking over my shoulder.

"Thanks for the flowers."

12

Danny

Four days and many video calls with our label later, our fifth album was available to the public. It never got any less nerve-racking, putting something new out there. Subjecting your art to criticism was exciting and terrifying at the same time. As much as we liked to stay true to ourselves and our signature sound, we still loved challenging ourselves and creating different music. But that always came with risk. Luckily for us, that risk had always paid off. None of our albums sounded the same, but the fans' reactions were always bigger and louder with each one.

There was still a part of us that always worried about disappointing the fans. They were the reason we were here in the first place, so letting them down was always our biggest fear.

Nikko filled us in throughout the day with how sales were doing and the reactions the album was getting. By the time the sun went down, it wasn't just our album release we were celebrating. We'd sold more albums for this release than we had any other day of our career.

I'd anticipated a smaller release party, but Nikko had invited over as many as he could after getting the news. It never failed to surprise me how many people didn't have plans on a Friday night and could be here at the last minute, but the house was crawling with people drinking to our name.

Top-shelf liquor was being poured into plastic cups while girls in tight dresses danced to our music playing through the speakers. Everyone kept handing me shots of fuck knew what, congratulating me, but I didn't want to be out of my head whenever Logan was able to show up.

"Danny! My man!" Nikko smacked my shoulder, holding out a cup of caramel-colored liquor. "Why are your hands empty?"

"I'm not thirsty," I shouted over the music.

He swayed and waved over two girls from the couch, whose asses were hanging out of skirts that looked like they'd been painted on. "Then, let me fill them with something more fun."

The two blondes clung to my sides like leeches, one stroking my arm while the other slid a hand around my waistline.

I quickly slithered out of their grasp, hoping their ridiculous body glitter hadn't rubbed off on me. "Not tonight, ladies. Someone else here will appreciate you more than I will."

They looked offended, but Nikko—being the opportunist that he was—welcomed them with open arms.

"Your loss, brother," he said, tipping his head at me as he led them out through the back toward the pool.

Lexie walked up beside me, tossing back a clear liquid in her shot glass. "Not into blondes anymore?" She bit into a lime wedge like it was an orange.

Liam joined us, sipping on a beer. "Nah, I think he's more into the dark-haired girl-next-door vibes nowadays."

I glanced over at him. "You haven't seen her?"

He shook his head. "Sorry, man."

I clenched my jaw, wanting to kick everyone out and take the bottle of tequila sitting on the table to my left up to bed with me.

"Hey, where's Avery at?" Lexie asked Liam.

"Nina got into some residency program in Los Angeles, so they went out for a drink to celebrate. She'll be here in a bit," Liam reassured her.

"LA? So, she's moving? What does that mean for you and Avery? Can she afford the apartment on her own?" Lexie pressed, a crease growing between her brows.

Liam shrugged. "She says she's got it handled. I'm not worried."

Lexie eyed Liam for a moment before a tall guy with dreadlocks caught her attention. "I'll, uh, see you guys later." She wiggled her brows at us.

Liam and I chuckled as Lexie approached a man twice her size, knowing she would chew him up and spit him back out.

The front door opened and closed, but the crowd was too thick to make out who it was. I could only see the top of a dark-haired head, and my heart pounded against my chest as I waited for them to reach a clearing in the room. But the familiar face I finally saw wasn't the one I wanted. Not at all.

"Fucking Hannah's here again?" My nostrils flared.

As if she had a tracking beacon on me, her eyes immediately found me across the room, and instead of them saying, *I wish you nothing but misery*, tonight, they said, *I want to fuck your brains out.*

I'd seen it enough times to recognize it, but it didn't have the same effect on me it usually had.

Liam elbowed me. "Ignore her. There are plenty of people here tonight to preoccupy her."

As Hannah strutted through the crowd toward me in a tight orange dress that matched all the others in the room, I knew it wouldn't be as easy as that.

I gave her the best uninterested expression I could manage when she landed in front of me.

Her hooded eyes raked up my body. "I believe congratulations are in order."

"Thanks," Liam mocked, tilting his head into her line of vision.

She flicked a middle finger up at him without taking her eyes off me.

"What are you doing here?" I crossed my arms over my chest.

She stepped closer, rubbing her tits on my forearms. "Looking for someone to fetch me a stiff one."

"Look somewhere else," I sneered, nearly gagging on her perfume.

"Don't be like that, Danny." She tilted her head and pouted. "You and I both know how tonight is going to end.

Let's not waste time arguing with our clothes on." Her sultry tone made my skin crawl.

"Pass."

She stroked her hand down the inseam of my jeans, ignoring my rejection. "I'm not wearing any underwear."

I caught her wrist before she could get too far and threw it away, relieved to finally have such a reaction to her. "Then, please keep off the furniture."

Liam nearly spat out his drink.

Her eyes narrowed. "Excuse me?"

"What aren't you hearing? I told you I was done, and there's nothing you can do to change my mind." I jutted my chin toward the door. "Leave."

Her brows shot up in disbelief. "You're serious?"

"As cancer."

She laughed, but it was devoid of humor. "Whatever, Danny. You'll miss this eventually, and when you do, you'll come crawling back, like always."

I stared at her, unfazed, until she grew embarrassed enough to walk away.

"I'm proud of you, man," Liam said after a moment.

I frowned. "Proud? What for?"

"It hasn't always been that easy for you to turn Hannah down. You two have a lot of history. It's nice to see you recognize what kind of people aren't worth your time. And I think a girl who *is* worth your time might be the reason for that."

Logan flooded my vision, and my jaw ticked. I didn't know why it mattered so much to me for her to be here, but she was the only one I wanted to see when the day was over.

Not Liam.

Not Tic or Lexie or Nikko.

Not fucking Hannah.

Her.

Liam squeezed my shoulder. "Maybe she's not into parties."

I looked around the hazy, smoke-filled room, watching people dry-humping and taking body shots off one another. If parties weren't Logan's scene, then this place definitely wouldn't convince a girl already on the fence about coming. She could probably hear the roar of music and people screaming from the street. If it had stayed smaller, more intimate, like planned, maybe she'd be here. There was no fixing that now. Not this late anyway.

Unless …

I smacked Liam in the chest as an idea came to me.

He choked on his sip of beer. "Jesus. What?" he snapped.

"Can you run downstairs and grab my Gibson?"

Coughing, he wiped the side of his mouth and frowned. "You want your guitar? What for?"

I grabbed a shot off a nearby table and threw it back to accompany the burn of adrenaline I suddenly felt. "I wanna liven up the place a bit."

Liam stared blankly and then shrugged, not caring enough to work an explanation out of me. "Fine. I'll be right back."

I looked around the room for my amplifier, finding it wedged between the couch and the wall.

Tic came walking over when he saw my struggle, trying to retrieve it. "What are you doing?"

I pulled on the corner of the couch. "Getting my amp."

He grabbed hold beneath my grip and helped me move the couch a good foot away from the wall in one swift push. The people sitting on it didn't even flinch.

Threading my hand through the handle, I hoisted the amplifier up onto the coffee table. Liam came back, handing me my guitar.

He and Tic exchanged glances as they watched me hook my guitar up.

"Is he drunk?" Tic asked.

Liam shook his head. "Nope."

I tested the volume and ran my fingers through the strings once. The girl sitting in front of the speaker quickly covered her ears in pain as the room erupted with the sound.

Perfect.

I climbed up onto the table, and the room cheered, thrusting their drinks into the air.

"That's a good way to get the cops' attention," Tic shouted.

My mouth curled up into a grin as I looked down at him. "They're not the ones I'm looking to get attention from."

13

Logan

"You're wearing makeup." Andre stared at the side of my face.

I ignored him as I shoved a spoon into my half-eaten pint of ice cream.

"For a movie night with me?" He gestured to the television screen my eyes were glued to.

"I'm not wearing that much," I argued. I lifted my blanket up to my shoulders, trying to hide more evidence of my almost night out.

I'd invited Andre over to watch movies … and possibly Violet for an hour or two while I went to Danny's release party. But right before he arrived, I stared at my reflection in the mirror at my long maxi skirt and lace top and felt butterflies in the pit of my stomach. I felt confident and pretty and … *me* for the first time in a long while. But my dad's voice echoed in the back of my head the moment I got excited, warning me to be careful.

After everything I'd put my parents through, my dad had come up with a simple solution to protect me from making more bad choices. He told me that if anything excited me enough to give me butterflies, it probably meant I shouldn't be doing it. I knew that applied more to things like drunk cliff diving or playing chicken with trains while high on pain meds, but after dinner on Monday night, it was safe to assume he wanted me to extend that safeguard to anything involving Danny as well.

"Does the makeup and"—he yanked my blanket away and pointed at my outfit—"the fact that you're wearing something you have to use a hanger for have anything to do with the party I saw going on across the street?"

I looked around the room at anything but him. "No."

"Logan, you're the fucking cling wrap of liars. The cheap, clear kind that's a bitch to deal with." Andre shook his head. "I can see right through your shit. Now, tell me the truth."

I snatched my blanket out of his hand and threw it back over my legs. "He might've invited me, but I changed my mind. Okay?"

"Again? Seriously? You're missing out on a killer party with rock stars to spend the night bingeing *Scream* movies with me?"

"Obviously." I shoveled a heaping spoonful of ice cream into my mouth, trying to force down the disappointment crawling its way back up. "I like movie nights with you better anyway."

"Well, it's a good thing you're not wearing pants because they would be on fire, liar." He touched the tip of his spoon to my nose.

"Andre!" I quickly wiped away the melted ice cream and gaped at him.

He laughed, licking off the remnants on his spoon. "You look nice, L. You shouldn't waste it on me."

I let my next bite melt in my mouth before I spoke. "I can't fall for a guy capable of destroying this life I've carefully placed back together. It's too fragile."

He circled a finger in the air. "How do you know he doesn't have a sword and shield in his armory, ready to protect all of this?"

"A knight in shining armor?" I side-eyed him. "Please."

"How do you know?"

"I don't. That's the point. I can't take the risk," I explained.

Andre groaned. "Everything in life is risky. Hell, *not* doing anything in life is risky."

I ran my fingers through my hair, creating a fist at the top of my head. "He's going to take her away from me if I mess this up."

Andre reached for the remote and paused the movie. "Who? Your dad?"

I nodded and squeezed my hand tighter until my scalp stung with the pressure.

"Did he say that to you?"

"He doesn't have to." I looked at him. "He brings Moose over here every time they visit, which just proves he doesn't trust me. And he's taking Violet to the cabin next weekend without me, and I can't help but think that he wants to give me a taste of what it's like to lose her."

Andre frowned. "He didn't invite you to go with them?"

I shook my head.

He pulled at my elbow, and I dropped my hand from my head. "Violet's not going anywhere. Stop thinking like that. Your dad can't take your daughter away just because you start seeing your neighbor. I don't care if he is a cop; that's not his right."

"It would be his word against mine. You don't understand the sway he has." My stomach clenched at the thought of how powerless I was.

My dad wasn't a monster. But he had left me in jail once to teach me a lesson. I doubted he would give me an opportunity to learn something from any mistake I made now that I had custody of Violet.

Andre stroked my arm. "What are you so worried about happening? Are you scared of relapsing?"

"God, no. I'm never going near anything ever again," I said. "And to make sure of that, I think it's best to stay away from hot rock stars who buy me flowers and say hot things while being totally sweet."

He blinked. "So, the ugly ones are safe then?"

I threw my head back. "There are no ugly ones. You should see their band. It's not fair to be that talented *and* attractive."

"I'd love to, but they didn't invite me. They invited you."

"Well, technically, they said I could bring friends." I shrugged.

His jaw dropped. "You are such a bish!"

"Hey now."

"Seriously, good luck finding a new best friend."

I rolled my eyes. "Can you just play the movie, please?"

He gave me all the dirty looks in the book for the next few seconds and then finally clicked the button on the remote again, resuming the slasher film.

In the next moment, the shrill scream of a guitar bounced off the walls of my house. Panic shot up the back of my neck, and I snapped my head in the direction it was coming from.

Danny's house.

"What the hell?" Andre stood up at the same time I did.

There was a moment of silence when I considered sitting back down, but the sound came back almost louder and showed no signs of stopping.

"Violet's going to hear that," Andre complained.

"I know!" I told him, marching toward the door.

It was Danny. It had to be. The sound was too meticulous, too perfect to be anyone else.

I growled under my breath as I shoved my feet into a pair of shoes. *What is he playing at?*

"You could just call the police and complain," he suggested.

"And wait twenty minutes for them to show up? No way. I'll take care of it."

The music amplified tenfold as I walked outside. The lights on Danny's front porch lit up half the block, and cars were parked bumper to bumper as far as I could see—in both directions. Anger fueled my feet as I marched faster, crossing the street and up their driveway. By the time I reached their porch, I was ready to scream. I threw their front door open so hard that it ricocheted off the wall and found Danny standing atop a table in the middle of the crowded room.

Danny's eyes locked on to mine, and his hands halted on his guitar, letting his last note ring through the speakers until it dissolved and all that was left was the dull roar of the crowded room. I pictured Andre in my living room, applauding at my speed of effectiveness.

"What the hell is wrong with you?" I screamed. My nostrils flared as I stepped toward him. "It's one o'clock in the morning! Violet is sleeping!"

Some of the conversations paused when they heard my outburst. A girl stumbled out of my way, seeing the rage on my face.

"Do you have any idea how fucking loud that is?" My mouth twisted.

Danny's lips curled up with amusement as he handed his guitar to someone beside him. I didn't take my eyes off him to see who it was, but I guessed it was either Liam or Tic. Tomorrow, I might be embarrassed that they were seeing me like this—their crazy new neighbor. But right now, I didn't give a damn what they thought of me. I had red tunnel vision, and Danny was at the end of it.

He jumped off the table and stalked toward me.

"Are you wasted or just inconsiderate?" I spat, narrowing my eyes at him.

Danny's eyes heated with every step he took closer, every word I yelled at him.

I stopped in my tracks, realization washing over me. "Oh my God! You knew exactly what you were doing, didn't you? You knew I would come over here to get you to stop!"

THE PIECE THAT BREAKS

He wasn't walking toward me now; he was charging at me. The sudden desire to smack the smug little grin off his face made my palm twitch, but he reached me before my hand could leave my side.

"Well, you got me here," I shouted in his face as I held my hands out. "Now, wha—"

His mouth was on mine before I could finish.

14

Logan

My fists clenched his shirt, and I pulled away, breathless. "You can't just—"

Danny shook his head and snaked a firm hand around the back of my neck, forcing my lips back to his. The impact and need in his kiss hit the reset button on my system, and my body melted into him, turning my anger into hunger and desire.

I could feel his mouth stretch into a smile against my own the moment I began kissing him back.

Whistles and cheers erupted around us, and some quieter party music resumed, but I barely registered any of it as Danny slid his tongue along my bottom lip.

I parted my lips at his soft, wet request and let him inside, feeling his hot tongue stroke in and out in the most toe-curling way. My core pulsed at the thought of what his skilled tongue would feel like all over my body, and a subtle moan escaped my throat.

Danny smiled again, pulling his mouth away from mine.

I whimpered and pouted my swollen lips.

"Come with me," he breathed out.

Sliding his hand into mine, he pulled me through the crowded room and led me to the basement door, keeping his body as close to mine as possible, like he thought someone would steal me away.

I wasn't sure what we were doing or where we were going, but I wanted his lips back on mine too much to care.

After he shut and locked the door behind us, we only made it three steps down the stairs before he slammed me up against the wall and devoured me again.

The pressure of his hard body and thick arms caging me in made my knees buckle, so I hung my arms around his neck for support.

His teeth teased my lower lip, and my body rolled against him.

"Fuck, Logan. You taste so good."

Feeling even more turned on with his deep, throaty words, I flicked my tongue against his chin and dragged it up his sharp jawline.

He couldn't get my legs up around his waist fast enough as he clamped his firm hands around my ass and pulled up. The moment my legs parted around him and he pressed himself against the thin layers of my skirt and cotton panties, I cried out.

Danny buried his head into my neck and rolled his hips into me, hitting the perfect spot once more.

"Danny," I gasped.

His hot breath hit the nape of my neck before he planted kisses up toward the spot below my ear. "Does that feel good?" he whispered.

I pinched my eyes shut and nodded.

"Tell me how good it feels, Logan. Tell me you want more." He looked at me through hooded eyes.

I dug my heels into his ass, hoping that was enough of an answer, but he didn't move.

"Yes," I finally said before begging, "I want more."

With a dark grin, he moved away from the wall and maneuvered us down the rest of the steps blindly.

When we reached the bottom and stepped into his studio space, he placed me back on my feet but kept his hands around my backside.

"Tell me to stop, and I'll stop, Logan," he pleaded, tipping his forehead to mine.

"Don't you dare." I peered up at him with a grin and shook my head.

He smiled against my mouth, dancing his fingers along the edge of my lace top. "I told you those lips would be mine."

I gave him what was his and kissed him again, stroking my tongue with his until he groaned. His erection grew and thickened against my hip, and my hands trailed down the deep valleys of his abs with excitement.

"Logan." My name rumbled from his throat as he caught my wandering hands at his zipper. "I'm fine just kissing you the rest of the night. We don't have to go there. This is enough for me."

Jesus. He was somehow possessive *and* respectful. That just made me want him even more.

His gaze dropped to my mouth, then flicked back to my eyes as our chests rose and fell together. "Maybe we should slow down. I don't want to scare you away," he murmured.

I tilted my chin up, gaze heated, and repeated his own words back to him, "I don't scare so easily, Danny."

My next move surprised the both of us as I walked into him and pushed at his large chest.

"What are you doing?" He let out a chuckle as he stumbled back a few steps, the back of his knees finding the chair behind him. He looked up at me as he sat, questioning and inviting.

"I'm really not sure," I answered honestly as I watched him watch me. I loved the attention his eyes gave to every inch of me as they raked up and down my body from his slumped, wide-legged position.

"I can't say I don't like where this is going so far. Come here." He crooked a finger.

My pulse skyrocketed as I climbed on top of him, placing a knee on either side of his muscular thighs. Throwing my hair to one side, I bent down and sucked gently on his soft skin, feeling his pulse hammer against my lips.

"Christ, Logan." Danny's fingers dug into my hips as he writhed beneath me. "That's such a turn-on for me."

I smiled and lowered myself down completely onto his lap, feeling just how turned on he really was. His hardened shaft pressed firmly against the restrictive fabric of his jeans, hitting me so good that I thought I was bare. That was when I realized that my skirt had bunched up around my waist and it was only my underwear rubbing against him now.

Liking the effect I was having on him while kissing his neck, I rocked my hips forward to try and amplify the soft moans I was eliciting from him, but the feeling of his cock rubbing my tight little nub sent a shock wave through me. I hadn't been ready for it. I threw my head back, gasping and clenching his shoulders.

His muscles flexed beneath my palms as he pulled my hips forward, creating the same motion again, only better.

I cried out.

"Fuck. That sound is so sweet," he said, guiding me into him again.

And again.

I moved with his slow rhythm and then a bit faster, needing more friction. I whimpered, "Oh, Danny. Oh—"

Danny's fingers grew more eager at my backside, motivating me to move. Harder. Quicker. He sat up straight, gliding a hand up to the back of my neck, capturing my lips with his.

My breaths were too labored to kiss him for long, and our mouths eventually hovered over one another, panting with each shameless roll of my hips.

"That's it, Logan. Keep going," he encouraged.

Our movements were frantic. Desperate. *Addictive.*

Every time his length hit me, the pressure built, and I rode him harder.

I gasped, my core tightening, "Oh God."

"Come for me," he rasped. "Come for me, Logan."

"I'm almost there," I breathed out, fighting to find my release.

He slid his warm hands up the inside of my thighs, beneath my skirt, and with a single stroke of his thumb over the center of my wet panties, I lost it with a sharp cry.

Danny didn't stop there. He continued to rub my swollen clit, letting me ride out my orgasm with moan after moan until I slowed and slumped forward.

"You are so damn beautiful." His drowsy voice vibrated against the crook of my neck. The tiny sensation made my flushed skin pepper with goosebumps. He soothed them away with a soft brush of his lips.

As my breathing began to even out, I sat up and looked him in his eyes. It might've been my imagination, but they looked bluer. Deeper.

My heart thumped against my chest as I came to, realizing what we'd just done. What *I'd* done.

Thump. Thump.

Danny's hands settled on the top of my skirt, rubbing soothingly at my sides as if he could see the panic washing over my face. "Logan ..."

"Oh my God," I said, eyes widening. "I am so sorry."

"Sorry?" He nearly laughed as he raised his eyebrows. "What are you sorry for, Logan?"

"I just, um ..." I chewed on my bottom lip, still feeling his erection below me. My gaze dropped to where our laps met, guilt rushing up my spine and embarrassment constricting my throat.

"Hey," he said, reaching up to cup my cheek. His expression was so sensual, so heated, that it was hard to look away. "Don't apologize for riding me. That was the hottest thing I've ever seen."

His words lit my skin on fire, and I climbed off his lap. My muscles were loose and achy as I found my footing.

"Where are you going?"

I blinked a few times. "I should get home. Violet—"

"Shit. Of course." He stood, concern pulling at his features. "Do you think she's okay? Do you want me to come with you?"

"Andre is there. She's okay." I shook my head.

Something about him steeled when I mentioned my friend's name. His eyes were no longer soft and reassuring. They were hard and ... hurt?

"I don't want him worrying, and it's getting late," I said, somehow making his expression more severe. I didn't know what to do. I was just trying not to bolt.

His throat bobbed as he swallowed. "Why do I feel like I did something wrong here?"

"You didn't," I said. *I did.*

He frowned. "You were just screaming my name a second ago, and now, you're backing away from me like you're afraid. I must've done something."

My stomach twisted at the pain in his voice. No, no, no. I was ruining everything. "You were perfect, Danny. I just need to get home," I explained.

He took a careful step toward me, and an alarm went off in my head. For some odd reason, my fight-or-flight instincts chose this moment to kick in, and I turned and ran up the stairs away from him.

So much for not bolting. I was like the Flash up those stairs.

Something stopped me when I closed the basement door behind me and entered the chaos of the party still going on.

Danny hadn't followed me.

It wasn't that I was looking for him to chase me, but I couldn't help but think of the look on his face right before I'd left him down there. He hadn't done anything wrong. He'd kissed me—God, he'd kissed me so fucking good—and then I ravaged him like a wild animal.

Oh God, had I *ravaged* him.

I could never look at him again. My entire body reddened like a giant tomato from the way I burned with embarrassment all over. Mortified didn't even begin to cover it. I wanted to crawl under a rock and never come back out. Maybe my dad had a point. I didn't need the big house. I should sell it and move to Ireland. Change my name to Lana or Ellen or maybe Amber—those were pretty names. And then I could enter the Witness Protection Program. My dad knew a guy.

Ugh. But I couldn't just leave Danny down there like that. Could I?

"I don't scare so easily." I thought back to the words I'd said before I ground on Danny to completion.

I don't scare so easily? Yeah, right. Way to bury that trait in the dirt, Logan.

I had gotten off on my neighbor, fully clothed, and then run away from him. Run. Like he was wearing a white mask and chasing me with a knife. Like he hadn't just given me the best orgasm of my life without even taking my clothes off. I couldn't imagine what he thought of me now.

I fisted the door handle to the basement. *Don't be a coward, Logan.*

A bathroom door opened behind me before I could muster up the courage, and I turned to look at the person walking out. A skinny blonde girl wiped her nose as she passed, paying no mind to me. But the brunette still at the sink made my heart drop into my stomach as I watched her slide a rolled-up bill across the countertop, snorting an all-too-familiar white powder.

Ice filled my veins, and my head suddenly felt dizzy with flashbacks. The oxygen around me thinned by the second. I needed to leave. Now.

My feet carried me toward the front door. The dancing and drunken individuals were a blur as I weaved between them.

"Logan, hey!" I heard Lexie call from somewhere behind me, but I didn't look back.

I couldn't look back.

I gulped in the night air when I stepped outside despite the tightening in my throat and ran for my house. My legs were burning by the time I reached my front door—I really needed to work out more.

As my shoulders fell back against the door, I shut my eyes and sucked in a breath. I had been so stupid for going over there. What had I been thinking? My fears and my dad's warnings had been right all along. How could I hang out with a bunch of rock stars and not expect to have my past come knocking on the door, asking for a do-over, like some toxic ex? The partying, the drinking, the drugs … that all came with the package, right? Of course it did. As much as I wanted that dark, sweet, tattooed, orgasm-filled package, I couldn't go near it.

I locked my door and the dead bolt for good measure. Not to keep anyone out, but rather to keep me in. My instincts couldn't be trusted right now. I could still feel the effects of Danny's hands on me. His lips. His tongue. My skin was buzzing.

I pressed my legs together, heaving out a sigh.

"Whatcha doin' over there, L?" Andre's voice pierced through the dark house, and I jumped.

"Nothing," I said with a pointed look, trying to make sure he didn't suspect anything. Anything at all.

The television barely illuminated his features as he raised his brows. "Why are you so flushed?"

I scoffed. "You can't see that. It's dark."

He snickered, and I knew I was busted.

I groaned, still out of breath. "Is Violet okay? She didn't wake up?"

He shook his head. "She's asleep. I just checked on her. Are *you* okay?"

"Fine. Just fine."

He nodded, pinching his lips between his teeth to cover up a knowing grin. "I heard the music stop quite a bit ago. I guess you handled it, huh?"

"Yep. Told you." I chuckled.

"You sure did," he said with a hint of mockery. "You plan on leaving the doorway tonight or …"

I glared at him and walked over to lean on the back of the couch, tensing under his stare.

"Spill," Andre ordered.

I crumpled instantly, twisting over the couch and falling into his side. "Goddammit."

15

Danny

I had dreamed about Logan for the last five fucking nights and thought about her every second I was awake. How could I not? Her scent lingered on me. Her moans still rang in my ears. And the way her body had moved on top of me was imprinted on my mind like a brand.

As haunting as those moments together had been, they had been fleeting. I needed to be near her again. Needed to feel her touch. To talk to her and ask her what I'd done wrong. It wasn't for a lack of trying—I'd knocked on her door every day since our release party and gotten no response.

Every day but today.

I'd told her I didn't want to scare her away, and that was exactly what I'd done. I wasn't sure how it had happened or how I could fix it, but I figured my persistence and stubborn effort in trying to gain her trust had run its course. I'd had it for a moment, and then it had been snatched away.

Maybe she was worried about me hurting her if we got too involved and had to explain that to Violet. I knew how much she meant to her. A guy like me didn't scream relationship security, but I wished she'd give me a chance to prove that looks could be deceiving and that her daughter was quickly becoming my weakness.

When Violet reached for me after I played for her in the recording studio, it was one of the best feelings in the world. Indescribable. Like I was the most important person to her in that exact moment. She didn't care who I was, what mistakes I'd made in the past, or how successful I'd become. She just saw me and chose to trust me completely. No exceptions or judgment. No one had ever made me feel that way.

The other scenario I thought of scared me more. That I'd pushed Logan too far. She'd given me no indication that she wanted us to stop, but I could've missed something. And it was driving me crazy, replaying every detail over and over in my head, trying to find it.

She wasn't going to open up to me again if I banged her door down and demanded an explanation. Maybe Liam was right. I needed to give her space. I just hated that option didn't come with answers.

With a growl, I rolled out of bed and made my way to the bathroom, taking another cold shower to soothe the ache of my morning erection. I'd forget about Logan for two seconds and find a moment of peace. And then I'd close my eyes and see her grinding on my cock. Her flushed cheeks and messy hair. Her short gasps as her orgasm crested.

Fuck. Me.

She was everywhere.

I twisted the shower dial all the way to cold and sucked in a gasp of air as the water turned to ice on my shoulders.

"Are you almost done in there?" Lexie's voice echoed.

As used to it as I was, I still flinched to cover my junk every time she came into the bathroom unannounced.

"Get out, Lex. I'll be done when I'm done."

"Well, my guest needs to shower before she heads to work," she complained. "You're going to use up all the hot water."

I shook my head, annoyed. "There'll be plenty of hot water. Now, get the fuck outta here."

"Ah. Taking another cold shower are we, lover boy?"

I snatched the shower curtain back far enough to pin her with a scowl.

Lexie held her hands up and grinned. "Look, I'm not complaining. I'm just saying, I've had a lot of hot showers lately, and I'm always the one to wake up last. That can only mean one thing. Someone's taking cold showers, and I highly doubt it's Liam."

I narrowed my eyes.

"You know, because he's boning your sister," she elaborated.

My hand fisted the showerhead and pulled it loose from the overhead handle, aiming it at Lexie.

She screamed and retreated behind the door for coverage.

I chuckled to myself and fixed it back into place, washing off some soap I'd lathered up.

"How are you not an icicle, you psycho?" she screeched. "Are you really that hard up for pussy right now?"

"Lexie!" I barked.

"I'm going; I'm going," she finally conceded. "Just hurry up."

She didn't have to tell me twice. It wasn't like I enjoyed freezing cold showers. I was just desperate to have some of the blood return to my head so I could think straight.

"I need your help with something."

My sister stared widely at me over her bowl of cereal the following morning. She had spent the night here last night with Liam and was getting ready to head to class. I wasn't usually up at the ass crack of dawn like this, but I wanted to catch her before she left.

"*My* help?" Avery asked with a mouthful of cinnamon cereal—the same shit she had eaten back when we were kids.

Liam turned around from the open fridge with an amused look on his face.

It wasn't like me to ask for help, let alone from Avery. But I was desperate. I needed someone to convince Logan I wasn't looking to just get in her pants and mess up her life, and I figured I'd have a better chance at doing that with someone who could actually vouch for me. Liam, Tic, and Lexie always had my back, no matter what, but I didn't want to mess this up if they decided to use this moment as a fun way to fuck with me. I might only have one shot, and Avery was good at being persuasive. Her words mattered to others. She had a way of making people trust her. Love her. It was annoying as shit, but

I also understood why. There weren't a lot of good people left in the world, but my sister was about as good as they came.

Besides, after choosing my best friend out of all the people to fall for, I kind of felt like she owed me.

I fisted the coffee mug in my hand and brought it to my lips. She was still frozen, waiting, when I finished what was left in my cup.

"There's this girl I want you to talk to for me," I finally said.

She laughed, nearly spitting on the table. "I'm sorry, but since when do you need my help with girls?"

I worked my jaw. "My usual charming ways aren't winning her over. I don't know what to do, okay?"

Avery raised a brow at me.

"Charming ways?" Liam smirked.

"Fuck you guys. Will you help me or not?" I asked, annoyed.

Avery shrugged and shook her head. "What exactly do you expect me to do?"

"I don't know. Just talk to her. Tell her I'm not a total piece of shit."

Her face fell. "No, Danny. Come on. If she really thinks you're a piece of shit, then she's not worth the effort. You're a catch"—she paused—"when you want to be."

"See. I knew you were the right one to ask," I said.

Liam leaned against the doorway and frowned. "Wait, wait, wait. Are you really into this girl, or are you just chasing her because she's the first girl to turn you down?"

Unfamiliar heat rose from my chest up to my neck. I didn't like that Liam thought this was just a game to me, but if my best friend thought that, then I was screwed in convincing Logan otherwise.

"You like her. A lot." Avery searched my face. "Don't you?"

I bit back a smart-ass remark and nodded. What a stupid question. I wouldn't be asking her to do this if I didn't.

"Who is she?" Avery asked.

"Our new neighbor," Liam answered with a smug grin.

"You've met?" Avery asked Liam.

He nodded.

"Her name's Logan," I said.

She looked up at Liam. "And you think she's good for him?"

He smiled and tilted his head. "Well, she's not Hannah."

Avery lifted her lip. "That's not setting the bar very high."

"I wasn't around her for very long, but she was sweet. She's got a cute little girl. Definitely had some dreamy eyes for Danny," Liam said.

"The little girl or Logan?" she asked.

"Logan." Liam chuckled. "But Violet adored him too."

That detail made me smile.

Liam settled into a chair next to Avery. "I think I like her more because she's turned him down so many times."

I gave him a dirty look but returned my attention back to my sister.

"I'll stop by her house after class," Avery finally said.

"Really? You'll do it?"

Her shoulders dropped. "Of course, Danny. Anything. She's important to you."

16

Logan

I stood in the red glow of my darkroom, sloshing a picture around in the developer and waiting for the image to slowly appear. It was my favorite part—watching nothing turn into something. It was the closest thing to magic for me.

When I finished rinsing the final solution off, I found an empty spot to hang the image to dry with the others. I was running out of room on the strings hanging above. Trying to preoccupy myself the last few days had meant a lot of trips to the park with Violet and several photography outings. The weather had stayed nice, so it was good to be outside, but I was pretty sure Violet was sick of going for walks at this point, and my inspiration was running low.

I kept my windows open every day to let in the fresh air, but I hadn't heard Danny's guitar melodies drift in since the party. I wasn't sure if that was normal for him after finishing an album, but I couldn't help but feel like he wasn't playing because of me.

I missed it. The sound had become familiar. Comforting even. But I knew it would be back again soon. Maybe tomorrow or a week from now. I hated the idea of having to wait to hear the sound of his guitar again until they all came back from their tour, but it *would* come back. Danny would forget about this thing between us and resume his habitual routine of sitting out on his front porch—half-dressed, no doubt—strumming his guitar.

And I would sit on my front step, listening, because I loved to torture myself.

Footsteps fell overhead, signaling the end of my short workday. Andre had offered to take Violet out for ice cream while I finished developing the pictures I'd taken this week. With three film rolls to choose from, I had thought I'd have something I'd want to bring in for Jennifer at the gallery, but I stared around the darkroom with the same disappointment I'd had for the last few months. None of them elicited enough emotion from me.

Andre stomped several times in the same spot on the hardwood floor above me, getting my attention.

"I'm coming!" I shouted up, chuckling.

It wasn't the most gracious way of communicating, but I didn't want him coming down here and letting in any natural light that could ruin my work.

When I got upstairs, Andre and Violet sat at the kitchen island, debating over whose ice cream flavor was better. Even with an almost four-year-old, Andre took his arguments very seriously.

"Uncle Andwe!" Violet whined, finally reaching her breaking point. The girl was going to take on the world someday, but she was going to have to improve her patience and stamina when it came to outsmarting men trying to outwit her.

"Bubblegum is clearly better than rocky road," I said, tossing in my vote.

Violet thrust a fist in the air, laughing in Andre's face.

"You're only taking her side because she's cute," he countered.

I shrugged. "And?"

"Don't be a sow lewsow, Uncle Andwe," Violet told him, her lips smeared with vegan blue ice cream.

He huffed and then nodded at the fridge. "I put your old-lady ice cream in the freezer, L."

"Pistachio is the best. You're missing out," I argued, reaching for the fridge.

The doorbell rang, and I paused.

"I got it!" Violet offered, scooting off her chair.

"No, baby. Finish your ice cream," I said, glancing at Andre.

"You think it's him again?" Andre asked.

The odds were high, considering he'd come by nearly every day over the last week. I thought that was why I'd tried to be away from the house as much as I could—I hated seeing his face on the other side of my door and not answering it.

"Are you going to ignore him forever?" Andre asked.

I sighed. "No. But you know I can't be with him."

"You're just answering your door, L. Not accepting his hand in marriage."

The doorbell rang again, and I begrudgingly walked over to get it, peering through the peephole first to prepare myself. To my relief, it wasn't Danny or anyone I recognized.

I opened the door, greeting the brown-haired girl on the other side. "Hi." I smiled. "Can I help you?"

Her striking gray eyes softened as she took me in. "Hi. You must be Logan."

Something was familiar about her, but I couldn't put my finger on it. The hair color? The bone structure? Something in the eyes maybe?

"Do I know you?" I asked.

"Not yet, but you know my brother," she answered.

Brother? Oh no.

"You're not related to Danny by chance, are you?"

She winced at the caution in my voice. "Guilty. I'm Avery."

I took a slow breath, trying not to get myself worked up. "I see he's sent in reinforcements."

Her smile was warm as she held up a coffee carrier in one hand and a paper bag in the other. "Can I bribe you for a little conversation?"

I racked my brain for excuses, coming up short. "Oh, I don't know. I have to—"

"She's free," Andre chimed in, appearing beside me. "Absolutely no plans whatsoever."

I flicked my gaze up to his, wishing he could hear the string of curse words running through my head.

He grinned.

"Perfect!" Avery said before introducing herself to Andre.

"Me and Vi already decided on a movie, but I'm sure she'll be in a sugar coma before the opening credits hit. Take all the time you need with her, Avery." Andre all but locked the door after he pushed me outside with her.

She smiled nervously, which told me this wasn't her idea. That eased my nerves a bit.

"Danny told me you had a little girl, so I took a guess and thought you might like a coffee."

I liked her already.

"Couldn't live without it." I grinned, taking the cup from her. "Thank you."

We sat on my steps for a few quiet moments, sipping our drinks and soaking in some of the afternoon sun.

"Thank you for letting me talk to you," Avery finally stated. "I'm sure you're not interested in hearing anything I have to say about my brother, given the fact that he enlisted me for help."

I frowned. "What do you mean?"

"Danny doesn't ask me for anything. Ever." Her brows twitched. "So, when he asked me to come over here and convince you that he's not the asshole you think he is, I figured he must've really messed things up with you."

"I don't think Danny is an asshole," I corrected.

"Well, whatever adjective you want to call him ..."

"Sweet. Thoughtful," I suggested. Some less innocent ones came to mind, but I kept them to myself.

Avery glanced at me, almost startled.

I arched my brow, adding one more. "Persistent."

"That he is," she said, a smile touching her lips. "I'm a bit lost as to why he wanted me to come over here then. It sounds like you like my brother. A lot. He made it seem like you wanted nothing to do with him."

"It's not that I don't want Danny." I shook my head. "It's that I can't have him."

"Um, I don't know if you know this, but Danny is crazy about you. He wouldn't have asked me to come over here if he wasn't. I've never seen him this way with anyone. You can have him any day of the week." She scrunched her face into a grimace at her last bit.

I smiled to try and ease the anxiety growing in my chest. Though her words made my heart skip a beat or two. "That's not what I mean. Danny is great. Really. Even my daughter loves him." I glanced back at the house. "But she's also the reason I need to stay away from your brother. And not just him, but that whole house too."

She looked back and forth, confused. "I'm not sure I understand."

My chest suddenly felt heavier, but her presence came with an ease that loosened my tongue. "I can't be a part of his lifestyle. It's too risky for me."

"I'm guessing by lifestyle, you mean his music career?"

I lifted my shoulders and nodded.

Avery thought for a moment and then shifted her body a fraction so that her knees were touching mine. "I get it, Logan. I've been with Liam for about a year and a half now, and it can be hard when he's gone touring. I was able to travel with him a little on their last tour, but then I started school and had to come back here. There were times when I didn't see him for weeks. And now, this tour is even longer, and I'm dreading him leaving, but we make it work. I know Danny would do anything to make it work with you too." She smiled.

I gripped my cup with both hands as I listened.

Her eyes lit up with an idea as she nudged my shoulder. "We could surprise them both and fly out together sometime while they're touring! It'd be so much fun—"

"I'm an addict," I blurted out. The familiar three words felt like a dry pill stuck in the back of my throat; I nearly choked on them.

Silence fell between the two of us.

"*Was*. I was an addict," I eventually clarified, hearing my pulse beating in my ears as I glanced over at her.

Avery's smile was gone, but her expression wasn't filled with judgment or confusion or even pity. It was kind and benevolent, and for some reason, that made tears well in my eyes.

"Logan," Avery said, placing a hand on my arm, "does Danny know that?"

I swallowed and swiped away a tear that had spilled down my cheek. "It hasn't come up."

"There are some things I think you should know about my brother." She took a careful breath, staring across the street. "I'm not sure if this will hurt Danny's chances with you or help push you toward him, but I'm hoping it's the latter."

I placed a hand on the step beside me to brace myself.

"My brother didn't have it as easy as I did, growing up. You could say I was favored a bit more than him. A lot more actually." She chuckled out of discomfort. "And our mom has never been the warmest person. She hated that he cared more about practicing his guitar than finishing his schoolwork. There were times she wouldn't talk to him for days if he failed a test or skipped class …"

My forehead crinkled. "Jesus."

"Little did she know, her cold-hearted ways were what fueled my brother's desire to be so rebellious." Avery took a sip of her coffee. "Academics weren't really his thing, but, God, did he love music. We both did. I'm glad he's stuck with it all this time."

"He told me your dad was a musician, right?" I stared at her.

She nodded and smiled. "He was a good teacher. If he were still here, he'd be at every single A Quiet Peril show."

"I'm sorry he didn't get a chance to see everything the two of you have done," I murmured.

I could see the emotions tensing her features as she grappled with her thoughts. "Danny was a couple of years older than me when he died. He was in high school and playing a small gig in town the night of the … accident."

It was my turn to offer her a comforting hand. What she was telling me was clearly not easy for her to get out. I remembered Danny saying that Avery was with their dad when the accident happened, so I was surprised she was bringing up such a traumatic moment for her when she'd only just met me.

"Danny, uh, ended up in the hospital the night of our dad's funeral. I guess he'd drunk too much." Her voice cracked. "Liam said he almost died."

My heart constricted at the thought of Danny lying unconscious on a hospital bed. "That must've been so scary."

Her eyes fell to her hands. "It would've been … had I known. You see, Danny and I weren't all that close—for obvious reasons. Liam told me all of this after we started dating. He mentioned that Danny struggled with drugs after that. I don't know to what extent or what kind." She looked up at me cautiously. "But it must've been pretty bad for how hard it is for Liam to talk about. And Danny doesn't exactly confide in me very often to ever bring it up. But I know he hasn't touched anything in years," she said confidently. "It's still difficult for me to wrap my head around, but I'm grateful he had his friends there to help him through it. Liam, Tic, Lexie, and Nikko … they were his family when my mom and I weren't."

"Why are you telling me all this?" I whispered because everything felt so delicate. "I'm happy he's okay now. Getting clean isn't easy. But it doesn't change my mind. I'm sorry."

She reached for my hand, and I let her take it. "Danny and the rest of the band would never put you in a situation where you would have to worry about that. Not after what Danny went through. They have rules."

The idea of the four of them having rules of any kind was difficult to believe.

"Rules, huh? What kind of rules?"

Her light chuckle broke through some of the tension. "Well, there's the *no drinking and driving* rule, which is pretty self-explanatory. And trust me, they won't tolerate even a drop of alcohol." She giggled, holding up a finger. She counted on another and said, "And then there's the *anytime, anywhere* rule, which basically just means they'll be there whenever another band member needs them, no questions asked. I know—cue the *Friends* theme song, right?"

I laughed and waited for the next one as she held up another finger.

"The last is the *no hard drugs* rule," she told me, locking her gray eyes onto me.

I shifted on the step uncomfortably. "Does that not include parties?"

"What?" She cocked her head.

"Where do they draw the line on that rule? Because I saw what I saw at their house the other night." I took a sip of my warm coffee and waited for her answer.

Her dumbfounded look told me she didn't have one. "What exactly did you see at the party?"

"Couple of girls snorting coke off the bathroom sink," I answered firmly.

She froze, color draining from her face. "That can't be right."

Anger churned in my stomach. It wasn't the first time someone hadn't believed me. "Maybe. It could've been some crushed-up pills now that I think of it. I didn't ask." I noticed my sharp tone and wished I could take it back. "I'm sorry for being so curt. You don't deserve that."

"No, it's okay. I'd be upset too." She pursed her lips in thought. "Most people who come to the house know that's not allowed, but there could've been some new groupies or something. I'm just surprised Nikko didn't find out. He's got a knack for that stuff. He would've kicked them out and made sure they weren't on any of the lists in the future."

I watched her scramble to find a reasonable explanation, and it dawned on me.

She was serious. These rules were absolute to them.

"I can talk to Liam and Nikko about it as soon as I see them. Do you remember what they looked like? Their names?" she asked, pulling her brows together.

"Look, you don't need to launch an investigation over this. I know it was a party and people have fun at parties. I'm just trying to explain why I can't be with your brother."

"No offense, Logan, but you're not the one I'm worried about. Danny has a history of substance abuse, and as much as Liam tells me not to worry about him, I can't help it. I want to protect him just as much as you want to protect yourself. Please. Is there anything you can remember about them?" she pleaded with me.

I thought back to that night—when I had been fighting the urge to run back downstairs to Danny, when I had seen the two girls. Everything after was all a blur. I only remembered a few details.

"Well, the first girl who walked out was blonde. I didn't get a good look at her. And the one in the bathroom had long brown hair. Pretty. I think she was wearing an orange dress."

"Was it mesh by chance?" she asked.

I frowned as that detail sharpened in my memory. "Yeah, I think so."

"Fucking bitch," she muttered under her breath.

"Not a new groupie, I take it?"

"Nope. Someone we can't seem to get rid of. Her name's Hannah. She's one of Danny's old … oh, I don't know what to call her other than toxic. Seriously, she should come with one of those neon warning labels. Danny's been asking Nikko to get rid of her for weeks, but she keeps popping up." She grabbed my hand again and squeezed. "Once I tell Liam about what you saw, she won't be back. He'll make sure of it."

I squeezed her hand back, feeling conflicted. Getting rid of Hannah wouldn't eliminate the risk altogether. There would always be another Hannah in Danny's world. But I also knew that there was a risk anywhere I went, with anyone I chose to associate with. And if I was as strong and smart as I believed I was, why couldn't I trust myself enough to know a wrong choice from a right one? Especially when being with Danny was the only thing that'd felt right in a long time.

"Why is this so important to you … me giving Danny a chance?" I asked.

She looked at me thoughtfully for a second before responding, "My brother has spent his whole life building up this hard exterior, protecting himself from the one thing he's wanted more than anything—a love that's not conditional. I feel like he has a chance of finding that with you."

The next breath I took felt funny. "You do?"

She gave me a soft, genuine nod.

"You really care about him," I said. "He's lucky to have you."

Avery laughed. "I'm not sure about that, but I care for him and want him to be happy. And the whole band has noticed how happy he's been since you and your daughter moved in."

I couldn't help the smile that grew across my face.

"I'm serious. They say he's been dancing around the house, baking cakes, and listening to Taylor Swift love songs. He's smitten, I tell you." She scrunched her face up in a teasing way.

"Stop!" I laughed, nudging her shoulder with mine.

"Just be careful when he starts writing you into his music." She winked at me. "That's when you'll know it's real."

We sat there for a moment, smiling and laughing, the air suddenly feeling lighter.

"Do you have anything going on tomorrow?" she asked, reaching into the paper bag she'd brought. She pulled out a couple of pastries, handing me one.

"Just working." I sighed. "My parents are taking Violet to their cabin this weekend so I can get some photography done. Why?"

"There's a music festival going on downtown—the Ex's and Oh's Festival." She glanced at me.

"I've heard of it." I nodded, taking a bite of the flaky, buttery goodness in my hand.

"We've all got tickets. My roommate, Nina, was supposed to come, but she's getting ready to move. So, we've got an extra ticket if you want to come with us."

I took a bigger bite, giving myself time to think about it. I needed to take advantage of my time without Violet and get some shots in, but I'd rarely gotten to have fun with people my age lately. And I did have the whole weekend to find some new places to photograph …

"You can bring your camera!" she added with enthusiasm, sealing the deal.

"Okay." My answer fell from my mouth before I even finished chewing, sending a bolt of excitement through me.

"Really?" Avery squealed. "Yay! Okay, it starts at four. I can pick you up around three, and we can ride together if you want?"

"That'd be great." I offered a smile.

"I won't tell Danny, just in case you change your mind," she told me.

I didn't think that would ease my nerves, but it did, and I wanted to hug her.

As if she could read my mind, she pulled me into her for a short embrace.

I hugged her back and couldn't help but laugh a little. "You know, I never really grew up wanting a sister, but I would've loved to have one like you."

Avery's eyes glistened before she pulled away with a smile that seemed like a front, covering up something deeper. She gathered her things and gave me her phone number before waving me goodbye, promising to see me tomorrow.

My throat constricted as I watched her walk away, knowing I had just made a decision that wasn't for Violet or my parents. It was for me. And maybe that was okay.

17

Danny

"What the hell is taking Nikko so long to get here?" I bounced my knee impatiently, sitting on the edge of the couch.

Liam came out of the kitchen, threading his arms through his jacket. "You didn't hear? He got stuck helping Nina move this weekend."

"Seriously?" I arched a brow. "They're back together again?"

"Probably just wants to spend as much … alone time … with her as possible before she's no longer a few miles down the road." He shrugged and then nodded upstairs. "Wanna yell up to Lexie and hurry her along? She chewed my head off when I poked my head in on the way down here."

"Lexie! Let's fucking go!" I barked, knowing I didn't need to be as loud as I was for her to hear me.

Her footsteps hit the stairs a second later, and she threw me a deathly glare when she reached the bottom. Her fishnets and tiny pink dress were going to put our security team to work tonight. "Yell at me like that again, and I'll cut the strings on your Fender."

Tic winced at her threat from his sprawled position on the other side of the couch.

I chuckled, knowing she was only half-joking. "You finally ready or what?"

"Yeah, yeah. I'm ready," Lexie said, applying lipstick in the hallway mirror. "Why are you all waiting on me? Avery's not even here yet."

Liam ran a hand through his freshly showered hair. "She's going to meet us there."

"You didn't tell me that." Lexie snapped her head around. "I wouldn't have taken so long if I'd known we weren't waiting on her."

"Yeah, right." I scoffed, pulling myself up off the couch.

We all piled into my car—Liam up front with me and Lexie and Tic in the back. Luckily, the drive to the festival didn't take more than thirty minutes, and we got there with enough time to get decent parking. When we got through the gate, Nikko shot us a text and told us where our security was waiting for us, and when we found them, they had already met up with Avery and … Logan?

Here.

With Avery.

Which meant … she was here with *me*.

I made a mental note to thank my sister later.

Logan hadn't seen me yet, so I took my time admiring her profile in disbelief. The soft pillows of her lips moved as she spoke to my sister, gripping the camera around her neck like it was a nervous habit of hers. Her hair was tied back with a few short black strands that hung around her face, blowing in the breeze. She wore an oversize sweatshirt I'd seen on her before. It was hiding whatever short bottoms she had on underneath, and my eyes drank in the sight of her long, bare legs.

I stepped toward her, taking advantage of how oblivious she was to my presence, and came up behind her. The chunky black boots she wore gave her an additional couple of inches, bringing the top of her head right below my chin. I only had to tilt my head a fraction to reach her ear.

"What a lovely surprise," I muttered deeply, fighting the urge to teeth her earlobe.

She tensed for a beat before she spun around and faced me. Her camera hit just below my beltline, and I was suddenly grateful for her choice of footwear.

I caught her waist and smiled widely. "I didn't know you were coming." I peered over her head at my sister, who was sporting a prideful grin.

"Oh, Avery said she had an extra ticket. I hope that's okay?" Her bright, almond-shaped eyes floated up to mine.

I cocked my head. "You don't have to ask if it's okay to be anywhere I am. My answer will always be the same."

Her face screwed into the cutest expression as she relaxed in my hold.

"Danny! Logan!" Lexie shouted after us.

The group was already ten paces away, heading into the massive field of thick crowds.

One of our security guys lingered behind, waiting on us.

I stepped beside Logan and offered my hand, hoping she'd take it.

She threaded her fingers through mine and pulled me toward our group without a second thought. "Aren't you guys just spectators tonight? Are they necessary?" She glanced back at the six-foot-four former kickboxer stalking behind us.

I chuckled and pulled her closer to my side to make sure she could hear me in the growing chaos. "They didn't used to be, but Nikko insists on having a couple on us whenever we're in large settings like this. Especially at a place where people might recognize us."

Logan glanced around at the vast amount of faces passing us by. "You think people will recognize you here?"

"Most likely. We used to play here." I nodded. "A lot of the music here is similar to ours, which means some of our fans could be here. Most of the time, when we run into them, they're chill, and they just ask for a picture or an autograph, but we've had a few … mishaps … since our last big tour."

"Like what?"

I looked ahead, mulling over whether I wanted to tell her on the off chance that it might frighten her away. But I didn't want to keep things from her either. I'd rather have her prepared than sidelined if something happened tonight.

"Last year, while we were touring on the East Coast, we decided to surprise another band that we're friends with and attend one of their shows. Some of the people around us knew who we were, and it became a little crazy. We thought it would die down after a bit, but it just kept getting worse. Next thing we knew, there were hands everywhere, reaching for us. Lexie ended up getting a black eye. Liam's shirt was torn off his back. Tic had scratches all over him from some of the girls' nails— so bad that they'd drawn blood. And some guy managed to get his hand down the back of my pants ..." I trailed off.

The concern on her face eased a bit at my last statement, and suddenly, she was rolling her lips between her teeth, trying to fight a smile pinching at her cheeks.

"Hey, that was traumatizing! He had my entire butt cheek in his grasp for longer than I'd like to admit, okay? Don't laugh."

Her smile only got bigger. "Definitely not laughing."

I poked a finger into her narrow side, making her laugh burst free.

The rest of the group stopped at a drink station and turned to look at us.

"What's so funny?" Lexie asked, eyeing the two of us curiously.

"Nothing," I said, clearing my throat.

Logan was still giggling. "He just told me about what happened to you guys at that concert last year."

The group gawked at her for a moment, confused, until she made a cupping-squeezing motion with her hands, and then the entire group was dying of laughter with her.

"Great," I muttered, pushing her hands down with a groan. "Thanks a lot, Logan."

Her eyes rounded with innocence as she rose up on her toes and kissed the side of my face.

My hand tensed around hers, letting her know how much her lips affected me.

"Do you want anything to drink, Logan?" Avery asked from the front of the line.

Logan looked behind the bar at what was available and then shook her head sheepishly. "Um, no, that's okay. Just a water is fine."

Avery turned around and put a gentle hand on Logan's arm. "You're safe with us. I promise," she said, giving her a reassuring nod.

I frowned at their interaction. *Safe with us?* Of course she was safe with us. What was she talking about?

Logan let out a breath and lifted a shoulder. "Okay, I'll have whatever you're having," she told my sister.

I watched Logan for a moment, trying to decide if I should press and ask what that was all about, but then she looked up at me and gave me this big, beautiful smile, and I knew she was okay, whatever it was. If I needed to know, she'd tell me.

Avery finished paying the bartender and handed Logan a canned cocktail with a wink, and then she headed toward one of the ten stages with Liam by her side.

I grabbed a few waters for us and our security, then started in the same direction as them with Lexie and Tic in tow.

Logan paused as she brought her drink to her lips. "Wait. You're not getting anything?"

Tossing back a third of my water, I wiped my mouth and exhaled. "Can't. I'm sober cab."

The side of her lips twitched up, as if she knew something I didn't, but her gaze fell back to the crowd as we began to weave our way toward the front of the stage, where the band had already started. I let go of her hand and placed mine on her lower back to help guide her as our security waved us through some barriers.

Logan gaped around at the private space we got to watch the set from and gazed up in awe at the singer towering just a few feet above her. She fumbled for her camera, and I couldn't help but laugh. As soon as she was done taking her pictures, Liam reached up and shook hands with the singer as he knelt to greet him. I offered him a respectful nod when he stood back up.

Logan snapped her head sideways at me, eyes wide. "Do you guys know *everybody*?" she shouted over the music.

I moved her in front of me so I could talk in her ear while still watching the band. "They opened for us on our last tour. They're good guys and really fucking talented. I can introduce you later if you want."

Some screaming amplified behind us, and I looked back to see why. Lexie had been spotted by some fans and was signing her name across some girl's tit.

Suddenly noticing me and the others, the group around Lexie began waving their pens aggressively and shouting our names.

I knew this was part of the job, and I didn't mind doing it, but, fuck, Logan had just cozied up in front of me, and I didn't want to leave her.

"It's okay." Logan saw the conflict on my face and patted my chest. "Go see them."

"I'm sorry. I'll be right back. Don't move, okay?" I waited for her to give me a nod before I walked over to pose for some pictures and sign a few autographs.

When I finished and turned back to find Logan, she had her camera raised at us instead of the stage.

"What are you doing?" I chuckled, wrapping my arms around her as quickly as I could.

"I like watching you guys with your fans. They adore you."

"I adore *you*, Logan Ellis."

She smiled and snapped a close-up photo of me before I could protest.

"C'mon now!" I nudged her and grinned. "What are you going to do with that?"

Logan tapped a finger on her chin. "Well, at first, I was thinking blackmail. But now, I'm considering selling it."

"Selling it, huh?" I asked, stealing a glance at her lips.

"Yep. I might just retire off this image," she teased. "People will pay big money for a rare picture of Danny Fox's nose hairs."

"Unbelievable. You just wanted me for my nose hairs all along. I knew it." I pouted.

She slowly raised her camera again and took another picture.

I didn't move. Her hips were right up against me, her body flush with mine, and I wasn't about to object to anything she wanted.

Pulling her camera out of the way of her golden eyes, the playful, doe-eyed look was gone and replaced with a sultry stare.

Panic erected in my chest as she leaned up toward my mouth with her lips slightly parted. I wanted to kiss her more than my next breath, but I didn't want her to run away again either. I was usually good at making hasty decisions, but this

… ugh. The odds were fucking with my head too much not to weigh my options carefully.

"Danny?"

I felt the vibrations of my name against my lips. I hadn't realized I'd pinched my eyes shut.

"You look like you're in pain." The warmth of her breath hit my lips, but she paused just short of a kiss, staring up at me. She had no idea.

"I'm sorry I ran," she said. "I was scared."

My hand slid up the side of her face, holding her close. "I thought you didn't scare easily?"

Her eyes flickered nervously. "I'm scared of everything," she confessed.

I almost didn't hear her amid everything happening around us. My thumb stretched up to rub the apple of her cheek, growing flush with vulnerability.

"But I no longer choose to be scared of this." She pushed up onto her toes and closed the distance left between us, kissing me hard.

I swiftly grabbed the back of her head and sealed my lips against hers, sliding my tongue into the soft warmth of her mouth. The moan I elicited from her throat made my knees nearly buckle.

Her back arched as our kiss deepened, and she dragged her teeth along my lower lip.

I cursed into her mouth and reluctantly pulled away, still holding her face. "You're going to have to stop that, or we're not staying for the rest of this thing," I growled.

Logan brought her wet lip between her teeth and smirked. "Okay, I'll behave."

When she turned back around in my arms, her ass hit my growing erection, and I growled again. She wiggled in my hold, laughing, but eventually stilled enough for me to focus on the band.

We stayed like that for the rest of their set, swaying together in sync with the music until it was time to move to another stage. Her closeness put my mind at ease. I thought I'd learned to ignore the loneliness I felt, never having someone to call my own, but that feeling eased every moment she spent in my arms.

The sun was beginning to set, painting the sky in orange and pink hues when the next band started. Lexie had found someone to dance with, who I was sure would be at the house in the morning. Tic made friends with one of our security guards and was chatting with him next to the stage. Liam and Avery had left for a few songs to check out another band. When they returned, Avery brought more drinks for her and Logan, and as the set progressed, I noticed the alcohol loosening her tiny limbs. She swayed and danced with less care, and that bright smile of hers began to show itself more and more.

It was nice, seeing her this way—carefree and unfiltered. It had me wishing I were up onstage, watching her in the crowd, dancing to my music. But then I wouldn't be able to hold her like this. If only I could be in two places at once. The thought of leaving her in a few short weeks had my stomach twisting itself, and I found myself drafting up ways to see her.

"Will you come to visit me on tour?" I asked next to her ear.

She swiveled her head and peered up at me. "Y-yeah. I'd love to see you guys play. When?"

"Whenever you want." I wrapped my arms around her tightly and brushed my lips against her neck. "I can have Nikko make the arrangements whenever it works best for you."

"Okay." She smiled and then shifted in my arms.

I loosened my hold enough for her to face me again. My Adam's apple bobbed in my throat as she wrapped her arms around me and planted the side of her head on my chest.

"I like it here." She closed her eyes and hummed.

"The festival?" I asked, folding my arms behind her shoulders.

She shook her head, squeezing me harder. "Here."

We stayed that way for a while—me resting my cheek on the top of her head and her clinging to my middle. If someone told me this was heaven, I wouldn't question it.

When she shifted her footing beneath herself, her feet got tangled up, and I had to hold on to her so she didn't slip through my arms.

I chuckled. "How did you manage to trip over yourself?"

"I'm clumsy and a bit of a lightweight. Sue me." Her eyes closed longer than normal as she giggled.

"Danny boy!" Liam called, lifting his chin. "We're headed to go watch Pacify. Are you two joining us?"

My eyes looked to where he pointed, and I held up a finger to signal him to wait.

I lightly stroked Logan's back with my fingers and looked down. "You okay to keep going? Or do you want me to take you home?"

"I'm not ready to go home yet. I'm having too much fun." Her words slipped off her tongue lazily.

"You got it. Let's get some food in you first." I started to drop an arm over her shoulders and led her to the nearest concessions when she rested her chin in the center of my chest and sighed.

I paused.

"Can you promise me something?" The golden flecks in her eyes brightened under the stage lights still gleaming above us.

"Anything, Logan." I smoothed a piece of hair behind her ear.

Her eyes grew hazy as she looked up at me. "Promise you won't ever touch me or do anything with me when I'm not sober."

Every muscle in my body tensed like I'd been doused in ice water. "Wh-what?"

"I like you. A lot," she said. "Like, *a lot*, a lot. I just want to make sure it's my choice."

My brows knitted, and I made sure she was looking at me again when I told her, "I would *never* take advantage of you or do anything you didn't want me to do. Sober or not. I promise. You hear me?"

She swallowed and nodded.

"Why did you feel like you had to ask me that?" I dared to ask.

Waiting for her to answer felt like an eternity.

She blinked up at me slowly and then finally muttered, "Because I don't know who Violet's father is."

18

Logan

The savory smell of bacon rattled me awake the next morning. My stomach rumbled, and my mouth began to salivate as I stretched beneath my fluffy blue duvet and squinted at the morning sun peeping through my bedroom shades. More sun than I was used to seeing when my alarm usually woke me. I glanced up at the clock and quickly ripped the covers off my legs, scurrying to my feet.

It's noon? How is it noon?

I suddenly realized that the obnoxious alarm on my phone wasn't what had woken me. It was the promise of breakfast and—

I caught a glimpse of my bed and stiffened. The right side of my bed I didn't sleep on wasn't tucked in the corner like it usually was. The covers were tousled, and the pillow had an indent from someone's head. My hands flew to the tank top and shorts I'd worn beneath my sweatshirt last night. They were still securely buttoned and wrapped around my body. I let out a breath of relief, but my nerves were still on edge.

The faint clang of silverware on ceramic broke me from my frozen state, and I made my way down the hall, following the delicious scent and sound of company.

Danny stood at the kitchen island, plating two servings of bacon and eggs. He lit up when he saw me. "Mornin', beautiful."

I sauntered into the kitchen and snatched the glass of orange juice sitting on the counter, downing half of it. "Morning? It's the afternoon," I eventually replied.

Danny eyed the glass in my hand and raised his brows. "That was mine."

"It was in *my* fridge!" I countered.

"Well, if that's all it takes, I was technically in your bed last night. Does that make me yours too?" He wiggled his brows playfully.

After taking another slow sip, I set the glass down and sank into one of the stools. "About that …"

"We just slept, Logan," he quickly reassured me as if he could read my mind.

"Yeah?" I asked, already feeling silly for needing more confirmation when I knew he was being truthful. Memories of last night were slowly breaking through the fogginess, and I vaguely remembered him removing my sweatshirt and tucking me into bed safely.

"I was a perfect gentleman."

I narrowed my eyes at him with a smug grin. "A gentleman who slept in my bed instead of on the couch?"

I enjoyed the way his throat worked as he tipped his head back and drank what was left in the glass.

"I never said I was a saint," he said, tossing a droolworthy wink at me.

There was a roll of excitement that followed his words, but I shook it off and chuckled.

"Besides, I made you a promise." He slid one of the hot plates in front of me. "And I keep my promises."

I eagerly shoved a piece of bacon in my mouth before I registered what he had said.

Promise? What promise?

And with a glance at his solemn face, the confession I gave him came flooding back too.

The muscles in his jaw twitched. "I'm sorry you have to ask for someone's trust like that, Logan."

My face heated. I couldn't believe I'd dumped all that on him last night. "I shouldn't have said anything. That was a long time ago and … not one of my proudest moments."

He leaned his elbows on the counter and frowned. "What do you mean?"

I sat back in my chair, feeling too seen.

"Wait, are you taking responsibility for the asshole who raped you?" he asked in disbelief.

I winced the moment the R-word fell off his tongue and shoved my plate aside, my appetite forgotten. An icky sensation slithered up my spine at the mere thought of *him*, and I tried to shrug it off. I sometimes got flashes of the man—his sweaty and thick arms, the roughness of his voice, and the way his hands had dug into me so deep that he left bruises behind.

But none of those haunting moments ever included me pushing him away or fighting him off.

"He didn't do … that," I eventually stated.

Danny clenched his hands into fists with a stunned expression. "I need some more clarification than that because that is not the impression you gave me last night."

"I was an addict," I clarified. "I didn't know what was happening at the time, but I doubt I told him no."

My pulse raced as Danny's face twisted in anger.

"He. Took. Advantage. Of. You," Danny gritted out slowly. "The fact that you can't confidently recall with one hundred percent certainty that you didn't tell him to eff off doesn't exempt him from that. And if you ever figure out who it was, I'll rip his fucking esophagus from his throat. That I *promise* you."

I shuddered at his protective threat. No one had ever held *him* responsible. The police couldn't do anything because I didn't have a name or a face to give them. There had been a ton of people at the party. Some I knew, some I didn't. It could've been anyone. All I had was a vague outline of a tattoo, which wasn't at all helpful. And my parents … they might not have ever said the words to my face, but I knew they'd blamed me for putting myself in that position.

"I'm not sorry it happened," I admitted, watching as horror quickly washed over his face. "Violet is the best thing to ever happen to me."

The crease between his brow softened. "I know that, but—"

"Danny, if I hadn't gotten pregnant, I wouldn't be sitting here with you. At the rate I was going, I'd be dead by now," I told him bluntly.

The heat on his skin faded and paled.

I stared blankly in front of me. "I was clean the entire nine months I was pregnant. I had no choice. My parents kept me under lock and key. Literally. The only time I left the house was for doctor appointments they drove me to. Going through withdrawal while pregnant was torturous. It was the longest year of my life. But I wouldn't have done it if she wasn't growing inside me." I breathed out a humorless laugh. "There were some days that I didn't care if I lived or died, and I honestly don't think my mom and dad cared either, as long as Violet was okay."

"C'mon, Logan …" Danny objected.

My shoulders sagged as I dropped my gaze to my lap. "They were angry with me. And I think they saw Violet as a second chance. That maybe if they helped bring her into this world and learned from their mistakes with me, they could redeem themselves. Whatever their reasons were, they kept me going and made sure I was healthy so Vi and I could be here. Together."

"You've made mistakes, Logan. That doesn't make you unworthy. It just makes you human."

"You don't know what I put them through. I owe them everything," I whispered, hearing my voice crack. "And even after all that, I still failed. I relapsed two months after Violet was born. My parents had to take out a second mortgage on their house to pay for my rehab and took care of my daughter while I was away. They didn't let me see her for a year, and that time away from her broke me. Changed me. Everything I wanted out of life suddenly became so clear." I choked on a sob. "Her. All I wanted was her. To be her mom. For her to know who I was."

Danny was beside me in the next second, brushing away tears from my cheeks and letting me cry against him. I mumbled an apology into his stomach, but it was incoherent, lost between my cries and gasps for air.

But he held me. He let me cry and fist his shirt, unbothered by the tearstains with day-old mascara I was leaving behind. His gentleness only made my tears flow that much harder.

Once my breath slowed and my tears dried, I traced the outline of his dad's guitar on his arm as he hummed a soothing melody to comfort me.

"I haven't cried like that in a long time," I finally managed to whisper.

He took a few breaths, grazing his knuckles along my jaw. "All I want to do is wrap you up and shield you from this pain you've kept bottled up. It kills me to hear you blaming yourself for this. You might not be who your parents wanted you to be, but you're *everything* I want, Logan Ellis." Danny bent down and touched his nose to mine. "You are who you are because of the things you've been through. You told me you wouldn't be here if it wasn't for Violet. Well, you *are* here. You made it. Don't ever dismiss the strength that took."

My eyes blurred again as he peered down at me with the utmost adoration. I gripped his neck and pulled him down, softly touching my lips to his. It was a whisper of a kiss, but it sent my pulse racing as if I'd just run a marathon. Leaning back enough to look at him, I smiled.

"I thought the butterflies would be gone by now," I whispered.

His brows etched with worry. "I will burn that red flag to the ground if I have to. You just tell me how."

I shook my head. "No. I don't think I want them to go away. It … excites me every time you touch me, but I've also never felt more myself than when I'm with you. And that's a safe feeling."

The corner of his mouth tilted up before he brought his lips back down to mine.

I wasn't in a hurry to let him go, but I needed to shower off the lingering smell of the festival from my hair and the emotions from this morning.

"I must look like a wreck. Are you okay hanging out for a minute while I go shower?"

"Of course. Let me just run home quickly and change. I'll be back before you're done."

"Okay." I smiled. "Just make sure you come back."

He hummed and smiled. "And here I thought, I was the clingy one."

I squeezed the water from my hair with a towel after throwing on a comfy tee and some shorts. There was rain in the forecast, and with how late we'd started our day, I liked the idea of a cozy day inside with Danny. He still wasn't back yet, so I headed downstairs to peek at some of my negatives from the Ex's and Oh's Festival.

I was looking through the focus finder at my first negative strip when I heard Danny's footsteps overhead. They trailed around the house—from the living room to the kitchen and down the hallway—before they stopped.

"Logan?" His voice echoed down into the basement.

"Down here," I called.

A few seconds later, he knocked. "Can I come in?"

I crossed the room and opened the door, smiling up at him with a fresh face.

"You lied," I said, crossing my arms over my chest. "You said you'd be back before I got done showering."

His shoulders shifted with a chuckle. "I was gone ten minutes, tops." He stepped closer, leaning against the doorframe. "Why? Were you waiting for me to join you?"

"No." I quickly shook my head, feeling heat spread into my cheeks.

He stalked around me with a smirk, gawking at my setup. "It turned out great down here. Much less serial killer–looking than the last time I was down here."

"Ah, then my plan is working. No one will ever suspect a thing," I teased, shutting the door behind me.

Danny peered around the room. "I thought it was supposed to be dark in here?"

"The safelights only need to come on once I start to focus and develop," I said, showing him some of the negative strips I was looking at. "I was just taking a look at some of the pictures I got last night. Trying to decide which ones I want to start with. I should probably have a few done to show my parents when they get back with Violet tomorrow."

"You think you got some good shots?" he asked, leaning over me from behind to observe.

The pressure and warmth of his entire front side resting against my back made my breath waver. "I'm not sure yet."

His chin brushed my neck as he tilted his head closer to my ear. "Can you teach me how it works?"

"You really want to learn?" I turned around so I could look at him. Something about him taking an interest in my passions lit me up inside.

He pulled back a step and grinned down at the infamous, faded emblem stretching across my breasts—my tattered Guns N' Roses T-shirt with a torn hem.

I noticed his eyes lingering on my shirt a second too long and rolled my eyes. " 'Paradise City,' 'Don't Cry,' and 'Patience.'" I counted each title on my fingers, pursing my lips. "Do you need more?"

He cocked a grin and raised a brow. "Excuse me?"

"Weren't you going to ask me to name three Guns N' Roses songs?"

"No." He laughed. "That T-shirt has been well loved. I didn't doubt you knew any for a second."

"Then, why were you grinning like that?"

That magnetic smile of his returned. "Because I can't wait to see one of my band tees looking the same way on you one day. All worn out and well loved."

My heart somersaulted. "I have to get one first."

He bent down and brushed his nose against mine, then straightened. Reaching a hand behind his shoulders, he fisted the back of his old shirt and pulled it over his head. "Here.

Take mine." The warmth of his body still lingered on the soft cotton as he handed it to me.

"Th-thanks." I clenched the shirt in my hands, looking up through my lashes at his naked chest.

It should be illegal to look as good as he did. It was distracting and doing something to my pulse that made me feel like I was on the downhill drop of a roller coaster.

Did he expect to just be half-naked the rest of the day? I knew he did that at home, but he was at my house now, and I wasn't sure I'd survive until tomorrow.

The hills of his abdomen tightened as he chuckled, noticing my wandering eyes.

I had to hold back a sigh.

Maybe if I give him my shirt …

A bold idea pushed its way into the decision-making part of my brain, and my heart rattled against my rib cage like it was trying to break free.

"You ready?"

I knew Danny's question was about the photography lesson, but I couldn't help but nod in response to what I was about to do next.

"Flip that switch there, on the wall," I murmured.

Danny did as he had been told, turning the room dark. It took a moment for our eyes to adjust. Only the faint glow of the red safelights illuminated his profile, and I suddenly wished I had my camera to capture how beautiful he was.

Danny watched me carefully as I set his shirt off to the side and gazed up at him.

Excitement fluttered in the pit of my stomach as I took the hem of my T-shirt in my hands and slowly removed it. The cool basement coated my skin in goosebumps and hardened the soft peaks of my bare breasts. I resisted the urge to cover them as I let him take me in.

Danny dropped his chin, the shadows around his eyes becoming darker as they fell down my neck, to my naked breasts, my stomach, and back up again. "Logan." My name echoed from deep in his chest.

His weighted stare was so intense that it nearly broke me in half.

"Yes?" I breathed.

"This is not how I envisioned a photography lesson going." He slid his lip between his teeth, wetting it with his tongue. "What are you doing?"

Regret crawled up the back of my neck the longer he went without touching me. "I … wanted to try it on," I blinked, reaching for his shirt again.

Danny caught my wrist and stopped me, caging me in. He locked eyes with me and shook his head twice, then leaned down to brush his lips along the side of my face. When he reached my ear, he released a ragged breath and pinched the lobe between his teeth.

Heat flared deep in my abdomen. I couldn't resist the urge to rub my thighs together as the ache grew.

"Can I touch you, Logan? I'll beg if you want me to."

With hooded eyes, I tilted my head and nodded.

.

19

Danny

Rolling my eyes back with a growl, I dropped my forehead to Logan's and slid my hands up the soft skin of her abdomen. Her stomach flinched with every slight movement I made.

When I reached the plump edge of her breasts, I halted, reminding myself to go slow. To ask permission even if it killed me. As important as it was for me to know I wasn't pushing her too far, it was crucial that she had full control over every move I made. To know she had the power.

And, *fuck*, did she have power over me. I was ready to devour every inch of her, every which way. But she needed to articulate her needs. Her desires.

Her chest rose and fell with sporadic breaths. "Danny, please," she whimpered.

"Do you want me to touch you here?" I stretched a thumb up and swiped it over her nipple.

Logan dropped her head back with a gasp.

"Remember to use your words," I said, my voice gravelly.

"Yes." She hurried out her response. "Yes."

I could smell the faint remnants of her soap, and I leaned into her neck, breathing in the intoxicating mixture of lavender and vanilla that was her.

Cock stiff and heart pounding, I finally slid my hands up over the swells of her breasts. My body shuddered at the contact of my rough hands meeting her delicate peaks.

She was so goddamn beautiful.

I touched my lips to her neck, licking and sucking my way down to the top of her shoulder.

She arched her back.

But I halted again.

"Is this okay?"

"Mmhmm," she moaned, tangling her hand in my hair.

"Logan"—I nibbled at her skin—"words."

"Yes." She let out a frustrated sigh. "Don't stop."

I continued kissing my way down her body, loving the way the red light reflected off her skin. She writhed beneath my touch, so I filed my leg between her thighs, letting her apply pressure whenever she wanted it.

My mouth moved lower to where she wanted it most, swirling my tongue just above her nipple. A delicious sting shot through my scalp as she fisted my hair.

"Danny!" she groaned, grinding her hips into me.

I flicked my eyes up to her and grinned. "Tell me what you want, Logan." My mouth watered. I wanted it just as bad as she did, but I needed to hear her say it.

"Kiss me," she begged.

Lifting my head back up, I gripped her chin and brought my lips to hers, knowing full well that wasn't what she meant.

She kissed me eagerly for a moment and then pulled away, breathless. "I'm so turned on. I feel like I could explode," she said, dipping her hand down to palm my aching erection through my pants.

I hissed at how perfectly she rubbed me. But this wasn't about me.

Stealing her hand away, I kissed the inside of her palm and put it back on the table so she could brace herself.

"Please, Danny," Logan pleaded. "I'm about to go feral on your ass if you don't put your mouth on one of my nipples and play with it."

Her growl of an order felt like a drug seeping into my veins, and when I sucked her nipple into my mouth, I knew I was addicted.

"Good girl," I rasped, swirling my tongue over the hardened bud.

"That feels … so good," she said, grinding her hips.

I pulled back gently, taking it between my teeth.

Her chest lifted as she hummed, letting me know she liked that.

I smiled and peered up at her as I moved to her other breast, giving it just as much attention.

Swirling.

Sucking.

Teething.

Pulling.

The pinch of her brows and the sharp bite of her lip told me she needed more, even though I was confident I could get her off on just this.

My hands dropped to the waistband of her shorts, and I fingered the drawstring, waiting for her to tell me to—

"Take them off," she called out without me even having to ask. "Rip them if you have to. Just take them off!"

I untied the knot at an unhurried pace, kissing my way down her stomach. I would do whatever she wanted me to do, but I'd do it at my own speed.

Logan cursed under her breath, and I chuckled.

Hooking my fingers under the fabric of her shorts and the tiny string of her thong, I knelt in front of her. My eyes lifted up her body, searching for that golden gaze before I shimmied them both over her hips and stripped her naked in the darkness.

"You're fucking stunning, Logan," I told her, looking up at her glowing red form. She looked like a work of art.

She bit down on one of her fingers with anticipation.

Trailing my fingers down the side of her leg, I reached behind her knee. "I'm going to open your legs wider. Can I take this?" I asked, applying a bit of pressure so she'd bend it.

It was too dark to see, but I could tell she was blushing by the way she nodded down at me.

"Yes, please," she whispered.

"That's my girl," I praised, hooking her leg over my shoulder.

I applied generous, leisurely kisses along her inner thigh while the hand not holding her leg firmly in place sprawled low on her stomach.

Her tiny, mumbled cries grew shorter and shorter, the closer I got to her core.

"What do you want, Logan? Tell me." I hovered my mouth right over her pussy.

She took my head in her hands and tried to push me down, but I didn't flinch.

"Fuck, Danny. Kiss me!" she cried out.

"Tsk-tsk," I said.

She released a breathy, surprised moan as my hands gripped her ass and lifted her up onto the edge of the table with her legs parted around me.

I smirked and kissed her mouth again, doing just as she'd asked.

Logan took the anger of her mistake out on my lip and bit down hard.

I fucking loved it.

"Ugh! You're driving me insane! I need a release," she begged.

Sliding one hand between us and gripping the back of her neck with the other, I felt my restraint slipping. "And I can give it to you. Just use your goddamn words, Logan."

She panted against my lips. "Fuck, just touch my clit already, Danny."

I teased my tongue into her mouth as my fingers glided against her wet center.

Her lips parted, too breathless to make a sound at first, and then she moaned as my rhythm increased in speed.

I pressed my lips along her jawline. "Like this, Logan?"

"More," she groaned.

I kept my thumb on her clit while I eased a finger inside her. "Does this feel good?"

She nodded frantically.

God, she was wet.

I nudged my head into her neck and panted as I pumped another finger inside her, feeling her wetness coat my fingers.

Logan rolled her hips, little by little, trying to make me go faster.

As much as it turned me on, it wasn't a vocal demand.

I brought my fingers out of her pussy and circled them over her swollen nub slowly.

"Your mouth," she gasped out. "Please."

"Tell me where you want it." I lent some encouragement instead of teasing her with another kiss because I knew she was growing dizzy with the need to come.

"Down," she said shyly.

I did as she'd asked and moved my lips down her throat to her heaving chest.

"Further," she told me.

I moved again, stroking one of her nipples with my tongue again. "Here?" I asked, taking a moment to nuzzle the peak.

She shook her head and shut her eyes. "Keep going."

I smiled as I pressed my lips down her belly and over her tiny stretch marks, and I fell onto my knees for the second time.

I dragged my eyes up her body, ready to proposition the same question when she gripped my hair.

"Kiss it, Danny. Kiss my clit." Her words were shaky but clear.

My mouth was on her in the next second, rubbing my tongue over her sensitive skin. That first taste of her was almost enough to make me come right then and there.

She screamed and fisted my hair, "Oh my—Danny!"

Hearing her cry out my name made my control slip, and I worked harder. Faster. Sucking her sweetness like I was starved.

She spread her legs apart further, bringing her peach of an ass nearly off the table. "Yes, just like that. Just—ah!"

Her high-pitched moans were music to my ears.

"You're so fucking soft. So perfect," I growled, thrusting two fingers inside her while keeping my mouth on her.

She was nearly there. I could feel the muscles pulsing around me.

"Danny … I'm—" Logan circled her legs behind me, digging her heels into my shoulders.

"Tell me what you want, Logan, or I won't give it to you."

"I want to come," she rushed out. "Don't stop, don't stop—" Her words cut off, and she took in a breath, arching her breasts up to the ceiling.

I worked my mouth faster, coaxing it out of her in just three flicks of my tongue.

Her legs trembled on either side of me, clenching, and she cried out with her release.

I couldn't deny myself of seeing the look on her face as she fell apart, so I quickly stood and watched, letting her ride out the end of her orgasm on the heel of my hand.

Her satisfied gaze locked on to mine, and it was so damn beautiful that it made me want to start all over again.

"I could do that every day, all day, for the rest of my fucking days."

She giggled breathlessly. "I think I'd like that."

I lowered my mouth to hers with a smile.

She reached up with a lazy grip, cupping my face as she kissed me back without protest.

Once her legs relaxed and her breathing evened out, I helped her off the table. As much as I wanted to explore her body with more light, I could see the faint goosebumps breaking out over her skin, so I reached for my shirt and held it out for her. I stretched it over her head and held the armholes open for her to thread herself into, letting it fall over her nakedness.

"How does it look?" she asked, twirling once.

The shirt was so big on her small frame that it covered everything, but my cock still twitched at the sight of my band name stamped across her chest and the knowledge of how every inch of her tasted beneath it.

"Beautiful," I said, feeling a sense of euphoria fill my chest.

She glanced around the darkroom and arched her brow playfully. "Are you ready for that lesson now?"

20

Logan

Danny had spent the night again.

In the back of my mind, I knew we could stand to pump the brakes a little, but after spending the last two days with him and the orgasm he had given me in the darkroom, I beat that thought with a bat and buried it out back with every other rational thought that I had when it came to Danny.

I'd hyped myself up the longer I went without that kind of physical touch that I'd grown scared of the idea of it. But even with my heart racing in my chest when I took off my shirt in front of him, it wasn't out of nerves or fear. It was the anticipation. I knew what I wanted for the first time and felt safe enough to ask for it. And he had coaxed every frustrating endorsement out of me, to be sure.

It was all I could think about.

His mouth. His hands. They had played me like they knew every melody and chord progression by heart.

I couldn't imagine what his performance would be like when he finally decided to join in on the orgasm train, but it made me ache, just thinking about it. He was skilled—there was no denying that. But that also meant he must have had a lot of practice with a lot of women. He was a well-known, talented musician and wildly attractive, so I knew it came with the territory. I was jealous, sure. But I was also grateful for their sacrifice—because however many women he'd been with before me, they'd made him all the more knowledgeable and calculated. And I was reaping the benefits.

Besides, they didn't get to wake up next to him this morning.

I did.

The fact that he hadn't tried to have sex with me yet made me think that whatever this was between us didn't only mean something more to me—it meant more to him too. And that left me feeling all sorts of happy.

My eyes crept open at the sound of a familiar click, and I found Danny kneeling on the bed, peering down at me through my camera lens in just his boxer briefs.

"What are you doing?" I smiled.

"Evening the playing field," he said.

I rubbed my eyes and yawned. "That's not fair. I was asleep and probably drooling over the naughty dream of you I had. The one I took of you looked perfect. Nostril hairs and all."

I hadn't really gotten a picture up his nose. I was lucky enough that the camera had focused on his handsome, bright blue eyes instead.

We had stayed in the darkroom for an hour or two after … everything … and I walked him through the process of developing an image from start to finish. The pictures from the festival turned out better than I'd expected. I still had a lot more to sift through, but the couple of shots I had taken of Danny were my favorite.

"You dreamed about me?"

I squirmed beneath his stare and nodded.

He lifted the side of his mouth up. "What was I doing?"

"You were between my legs with that skilled tongue of yours," I said, wetting my lip.

His eyes heated. "Did you use your words?"

"Oh, I was very vocal." I smirked. "It wasn't as good as the real thing, but at least fantasy Danny was willing to go another round."

His brow arched. "Don't insult my stamina. You might regret it."

The curiosity made my heart skip. I had been spent after the darkroom, but that hadn't stopped me from trying last night.

"I wanted to take it easy, seeing as how I haven't even taken you on a date yet." He shrugged.

"Ah, yes, I forgot you're a gentleman."

"That's right."

"The kind that will eat me out before he takes me out, but is too cheap to buy dessert," I taunted him playfully.

He worked his jaw and then flung my camera to the other side of the bed before crushing my body with his. "Cheap, am I?"

I giggled as his hands poked at my sides. I tried fighting him off, but he managed to capture my wrists and pin them above my head.

"You have no idea the kind of sweet tooth I have," he muttered, pressing his hips between my legs. The comforter was too thick, and I wished I could remove it. "Dessert is my favorite part of the meal, but I sometimes like to watch you enjoy it first."

"Well, I like to *share*," I countered suggestively.

He chuckled. "Oh, yeah?"

"Yep. I'm the kind of person who always asks for two spoons instead of one." I wiggled my brows.

"Hmm, how considerate of you. I prefer using my hands when I can." He gripped my wrists tighter for effect.

"What are your thoughts on dessert for breakfast?" I proposed, rolling my body underneath his weight.

Danny groaned, dropping his forehead to mine. "Tempting. Fucking tempting."

I lifted my mouth to kiss him.

"We've got plenty of time, Logan." He smiled against my lips and then kissed me once. "And I'd still like to take you out."

I groaned. "Fine. Let's go."

"What?"

"Right now. Let's go. You and me. Date time." I nodded my head sideways.

"You really want my cock that bad?" he husked.

My tongue swiped my bottom lip of its own accord. "I need to practice using my words."

His eyes flared as he stared at me. "You're making this really difficult to say no."

"Then, don't."

He shook his head after a moment. "Not today."

I jutted my lip out. "First times are always so nerve-racking though. Don't you want to just rip the Band-Aid off?"

His brows scrunched as he pulled back and rested on his elbows. "That's not exactly the phrase I'd use to describe the first time I fuck you."

I rolled my body again, unintentionally.

"Wait, *first time* ..." he muttered.

I searched his face and then rolled my eyes playfully. "I'm not a virgin, Danny."

He made a face at me that told me he wasn't entertained by my joke. "Logan, have you had sex with anyone since—"

"Violet?" I asked, feeling my cheeks burn. "No."

Danny brought a hand to my face, holding my chin with his fingers. "Then, the answer is *hell* no."

I sighed. "Danny—"

"No," he repeated, growling. "I'm not ripping the Band-Aid off—as you so politely put it—and screwing you just so you can get it over with."

I widened my eyes, horrified. That was not at all what I'd meant.

"You deserve so much better than that," he said firmly. "And so do I."

I couldn't understand why, but my view of Danny began to blur with the burn of fresh tears. "I'm sorry. I didn't mean—"

"Fuck, Logan. I'm sorry. That wasn't supposed to sound angry or make you cry." He held my face.

"I'm not," I lied, reaching up to wipe a tear away.

He placed a gentle kiss on my cheek. "I'm so sorry."

"No, don't apologize. You're right. It's just … you're so much different than I thought you'd be."

"How's that?" he asked.

"I think you're … good for me."

A smile touched his lips. "I think we could be good for each other."

I gazed up at him, letting his blue eyes pierce into me. *Through* me. Touching me better than his hands or mouth could. And then, suddenly, they disappeared behind closed lids as my doorbell echoed throughout the house.

I frowned. "What time is it?"

Danny grabbed his phone from the bedside table and lit up the screen. "Almost nine. Why?"

Loud knocking ensued, and I reached for my own phone, checking the camera. "It's my parents with Violet. They're early."

I pushed Danny off me and scrambled to my feet.

Danny ran a hand through his messy hair and quickly pulled his pants on. "Why are you acting like you're in trouble?"

I sighed. "I … don't know. I just feel like they won't be happy if they find you here."

He smirked. "Are you planning on having me hide in your closet? Because that's not really my style."

"It wouldn't make a difference anyway. They have Moose with them. He was a police dog and would find you in a second."

I looked around the room in a panic. The judgment on my dad's face appeared in my head, forcing out all reason.

The doorbell rang again. And then a third time.

"The window?" I pointed.

Danny raised a brow. "Logan, you're an adult. Are you not allowed to have other adult friends over?"

I knew that I wasn't a stupid teenager anymore, but the fear of disappointing them still filled me with anxiety just the same. "It's just not a good look for me with them. It's early, and"— I glanced down at my A Quiet Peril T-shirt and gestured to his naked torso—"you don't even have a shirt."

"All right, fine. But this is a onetime thing." He shook his head and smiled.

"Thank you." I pecked him on the lips and ushered him out the window.

When he made it out of the bush below my window, I hurried toward the front door, snatching a towel from the bathroom to tie my hair up on the way.

Moose came through the door first, smelling me carefully before doing his perimeter check.

"What took you so long to answer?" Dad frowned.

"I was in the shower," I lied. "I wasn't expecting you guys until this afternoon."

My mom finished helping Violet from her car seat, and she came running over.

"We went to stop for breakfast, but Vi insisted that we drive back so you could join us," Dad explained.

"You did?" I scooped Violet up into my arms for a hug when she reached me. "Thanks for thinking of me, baby."

Violet squeezed me back with her little arms. "I missed yew, Mommy."

"I missed you too. Did you have fun with Grandma and Papa?"

She nodded, but I could tell she was tired from the drive.

"I caught a fishy," she told me through a yawn.

"You did?" My heart constricted. "Was it a big one?"

"Huge," she said.

My dad shook his head and held up his thumb and index finger to reference just how small it was.

"I few him back so he cewd swim with his fwends," Violet added.

There was a sour feeling in the pit of my stomach as my parents chuckled together. I'd missed seeing my daughter catch her first fish. I still remembered the first time my dad had taught me. He had been so happy and proud of me when I reeled in the tiny trout. Now, Violet had her own memory of that forever, only I wouldn't be in it. I'd already missed her first steps and her first words when I was in rehab. This was just one more thing I couldn't share with her. I knew I couldn't be there for all of her firsts, but I could've been there for this one.

"What's that doing here?" Dad asked, looking over my shoulder.

I twisted to see what he was referring to and saw Moose sniffing Danny's guitar, leaning against the side of the couch.

My stomach sank. I'd forgotten that he'd brought it over after he ran home to change yesterday. He'd played for me while I cooked us dinner last night.

"Danny's hewe?" Violet's sleepy eyes grew wider in excitement when she saw the guitar.

"No, baby." I turned back to my dad, three shades paler. "He came by yesterday."

"What for?"

Out of the corner of my eye, I could see movement from Danny's porch, and I had to fight the urge not to look over at him.

I shifted uncomfortably under the weight of my dad's stare. "Why don't I go change and get ready real quick, and we can go? You want waffles or pancakes, Violet?"

"What was he here for, Lo?" My dad crossed his arms.

My mom swatted at him. "Stop grilling her, John."

I wasn't sure if it was his tone or the lingering jealousy of missing Violet's first fish, but my fear of disappointing him was quickly changing into annoyance. "We had dinner together."

He didn't say anything. He just stared some more. I swore I saw a muscle below his eye twitch, but I couldn't be sure.

"You did?" My mom smiled. "That's great, honey."

"He also spent the night," I added, feeling my pulse in my throat.

I kept my focus fixed on my dad. I was sick of faltering under his judgment. I hadn't done anything wrong. And maybe he wouldn't approve—I didn't think there would be many guys he'd approve of for me—but hopefully, I'd get points for honesty. I was trying to win back his trust after all.

"A sweepovah?" Violet tilted her head and then pouted.

I finally blinked away my dad's hold and looked at Violet. "Don't worry, baby. He'll be coming over a lot more often."

"Yay!" Violet's smile returned. "I wike Danny."

"Me too, Vi." I dared another glance at my dad's stone-cold expression. "Me too."

21

Danny

"So, what's up? What was so important that you didn't want Tic, Lex, and Nikko here?" I asked Liam, bringing my beer to my mouth.

After some phone call interviews with a few radio stations around California, Liam had pulled me aside and asked to grab drinks at Eleven's—a bar we frequented often and used to play gigs at back in the day. Matt, the owner, let us drink for free when we announced we were stopping in because it brought in more customers. Today wasn't like the others. Matt wasn't even here yet because it was so goddamn early. The sun hadn't even set, but I was down for a beer or two. I needed it to ease the nerves eating away at me from the ride over here.

Liam settled into the seat across from me. "I want to ask your sister to marry me," he said like it was the most casual thing in the world.

I paused and then pulled my bottle away from my lips slowly, processing.

They'd been together for nearly two years. I didn't know why I hadn't expected him to want to put a ring on my sister's finger at some point. Maybe I had, but I guessed I'd thought I'd be the one to marry first since I was older. It definitely wasn't a modern idea, and I hadn't been very good about finding a girl who wanted to spend more than one night with me, let alone spend a life with me. The thought of marriage hadn't really crossed my mind until the last year or so. A hope of it happening for me one day anyway. And now that my best friend was sitting in front of me, talking about taking the big step, I couldn't help but wonder if that future was in store for me sooner than I'd thought.

Jesus.

I spend two nights with a girl, and I'm already thinking about a future together?

Don't be stupid, Danny. Happy endings aren't your thing.

I frowned after a moment. "What's stopping you?"

Liam's lips twitched. "I've never been a formal kind of guy, but I wanted to ask for your permission, I guess."

"Why?"

"Because it's important to me. And I think it would mean a lot to Avery to know that you wouldn't hate her for this. You haven't ever really had a say in much of her life, and she values your word."

I scoffed and twirled my beer on the table. "Funny."

"It's not a joke." Liam raised his chin slightly. "You have no idea how much she loves you."

My throat felt uncomfortable as I swallowed, and then I finally looked at him again. "What about our mom? Shouldn't she be the one you ask?"

He shook his head. "Avery doesn't talk to her all that often anymore. She checks in on your mom every once in a while, but she is done asking her for anything. That includes her opinion on who she spends the rest of her life with."

"Ah, so you're asking me because you already know our mother won't give you the answer you want."

His jaw ticked. "C'mon, Danny. I'm doing this out of respect for you and your sister. I wish your dad were here so I could ask him, but he's not. She's only got you."

There was a strange tightening in the pit of my stomach. "Okay, man. Yeah. If you really need it, then you have my ... permission or whatever."

"Yeah?" The tension in his eyes softened, and he grinned to himself. "Thanks, man. I mean, you know I'd marry her anyway ... but thanks."

"Sure," I said, sipping my beer.

It had taken me a while to get used to seeing the two of them together. Hell, I still wasn't fond of the times I caught Avery walking out of his room in the morning. But Liam was my best friend, and I was glad my sister had found someone that I knew would treat her right.

He tipped his drink at me and cocked his head. "I'll finally get to be your brother."

"I thought we already were brothers?" I glowered.

"Well, yeah. But now, it'll be legal."

"Hey, she has to say yes first, dumbass." I chuckled.

He held out his hands in shock. "Why do you have to put that out into the universe?"

"I'm just kidding," I said. "When are you going to do it?"

He looked down at his drink in thought, then back up at me. "I'm not sure I want to plan it. I kind of just want it to happen when it happens, you know? But I hope it's soon. The ring is burning a hole in my pocket. I keep thinking she's going to find it."

"You have it already?" My forehead creased.

He nodded. "I went and picked it up that day you met Logan and Violet actually."

"Huh. You've had it for a minute, then. Does anyone else know? Tic? Lexie?" I asked.

He sighed deeply. "I was trying to wait to tell everyone until I talked to you first, but Tic thought I seemed off and was worried about me, so I had to tell him to get him off my back. And fucking Lexie caught me hiding the box in my nightstand."

I laughed, not surprised.

"That girl moves like a fucking Prius, I swear. She's everywhere." Liam took a swig from his glass and shook his head in disbelief.

"You think she was, like, a cat in another lifetime?"

"Yeah. One of the annoying ones that knocks shit off tables all the time."

We both laughed and clanked our glasses together.

"I'm happy for you, man. Really," I said. And I was. I just couldn't help but worry about how things would change after this.

"Thank you." Liam peered up at me with a look of relief. "Avery's great, man. I love her, and I can't fucking wait to marry her."

"Good for you." My brows twitched. "You two are gross."

He threw his head back with a laugh.

I shifted taller in my chair and cleared my throat. "I should probably make some protective-big-brother speech … right?"

Liam crossed his arms mockingly. "I think we're past the point where that's needed, but sure. Let's hear it, Danny boy."

"Uh, okay. What about …" I lowered my tone and spoke from my chest. "If you hurt my sister *ever*—"

"Ooh, nice. Threatening me from the start. I like it so far." Liam listened, amused.

"I'll take a baseball bat to your truck. How's that sound?"

"Pretty solid. You know how much I love my truck. I'd probably go with some bodily harm too. You know, make it impactful enough that I don't walk straight ever again," he suggested.

Smiles crept up our faces.

"Baseball bat to the kneecaps?" I offered.

"Aye, that's more like it. I'd expect at least that if I ever broke Avery's heart."

"Agreed." I held my hand out. "Shake on it?"

Liam's hand clapped mine in a firm grasp and shook it. "Love you, man."

"Love you too, brother."

22

Danny

My life was now reduced to two things. Playing music with my band and seeing Logan as often as I could. The only problem was, in just two weeks, one would keep me from the other. As excited as I was for the tour and to play our new music for our fans, I hated the idea of leaving Logan and Violet here while I was halfway across the country. Especially after how much effort it had taken to get to where we were and how much further we had yet to go.

What if she got smart and realized I wasn't worth it? Or couldn't handle the time apart? There weren't a lot of musicians I knew in relationships that came with strings, other than Liam and my sister. Sure, I knew a couple of married guys, but their wives were usually on tour with them. Logan couldn't do that. Not with Violet.

Five months of buses, stages, and hotel rooms meant there were seven months I got to spend here with her during the year. At least until our tours grew longer. I'd already worked out a few times where I would have an extra couple of days to fly back, and we had some shows in Northern California that weren't too far to travel from. With a little patience and effort, we could make this work. We had to. I was already in too deep to lose her.

I knocked on Logan's front door and waited, my hands resting in my front pockets. With the tour coming up, there had been a lot of interviews, promotional shit, and meetings that kept me from taking her out any sooner this week, but I had the night off, and she was able to get her friend to watch Violet.

"I got it," I heard a deep voice call from the other side.

The door opened to fucking Mr. Tall, Dark, and Handsome himself, and I felt a little uneasy that this was the best friend Logan spent so much time with.

"You must be Andre. I'm Danny." I extended my hand to him.

He clasped it, pulling me in for a shoulder bump. "Hey, it's nice to meet you, man. I've heard a lot about you."

"You have, huh?" My mouth tilted up. "Good things, I hope."

"Oh, yeah," he said, flashing a wide, knowing smile. "Logan hasn't shut up about you."

"Andre!" I heard Logan scold him from somewhere in the house.

We both laughed as he invited me inside.

"Danny!" Violet came running at me from the kitchen, arms stretched wide. Her fluffy yellow dress and braided dark hair bounced with her tiny strides.

"Look at you, sweetheart." I scooped her up into my arms. "You look like a small princess."

"Wait until you see Mommy," she said, looping her arms around my neck.

She pulled back and planted a peck on my cheek, and my heart was a goner. Done for, shattered into a million little pieces.

The powerful clack of heels hitting hardwood made my eyes lift as Logan entered the room, and my balance wavered.

What were these Ellis women doing to me?

My heart sped up in my chest as my gaze wandered over Logan's body, taking my time on the tight black dress hugging her shape like it was a second skin. The long waves of her hair hung loosely over her shoulders as she fussed with the ends of the sheer sleeves nervously.

"Wow." The pathetic word almost got stuck in my throat. I cleared it and tried again. "Logan, you look ..." *Better than I deserve.*

"Thank you," she muttered quickly when I still couldn't find the words. Confidence brightened her smile.

"You've stunned the man silent." Andre clapped a hand over my shoulder and looked at Logan with pride, but only that.

It was hard to believe that anyone could look at her and not fall at her feet, no matter what she was wearing. But I didn't know the history the two of them shared.

A lot of people found Lexie attractive—hence the number of people who shared her bed with her—and I could admire her taste in style and music and even admit she had a cute face, but she was my bandmate. A sister. I'd never seen her as

213

anything more than that, and I was confident there was nothing that would ever change that.

Logan and Andre's relationship could be like that. That thought soothed the near-jealous feeling in the back of my neck with the comfort that she'd had someone like him to stand by her side for so long.

"Glad to see you finally found something buried in the back of your closet," Andre teased her. "Did it have cobwebs on it?"

My brow ticked at him, but Logan was quick to hold up a feisty middle finger in his direction when Violet wasn't paying attention.

"I think I'm underdressed. I'm going to look like a schmuck next to you," I said, gesturing to my all-black attire. I was grateful for my last-minute decision to ditch the plaid shirt, but I certainly didn't match her efforts by swapping it for a leather jacket.

"Not at all. You look great, Danny," Logan said. "I just wanted to try something different for myself tonight."

"You guys match," Violet stated, still comfortable in my arms. "Bwack and bwack." She pointed at the two of us.

Logan walked over and kissed her forehead. "You're right, baby. We do match. Good job." She smiled and flicked her eyes up at me.

Now that she was standing closer, I could see the faint shadow and liner she had on made her eyes pop more than usual. Her freckles hid beneath a thin veil of makeup as well, but I could still see them. And her lips … fucking hell. I wanted her to stamp her soft lips in that rosy shade of lipstick up and down my body, so everyone knew I belonged to her.

"You ready to go?" she asked me, unaware of where my mind was wandering.

I blinked and set Violet down, giving her a nod.

"Okay, Vi. Have fun with Uncle Andre. I won't be gone too long, okay?" Logan bent down and hugged Violet and then Andre. "Thanks again, Andre."

"No problem." He shrugged. "Stay out as late as you guys want. I don't have to work tomorrow, so I can crash on the couch if you need."

Andre and I exchanged another handshake, and then I left with Logan.

"You didn't have to drive across the street. I could've walked to your car," Logan stated, spotting my cherry-red Audi in her driveway.

I waited until her front door latched behind me and then caught her wrist and pulled her into me until she collided with my lips. Her mouth was parted slightly, and I plunged my tongue inside with a groan.

Her hands, once still, dived inside my open jacket, rubbing up and down my abdomen.

I pinched my eyes shut at how her greedy hands made my dick twitch, but I grabbed hold of them and folded her into my chest. "I don't think I can make it through dinner with you dressed like this," I growled.

She looked up at me slowly. "Should I go change?"

"Fuck no." I shook my head and grinned. "This will just be a good test of my self-restraint."

The drive to the restaurant wasn't all that long, but when I placed my hand on her thigh and she parted her legs a fraction, I considered taking a loop around the city. But if anything, I was a determined man, and I only had so many nights to take her out, just the two of us, before I left. I was going to take her on this date even if my erection was threatening to pierce through my jeans in protest.

When we finally made it inside and sat at the round table I'd reserved, I couldn't help but stare over my menu at Logan as she decided what to order. Her teeth pressed into the pad of her thumb. She had been completely unaware of the way she turned the head of every guy in here when she walked in. Some of them still had their heads craned in her direction despite their own company.

"Are you two ready to order?" Our waiter appeared between the two of us.

His eyes lingered on Logan longer than I was comfortable with, but she didn't seem to notice. Besides, if I was going to beat someone up for having an eye for a beautiful woman, I'd have to take on half the restaurant. And I didn't want to bust my knuckles up before the tour.

Logan ordered some dish she could barely pronounce the name of, and I asked for the same thing because I hadn't even glanced at the goddamn menu.

The waiter noted the unpleasant look I gave him after a stern clearing of my throat and hurried away to bring our order to the kitchen.

"This place looks great," Logan said, scooting her chair in with excitement.

"Yeah, Lexie said it's the best Korean steak house she's found out here. Thought we could try it out together." I smiled nervously.

Why it made me nervous to simply sit across from her and eat a meal after I'd had her pussy in my mouth only a few days ago was beyond me. Maybe it was because this whole date thing was new territory for me. I hadn't ever done this with any of the girls I was with in the past. I never saw the point. The ones who had wanted to stay longer than one night with me never caught my interest, and for some reason, the only girls I'd ever found myself drawn to were the ones who didn't want me back. Logan was the first person to ever have enough valid reasons not to be with me, yet she still found even more reasons to ignore them.

We made small talk to combat my nerves, and by the time our waiter returned with our drinks, Logan was laughing at something I'd said, and I'd forgotten about why my guard was up in the first place.

"Can I ask you something?"

Her lashes fluttered as she peered up at me, a grin still stretched across her face.

"What did my sister say to you that made you change your mind about me?" I asked curiously. "It seemed like you'd written me off after that night at the party."

Her wide smile from laughter fell into a soft grin. "It wasn't any one thing in particular. She eased my mind about a lot of things."

"Such as?" I pressed.

"She told me you two haven't always been amiable toward one another, but your sister cares a lot about you, Danny," she started as if she was easing into something she wasn't sure I'd want to hear.

"You're not the first person I've heard that from this week." I arched a brow. "But, yeah, Avery and I have had our differences."

Logan's eyes fell to the table and then inched back up to mine. "I told her about my struggle with addiction when I was younger and my concern about being around you after seeing those girls at the party, and she sort of filled me in on your own past with ... well, everything and told me about your band's rules and how I didn't need to worry about any of that. And I guess I believed her."

I blinked, trying to decipher which part of that statement I wanted to dissect first. "What about my past does she know about? And ... and what girls?"

She twirled her thumbs anxiously, and it reminded me of the look she'd had when her parents showed up at her door after I spent the night.

I took a slow breath and smoothed my frown lines. "Sorry, I'm just a bit confused. None of my past is a secret. Not to you," I told her. "I just feel like there's a lot of information I'm missing here. Can you start with the girls you mentioned?"

"Avery didn't tell you about it?"

I shook my head.

Logan sighed. "When I came upstairs after we—"

I smirked at the memory of her grinding on top of me and then nodded so she'd continue.

"Well, there were two girls doing drugs in the bathroom across the hall. I described one of them to Avery, and she seemed certain that it was a girl named Hannah that you used to date." She looked at me warily.

"You're fucking kidding me," I muttered under my breath and clenched my fist.

Hannah was who I used to get my supply from a few years back. She sold on the side for extra money, but I'd thought that was over. *Fuck.* And now, she was doing it in my house?

"Yeah, no one told me anything about that."

Logan reached across the table for my hand, and my grip loosened. "I know it doesn't seem like it now, but they probably didn't tell you because they wanted to protect you."

"Protect me from what?" My jaw tightened, but I found the answer in Logan's eyes. "Jesus. Liam must've told her everything."

"Not … everything. Just enough for her to worry. Like I said, she cares about you."

"I'm not made of glass. I won't break."

"She probably didn't want to concern you with something that she was sure Liam would take care of."

A humorless smile stretched across my lips. "Let me get this straight. I sent my sister over to talk to you, and she decided to tell you about my substance abuse and overdose to try and win you over?"

Logan winced. "She didn't tell me about your past to harm your chances, Danny. She wanted me to understand you better. To know how you needed to be loved. In fact, it was the way that she spoke about you and the people around you so highly that made me feel like I would be safe with you."

My gaze flitted up to hers as my hand unfurled and interlocked with hers. "You will always be safe with me."

She smiled. "I know that now."

"So, I guess I should thank my sister?" I circled my thumb over the top of her hand. "Even if her tactics were questionable."

"If you don't, I will." Logan laughed right as her phone buzzed on the table beside her. She glanced down at it and quickly picked it up, giving me an apologetic look before answering. "Andre? Is everything okay?"

Our waiter returned, setting our plates down in front of us, but I could tell by the look on Logan's face that something was wrong at home.

"Can you actually box these up for us, please?" I softly asked the waiter, and he swiftly took them back to the kitchen.

"Okay, just tell her I'll be home soon and put a cool washcloth on her forehead." She paused, listening. "Don't apologize. It happens. Okay. Okay. Bye."

"Violet all right?" I asked immediately after she hung up.

Logan ran her fingers through her hair. "Andre ordered some food from a pasta place in town, and there must've been some dairy in the sauce. She's got an upset stomach. I'm sorry to cut the date short, but—"

Our waiter was back with our food in a to-go bag. I quickly pulled out a few large bills and placed them on the table, knowing it easily doubled our tab.

When we got out to the car and backed out of our parking space, I shifted the gears and took off.

Logan squealed, gripping her seat. "She's in good hands, Danny. You don't have to break the law to get me home."

I pushed my foot down further, lurching my car through an intersection just before it turned red.

"Danny!" Logan scolded, but a smile spread across her soft pink lips.

"My sister told you about our band rules, right?" I asked, grabbing her hand and placing it under mine on the stick shift.

Logan nodded, looking down at our hands as I moved them from second to third gear.

"Then, you're aware of the *anytime, anywhere* rule," I said, shifting again as we whipped around a corner. "That rule pertains to you and Violet now too."

23

Logan

I'd already started a load of laundry, changed clothes, brushed my teeth, and washed my face when I sauntered back to the couch alone, waiting for Danny to return so we could finish our date on a better note with movies and popcorn.

After we had gotten back from our interrupted dinner, Andre had left, and Violet had insisted on Danny reading her a bedtime story. I was beginning to think I was just chopped liver to her whenever Danny was around, but I also didn't mind watching the two of them together. As much as I hated Andre comparing my daughter to an animal, he was kind of right about Violet. She had a good sense of character, and she had attached herself to Danny the moment they met. She trusted him. *I* trusted him. And that made the cautious side of me loosen its hold on my soul, and everything felt a little bit … lighter.

I knew Violet could be persuasive—when you told her two bedtime stories, she usually suckered you into reading three—but Danny had been in her room for over forty minutes. That was twice as long as it usually took her to fall asleep, especially at this hour.

Curiously, I stood back up and made my way down the hall to her bedroom, peeking my head through the cracked door.

To no surprise, Violet was asleep on her stomach. Her butterfly night-light sent a warm glow throughout the room. Her arm was stretched out, and she was holding hands with Danny, who was on the floor, slumped beside her bed with a book in his lap.

Sucker. I smiled.

An ache behind my eyes blossomed and grew the longer I stood there, taking in the image of the two of them. I had no reason to cry. Andre and my father read Violet bedtime stories all the time, and I never cried over it. But the image of my gentle, brown-haired three-year-old asleep next to my guitar-playing, seemingly jaded, tattoo-covered bad boy, holding a giant hardback with a unicorn on the cover, made a pleasant warmth pool in my chest. A warmth that spread throughout the rest of my body, filling in all the cracks and jagged edges I hadn't thought would ever heal.

I opened the door wider and tiptoed into the room, reaching down to tap Danny on the shoulder.

His eyes blinked open as he positioned himself back upright. He lifted his gaze to meet mine and then glanced around the lavender-painted walls, realizing where he was. With a careful release of Violet's tiny fingers, he slowly stood and followed me out of her room into the hallway.

"How long was I out?" He chuckled deeply.

I quietly shut Violet's door behind me and gazed up at him. "Hard to say, but you must've fallen asleep before you got to the part where Glitter, the unicorn, gets to Unicorn Mountain because that's when it really gets exciting," I teased.

"Ah, what a shame," he said, smoothing a piece of hair behind my ear.

The softness of that simple gesture and his mesmerizing blue stare made the ache behind my eyes intensify, and I pulled him toward my bedroom.

He followed me until my door was shut, and then I pressed him up against it, kissing him deeply.

Danny pulled away after a beat, cupping my jaw with his large, rough hands. "What's all this about?" he asked, smiling.

My eyes glistened with tears, but they never reached my cheeks. "I want you." My voice wobbled. "All of you."

His hands stilled and then curled around the back of my neck, holding me gently. "Logan ..." My name echoed from his throat in a pleading yet guarded way.

I placed my hands on his forearms, wanting to give him reassurance. "I *need* you, Danny," I corrected.

His hold on me tightened right before he crashed his lips to mine.

My hands fell down his hard abdomen, landing on the bottom of his shirt as he slowly backed me into the room.

Lust and anticipation fueled my hands. My mouth. My feet. Until the back of my legs hit the edge of my bed and his shirt was gone.

Danny was just as eager, but his movements were more graceful. Deliberate. His tongue explored my mouth, taunting me, as his fingers trailed down to the bottom dip of my spine. When he hitched his thumbs beneath the waistline of my bottoms, I was glad I didn't have to give him verbal confirmation for him to slide them down over my hips.

A groan escaped his lips when he discovered I wasn't wearing underwear. "What are you doing to me, Logan?" he rasped, looking down at my half-naked body.

I grinned and tore my shirt over my head, dropping it to the ground next to me.

His eyes dragged over my body greedily, like he was seeing it for the first time again. Under better lighting than the safelights of the darkroom, I felt so much more exposed and bare. But his darkened stare heated every inch of my skin it gazed upon and inspired more confidence in me than I'd ever possessed.

"Kiss me," I demanded.

The words barely left my lips before he brought his firm mouth down to mine again.

"You tell me to stop at any time, and I'll stop," he said, breaking away long enough to meet my eyes. "Understood?"

I nodded, already undoing the button of his jeans. "I don't ever want you to stop."

He stilled my hands and repeated firmly, "Do you understand, Logan?"

"Yes, I understand," I whispered.

He quickly captured my mouth in another hungry kiss and tugged gently on my nipple with his callous fingers.

I moaned at the surprised pleasure shooting through me, but Danny seized every loud note before it could pass through my lips.

"Shh." His teeth pinched my bottom lip and pulled. "We have to be quiet." He dragged his hand further down and swiped his fingers through the wet heat of my core.

My back arched as I gasped up at the ceiling.

"Fucking hell, Logan. You're so wet for me," he said, pushing a finger inside me and covering my cries with another kiss.

My hands were useless with his pants, so I clumsily brought them up the hard valleys of his abs, over his chest, and to his broad shoulders, and then I threaded my fingers through his thick hair—the only thing I had to hold on to.

With his fingers pumping in and out of me and with one arm around the center of my back, he lowered me down onto the mattress carefully. When I was fully situated, my ass near the edge and my knees propped open, he stood back upright and watched me writhe to the workings of his skilled hand— circling, pumping, and curling in the most delicious ways.

"Danny." The two syllables were my next inhale and exhale as the ache built. My hands fisted the sheets.

"Not yet." He shook his head and removed his fingers all too soon, denying me my release.

I panted and watched him first take off his pants and then the tight briefs. As soon as the elastic band dropped below his hips, his erection sprang free. My mouth dropped open when I saw it bob between my parted thighs.

There is no way in hell—

"It'll fit, Logan. Trust me," he growled, dropping onto his knees.

I quickly clapped my hand over my parted lips as his tongue flicked my clit a few times before he covered me completely with his warm mouth.

He flattened his tongue and stroked until I was on the edge again, hot and ready, and then pulled away just as stars began to enter my peripheral vision.

"Please, Danny," I begged breathlessly, my entrance throbbing. I crawled backward on the bed as I watched him stretch the condom he'd fetched from his pocket over his thick erection.

"Please what?" He looked up at me through dark lashes, and it was the sexiest thing I'd ever seen. "Make you come?"

I bit my lip and nodded as he climbed on top of me.

"I'd ask you how, but I think I already know." He kissed me thoroughly, and I could taste my arousal on his tongue as he lined the head of his cock with my entrance. "Are you ready?"

"Mmhmm." My heart thrashed against my rib cage.

"Look at me, Logan," Danny told me.

I wanted to close my eyes and succumb to the pending pleasure I was waiting for, but I met his blue eyes, and they held on to me as he slid his hips forward.

I sucked in a breath, slowly stretching around him. "Oh my … Danny—" I gasped out.

He continued to ease into me at an agonizingly slow pace, all the way down to the hilt, and then stilled, shutting his eyes to savor the contact of my walls flexing around him. When he opened his eyes again, he reached up and stroked my cheek. "Are you okay? How does this feel?"

"Good. So good," I whimpered and wet my lips, desperate for him to move again.

With a crooked smile, he pulled out slowly, letting me feel every inch of him before he thrust into me again.

"So fucking beautiful," he gritted through his teeth, his arms trembling on either side of me with restraint.

His next thrust came faster. Harder. Hitting every nerve just right.

I sucked my bottom lip between my teeth to muffle my cry. "I don't want you to leave," I said, arching my back as spots began to fill my vision. "I want you to stay. Here. Forever."

His mouth met my raised chest, savoring a pebbled peak with a restless tongue. "*Need.* You need me, don't you?"

My body rocked as his weight pressed into me again and again. I dragged my hands over his tense shoulders and up to his face, making him look at me.

"No one has ever made me feel the way you make me feel. I need—" My voice broke off as my mouth dropped open with a silent cry when Danny reached a hand between us, circling my clit.

"Tell me, Logan. Tell me you're mine," he whispered roughly, thrusting into me.

"I'm yours," I finally breathed out, the increasing wave of pleasure building in my core. "I'm all yours, Danny."

His eyes sparkled at my response. Without warning, he sat upright on his knees, gripped the apex of my thighs, and continued driving into me.

I leaned up onto my elbows and bucked my hips, meeting his rhythm as he slammed into me faster. The image of his hard stomach flexing and his corded arms gripping me into him was nearly enough to send me over the edge.

He lowered his chin, giving me a dark, hooded stare as he watched where our two bodies became one. "I belong here"—*thrust*—"with you"—*thrust*—"clenching"—*thrust*—"around"—*thrust*—"my cock."

"Danny." I moaned out his name, overwhelmed with his throaty words, his touch, and the way he filled me so fully. "I'm so close."

He suddenly lifted me up and placed me on top of him like I weighed nothing. "Find it, Logan," he said, swiping aside a strand of hair from my sweat-glistened forehead. "Ride me."

I looped my arms around his neck and rolled my hips forward, slowly at first to adjust to the deeper sensation of being at a new angle and then quicker to satiate the low ache begging to be set free.

He buried his head in the crook of my neck and dug his fingers into my ass, cursing under his breath. "Fuck, that's right. Just like that."

There was something so powerful about riding him and chasing my orgasm at my own speed. I'd never felt more desired or in control of anything in my life. That feeling—one I'd only ever felt with him, *because* of him—dangled three bold words on the edge of my tongue. It was strange how the idea of saying them after so little time together didn't scare me, but not saying them scared me more. Like I'd lose him if I didn't.

"Danny, I—"

But I was already there. Falling over the edge. Too consumed to finish my words.

Danny clamped his hand over my mouth to stifle my cry right as I exploded around him. "I know," was all he said before he tensed around me, finding his own release. "I know," he repeated through a guttural moan.

I continued rocking my hips into him, letting us both ride out the end of our orgasm. My movements became shorter. Shallower. Until we both just held each other and collapsed onto the bed.

We lay there, letting our breaths even out, looking at one another for as long as we could before our eyes drifted shut.

I nestled forward into his warm chest and fell asleep to the sound of his steady heartbeat.

I found myself conflicted the next morning when I woke up to the smell of breakfast again. Violet was my whole world, and I didn't want to confuse her or get her too attached to Danny if … well, if we didn't last. It would already be confusing enough that he was going to be gone for the next several months on tour. I knew she'd ask about him, and I'd have to remind her that he wasn't across the street anymore. He would be across the country.

But there was another part of me that truly believed this could be the forever sort of thing, and if that feeling in my gut was right, what was wrong with starting forever *today?*

Life was short. Danny and I had already had a few near-death experiences to prove that. So, maybe taking a chance on this wasn't so crazy. It was just finally … living.

I glanced down at my wrist resting on the empty pillow beside me, dragging my eyes across the tattooed letters. A smile touched my lips, and I climbed out of bed, feeling grateful. Grateful that the old me had made a permanent decision that helped the new me in a moment when I needed a little encouragement.

It was still too early for Violet to be up, so I quickly dressed, and followed the smell of butter and pancakes toward its source. My bare feet padded to a stop at the kitchen entrance when I discovered Danny dancing. *Dancing.* To the faint melody of one of The Beatles' greatest hits.

"I could get used to this," I said, biting my thumb with a grin.

Danny spun around with a bowl and whisk in hand. "You're up," he said, surprised. His striking gaze fell over my lacy underwear set and an open flannel shirt. "How'd you sleep?"

I answered him with a playful, knowing grin and grabbed some blueberries out of the fridge. "Add these in there if you really want Violet to love you."

He stepped closer, lifting the side of his mouth up. "And what about you? What kind do you prefer?"

"Chocolate chip," I replied, my cheeks flushing. "But we don't have any, so regular is fine."

He set the bowl down and pulled me into him. "I can run into town if I have to."

I pressed up onto my tiptoes, bringing my mouth to his. "You're not allowed to go anywhere. At least not for another thirteen days."

His thumb brushed over my cheek as he hummed. "Okay, fine. But only because you're using your words like a good girl." He claimed my lips once more before returning to his diligent breakfast-making.

Danny was no chef—his dairy-free-milk-to-pancake ratio was a little on the thin side, and the pour was uneven at best—but it was so incredibly sexy, watching him enjoy doing something for us.

Having him read bedtime stories to Violet, waking up next to him in my bed, watching him comfortably cook breakfast in my kitchen for the three of us—there was a domestic feeling about it that I didn't mind one bit. In fact, I wanted to hang on to it tightly and never let it go. But that thought only reminded me of how soon he'd be leaving, creating a sinking feeling in the pit of my stomach.

"Hey, where'd you go?" he asked, turning his head toward me from the kitchen stove.

I blinked away my frozen gaze and met his stare. "Hmm?"

"You went and got sad on me."

"I did?" I tried to make my face return to the way it had been, but there was no use. I was hating the idea of him jumping on that tour bus more and more.

He nodded. "What's the matter?"

"I'm just going to miss this." I sighed. "Having you so close to me."

He dropped what he was doing and pulled me into him.

"Why can't you be a gardener or a plumber or something?" I pouted.

He chuckled, raising a brow. "Because I look a lot better with a guitar in my hands than I would with a shovel or a wrench."

He was right. I couldn't imagine him doing anything else. But I had a hard time believing that he couldn't pull off any occupation.

"I'm going to come back as often as I can, and I'll call every day. I promise." He pulled a folded picture out of his back pocket and showed it to me. It was the one he had taken of me in bed.

"When did you develop this?" I asked, looking down at the black-and-white picture of me.

"This morning." He shrugged. "I snuck down into the darkroom while you were still sleeping." The exposure was far too light, but other than that, he'd done well, considering he'd only had one lesson with me. "I wanted a way of keeping you with me when I'm gone," he added before folding it back up.

And just like that, the seam of my chest slowly unraveled, freeing a thousand butterflies from their tiny, dark cage.

24

Danny

S he needed me. I'd never been needed by anyone in my entire life. Not in the way Logan did. But she only needed me. Not my talent with a guitar, my money, or the bragging rights of getting to ride me for a night.

Me.

Walking away from Logan was nearly impossible when our two weeks together came to an end and it was time for me to get on the tour bus. It was like we'd finally made it, and in a blink of an eye, it was over. Okay, it was far from over, but I felt like it was no longer in my grasp, and I hated it.

Logan and I had spent our time together wisely when I managed to escape from Nikko's million little last-minute tasks. We went driving down the coast for a few hours together, searching for new spots for Logan to take pictures. I went with her to a dealership and helped her pick out the car she was going to buy when she saved up enough money. I wanted to buy it for her—surprise her and park it in her driveway with a big red bow—but she saw the idea spark in my eye and made me promise not to. She insisted on purchasing the car herself, and I respected that. We went to the park with Violet on days the weather was nice, and they showed me their favorite ice cream place in town. Andre let me join in on one of their horror movie nights. I couldn't fucking get to sleep after it, but it was fun to get better acquainted with Andre and gain a new friend.

Last Monday night, I joined Logan and her parents for dinner again. Unlike our last dinner together, Mr. Ellis didn't talk much. I thought the lack of grilling questions and rude comments would make the night more bearable, but it was somehow even more tense. His cold, dark stare had a weight to it, and I could feel it on me from the moment he got there until he left. Logan told me that his trust was hard to earn and that we'd get there eventually. The idea of her wanting me to be around long enough to earn it tugged on my heart a little.

Rehearsing for the tour had taken up more time than I would've liked, but the rest of my free time that wasn't filled with car rides, ice cream runs, scary movies, or dinners had been spent giving Logan orgasms.

Lots of orgasms.

Logan had a higher stamina than I'd thought she would after being out of … practice for so long. She had a craving for me that I was happy to satiate. Our need to be with one another was nearing an obsession, but I didn't care how unhealthy that might be. There were worse things out there—things we were both too familiar with that had come close to destroying us. But we had been alone then, desperate to numb the emptiness of our existence. Logan was a different kind of drug. One that made my soul catch fire and the pain fade. She wasn't numbing the loneliness. She was healing it.

"So, she's your girlfriend now?" Tic asked, settling into the sofa cushion next to me.

Liam sauntered up from the middle of the bus, where our bunks were. "Never thought I'd see the day Danny Fox had a woman he labeled his own."

Lexie was somewhere in the back with a couple of groupies she had picked up at our show in Reno. With Liam and me off the market, Tic and Lexie had twice the number of options for one-night stands. Lexie shouldered that burden with ease while Tic stayed the same old Tic. He had his fun, but he was very particular about who he shared his bed with, and he didn't talk much about the ones who were so fortunate. That part of his life he liked to keep private. It was understandable, considering how much of our lives were becoming more public.

I pulled my gaze away from the window and strummed my fingers through my guitar strings. "What of it?" I asked the two of them.

"Nothin', man. You've just been moping around for the last five shows," Liam said.

"We've only played five shows," I noted.

Liam pulled a water bottle out of the fridge and twisted the cap. "Exactly."

"Whatever. I have not been moping." I rolled my eyes and then set them back on the passing cars outside.

Storm clouds rolled overhead, casting a faded green hue through the midday light.

Tic propped his elbow up on the back of the cushion and rested his head in his hand. "You have. And I think it's because you miss your girlfriend." He dragged the word *girlfriend* out with a mocking tone.

I covered the strings on my guitar with my hand to silence them as I pierced Tic with a glare.

Tic gave a playful grin. "Hey, man. I'm just teasing. We're all happy for you. That's why we bought you a flight home from Seattle after our next show."

My eyes shifted between the two of them. "How? Our Seattle and Portland shows are back-to-back. There's no time."

Liam shrugged. "They're two days apart."

"We sent the ticket info to your phone." Tic nodded at my phone sitting on the table beside me.

Liam leaned against the fridge. "After we finish up in Portland, we'll drop you off in Seattle the next morning. You'll have about twenty hours before you have to be onstage again."

"There's no way Nikko cleared this," I challenged. "I already booked flights for any long gaps in our schedule, and the first one isn't until we get to Colorado."

Tic chuckled. "Nikko doesn't have to know."

"He'll know when I'm not there for sound check."

Liam smirked. "Well, by then, he won't be able to do anything about it."

"Just take the ticket and say thank you. We're sick of the sad songs you keep playing on that thing." Tic jutted a finger out at my guitar.

"Screw you." I smiled. "And ... thanks. Thanks a lot, guys."

Seattle was our best show yet.

After Portland and my quick trip home to see Logan, I had flown back, ordered a ride from the airport to the venue, and gotten to the greenroom with thirty minutes to spare. Our opening band was halfway through their set, and Nikko was ready to murder me, but the adrenaline of making it back in time for the show after seeing my girl made me play better than I had since we had started our tour. Which, in turn, made Nikko's angry rant afterward shorter than it would've been had he noticed any signs of me being distracted onstage instead. I'd thought he was just glad I was staying away from late-night skinny-dipping and strip clubs.

I slept through most of the ride to Spokane. The curtains to the bunk area kept enough of the early morning sunlight out, but after a few too many jostles from bumps in the road and Tic's incessant drumming on God knew what, I climbed out of bed and joined my three bandmates for some breakfast.

"Fuck, Tic. Ever thought of pounding those things on some pillows or couch cushions instead?" I squinted and rubbed my eyes.

Tic raised his drumsticks in the air like he hadn't realized he'd been tapping them on top of our tiny kitchen table. "Shit, sorry. Did I wake you?"

"It's good you're up," Liam said, eyeing me. "We need to have a band meeting."

"At ten in the morning? Really?" Lexie asked, her last night's eye makeup smeared in the corners.

Liam sighed, running a hand down his face. "Well, we get to our hotel in thirty minutes, and you're all going to get to your rooms and sleep a few more hours until sound check. And then we have a radio interview, our meet and greet, and we all know Lexie will disappear as soon as we get offstage tonight. I'm sick of putting this off. We need to be on the same page."

Tic nodded and looked between Lexie and me.

Unease filled my empty stomach. "What's this about?"

Liam gestured for me to sit with the group, and I did, cautiously scanning each of their faces to see if they were as worried as me.

"Tic and I have been talking, and once the tour is over, we think we should put the house up for sale."

Panic shot up the back of my neck. "What?"

Lexie shrugged, unfazed. "I'm down."

How was I the only one who seemed surprised by this?

"Why?" I pressed, pinching my brow together.

Tic shifted his eyes to mine. "Well, for starters, your sister and Liam are going to want a place of their own once they get married."

"He hasn't even proposed yet!" I said.

Lexie leveled her eyes at me. "What? Like she's going to turn him down?"

"I mean, if this thing with you and Logan works out, won't you want a place of your own too?" Liam asked.

I chewed on that for a moment. I hadn't really thought much past where Logan and I were now. I liked having her right across the street. But, yeah, I guessed I'd want a place to call home with her someday. A place that was neither hers nor mine, but *ours*. That didn't mean I was ready to say goodbye to the house I currently called home. We'd produced three albums in that basement and moved in together when we could barely afford ramen noodles or a six-pack of beer. It had too many memories attached to it to simply slap a For Sale sign on it without so much as a second thought.

"Tic, this was your home growing up. How are you okay with this?"

He nodded and sighed. "A lot of good shit has happened there, Danny. But I can't keep it forever. We knew it was only a matter of time after we signed with our label. Besides, did you really think we four were going to live together our whole career?"

"I don't know. Maybe." I swallowed.

"We're selling out huge venues now. We need more security," Liam explained. "You already had a stalker break in last year, and another one attempted it just a few months ago."

"Some guy asked me to sign his gut when I got out of Liam's truck the other day." Lexie scrunched her face and then added, "And I'm sick of sharing a bathroom with you boys."

Liam and I craned our heads to look at her.

"Yeah, we're not too fond of having to share with you either, Miss Uses All The Shampoo And Doesn't Replace It." Liam scowled, and she rolled her eyes.

"So … that's it then?" I asked. "You guys have already decided on this?"

All three sets of eyes landed on me with a pitiful look.

"I'm really sorry, Danny boy," Liam said.

Tic placed a hand on my shoulder. "It's for the best."

"It's not like we're breaking up the band." Lexie chortled.

"Yeah, quite the opposite actually," Liam agreed. "We're doing so well. We kind of have to take this next step."

Everything they were saying made sense. I just couldn't help but feel like I was losing my family. I was sure it was for the best, but the sinking feeling in my chest kept getting deeper, and that familiar emptiness rose from the depths.

25

Logan

Seven weeks had gone by since Danny had left on that monstrous bus. It had been parked outside on the curb for two whole days before they left, and I would stare at it while I sipped my morning coffee, cursing under my breath. But now, I'd give anything to see it again. To look down the street and see it coming over that small hill at the end of our neighborhood. Instead, I was left with the view of Danny's empty driveway and a quiet porch.

Danny had called me from the road last night from somewhere in the middle of Utah. It was hard for me to keep track of where he was from one city to the next, but he called me every night to tell me exactly where he was and how his day was. During last night's conversation, I'd heard a few unfamiliar voices trail off in the background, but he'd assured me they were more of Lexie's guests. Not that I was worried. You'd think with all the girls I'd seen practically throwing themselves at him at the music festival and the ones I was sure were doing it in every city they visited, I'd be more concerned. But that wasn't the case. Danny had promised me that I could trust him, and so far, he hadn't given me any reasons not to. Hell, he had flown home two weeks ago for less than a day and taken Violet to the zoo even though Andre had offered to watch her for us. He didn't only miss me, but he missed my daughter too. If that wasn't a man worth putting my faith in, I didn't know who was.

"These are wonderful, Logan," Jennifer said, analyzing the photographs I'd brought with me to the gallery. She spread the prints out on the table like she was searching for something more. "Is this … everything?"

I nodded, chewing on my lip with a dreadful sigh.

She gave a soft smile and pushed a dark curl out of her face. "They're stunning. Really. They're just lacking … originality."

And there it was. Her honesty stung, but I couldn't disagree. I'd seen a million photographs like the ones I'd taken before—the crashing waves on the shoreline, people looking off into the distance where the ocean met the sky, views of where the city stopped and nature began. Sure, I had a different eye, but it wasn't enough to have an entire collection of it up at the Simonet Gallery.

What was I thinking?

"I see beautiful pictures, Logan, but none of them make me feel anything."

Double ouch.

She continued to page through my folder toward the back.

"I know," I said, trying not to sound too defeated. "I'll find something—I'm sure of it."

"What are these?" she asked, pulling out a couple from the music festival.

"Oh, those." I smiled, thinking back to that day. "I went to the Ex's and Oh's Festival with some friends and brought my camera along. I was just having some fun."

She shifted her focus from the pictures to me. "See, now, this is what I'm looking for."

I blinked up at her. "Really?"

Her lipstick-framed smile stretched up her face, making the crinkles by her eyes deepen. "Absolutely. If it elicits emotion from the artist, it will translate into the art, my dear."

Her warm eyes fell back down to the image of the lead singer I'd quickly snuck a shot of, belting his lyrics out into the microphone. The veins in his neck popped, and his eyes were squeezed shut. You could almost hear the note screaming from his throat from the effort and power he was forcing out in that single moment I'd caught on camera.

"I think you've found what you've been searching for, Logan. Do you have any more?"

I'd sifted through hundreds of images from that night, but I hadn't had enough that I thought were worth showing to make a full collection. "None that are like these, but I can get more."

"Please do. I'd love to see them." She patted the top of my shoulder and handed me back my photographs. "I have a weekend open in a couple of months. Bring me something that makes you light up the way these did, and the spot is yours," she said with promise before disappearing into her office.

When I stepped outside the large glass doors of the gallery, I pulled out my phone and double-checked the band's schedule before I called Avery.

She answered on the second ring.

"Hey, Avery. I hear there's a really good band playing at the Fillmore next weekend. What do you say we make a trip to Denver together and surprise Liam and Danny?"

My father carried a folded-up piece of paper in his back pocket to dinner on Monday night. He took it out just before he sat down to eat and left it in the middle of the table, face down, right beside the roast and peas. When I asked him what it was, he told me he'd talk about it later after Violet went to bed, which set off a panic button in my nervous system.

I watched those papers like a hawk for the entirety of our meal, only looking up from it when my mother would ask the occasional question about what I'd been up to.

My dad knew exactly what he was doing when he set it down the way he did. It was cruel really. He knew I'd sit there and overthink what it could be, but he enjoyed watching me squirm. For all I knew, it was a recipe my mom wanted to give me. Or maybe it was a receipt for all the bills I'd racked up over the years and they were finally coming to collect my debt. Either one seemed likely.

An hour later, my mom went to put Violet down, and I couldn't stop my pulse from quickening when I was left alone in the living room with my dad. I wasn't sure if I was more nervous about asking them to watch Violet while I flew halfway across the country to take pictures of my very hot boyfriend playing guitar or to find out what the mysterious papers were.

Definitely the papers.

I started with something exciting I'd suddenly thought of to help ease into the more pressing questions. "I'm buying a car next week."

Dad tore his gaze away from the basketball game on the television. He didn't even like to watch basketball; he just wanted me to be the one to lose my shit and beg him to tell me what it was he was dangling in my face this time.

"Oh, yeah?" he asked, raising the corner of his mouth. It wasn't a full smile, but I'd take it.

I nodded. "Danny helped me pick it out when he was here a couple of weeks ago. He knew all of the questions to ask about safety and performance."

"And you've saved up enough for it?"

I nodded again. "More than enough, Daddy."

"That's great, Lo," he said, patting my knee. "Great job."

"Thanks."

His eyes shifted back to the screen, and I chewed on my lip as Moose jumped up to lay beside me on the couch.

"Speaking of Danny …" I waited until he looked at me again before I continued, "I was wondering if you and Mom could watch Violet this weekend while I go and visit him in Colorado."

"Lo—" He started to shake his head.

"It's for work," I argued first, petting Moose to ease my nerves. "Well, sort of. Obviously, I want to spend time with him, but I'm also going to take some pictures. I spoke with Jennifer on Saturday, and she loved the images I'd brought in of some of the bands I'd photographed at that music festival I went to."

"I don't know, Lo." He stood and fetched the papers he'd brought with him and then sat back down next to me. "I had Johnny from work run a background check on your new neighbor, and I found some things I don't like."

I wasn't sure if I was more surprised that he had actually had someone at the station run a background check on Danny or the fact that he had waited this long in the evening to bring it up if he'd found something on him. He loved a good told-you-so moment.

"Dad, seriously?"

His eyes scanned down the page, unfazed by my deadpan expression. "A DUI before he was even eighteen … minor possession charges … overdose of a narcotic …"

I sighed. "I know about his past, Dad, and I don't care."

"You don't care?" He frowned, lowering the paper into his lap. "How could you not care?"

"Because that's not who he is anymore."

"Oh, you barely know the guy." He scoffed. "This list goes on for years of his life. It wasn't just a phase or some teenage outburst."

"Neither was mine, but you still gave me a second chance. Why can't you give him one too? I bet there's nothing on there from the last two years." I hit the paper in his grasp, hoping I was right.

He looked down at it again. "Ah, but there is."

My stomach twisted. Had Danny lied to me?

"Let's see here. There were multiple noise complaints from Kansas City to New York and Milwaukee. Oh, and an indecent exposure charge from two summers ago near some lake in Minnesota."

The muscles in my shoulders unraveled. "That's it?" I chuckled.

The crease between his brows grew deeper. "What do you mean, that's it? The boy is a troublemaker. I don't want you and Violet to get caught up in his … ways."

"Dad, he's a musician. If he's not getting in trouble for being too loud, he's probably not a very good one."

"It's more than that, Lo. Something that's not on here." He set the paper down on the coffee table and sighed.

"What then?"

He interlocked his fingers in front of him. "I thought his name sounded familiar, which is why I looked him up in the first place. And I was right. I didn't know Danny, but I knew his last name. As an officer, there are some cases that stick with you, even through the years. And I remember being at the scene that day—fishing David Fox's car out of the river."

My face paled. "You were there after his sister and dad's accident?"

"I was." He raised his eyes to mine. "I met Danny's sister. She's a tough one, that girl. She managed to survive the fall, get herself out of a sinking car, and swim to safety despite her injuries."

My throat bobbed at the thought of a smaller Avery going through all that. She must've been so scared.

My father's eyes rounded with sadness. "Poor thing had a terrible concussion and couldn't tell me much about what happened. That's why we had to rule it an accident. There wasn't enough evidence to prove … well …"

A cold rod shot up my spine. "What are you saying? That it wasn't?"

"I interviewed several witnesses, Lo. A bicyclist claimed to have heard a girl screaming in the front seat of the car way before they even went over the guardrail. Another person who had been driving behind them said he was driving erratically and speeding."

"That could mean anything. Maybe something was wrong with the car," I offered.

He shook his head. "We had tests run on the vehicle after we recovered it. There was nothing wrong with it."

Moose moved his head into my lap, sensing my unease.

"Had he been drinking?"

"Toxicology came back clean."

My eyes burned. "That can't be. That's too—"

"Terrible? Yeah, it is."

I took a moment to digest what he had told me. It was too much. Too dark. Danny couldn't have known, and if that was true, I hoped he never found out.

Oh, Avery. Did she remember everything? I hoped not. How could a parent ever—

I cut off that thought, immediately feeling the urge to run into Violet's room and hold her.

"Even if that is true, what does that have to do with Danny?" I asked. "He wasn't even there."

"That doesn't mean he's not dangerous."

"Dangerous?" I snapped. "Dad, it's not like killing your kid is a hereditary trait. Jesus."

"You told us the other night that he's just like his father."

"In regard to their passion for music, yes. But it's not like I knew the guy." I shook my head, growing angrier by the second. "This is a ridiculous argument. Stop it."

"I don't want him around Vi. Or you." He lowered his tone in warning, but it didn't scare me.

"Too bad. That's not your decision to make."

He scowled at me. "I don't understand how a boy could mean so much to you that you're willing to turn a blind eye and—"

I rose onto my feet. "Because I love him! Okay?"

His eyes widened at my outburst. Or maybe it was my proclamation—I wasn't sure. I was too busy repeating the words in my head, realizing they were true.

I loved Danny.

I loved the way his blue eyes looked at me like I was the most important person in the world to him and the deepness of his voice. I loved his possessive touch and how his hands were both gentle and rough at the same time. I loved how he could get lost in a song when he was playing guitar and the way his eyes softened when he spoke to my daughter. Most importantly, I loved how much I'd started to love myself again since he'd entered my life.

"Logan, you don't know him—"

"I do. I love him, Daddy," I told him again. "I'm not turning a blind eye to anything. I love him, and I trust him. Now, you need to trust me. I know that's asking a lot after everything I've put you and Mom through, but I really need you to dig deep and trust my judgment on this. Okay?"

I realized the weight of all this and the possible repercussions if I turned out to be wrong about Danny.

But I wasn't.

I'd never been surer about anyone or anything in my life.

My dad finally gave a single nod and muttered, "Okay, Lo."

26

Danny

"Hello, Denver!" Liam shouted into his mic from the darkness. "You all look fucking beautiful tonight!"

Lexie ran her fingers through her bass guitar, sending a low hum throughout the theater of thirty-six hundred screaming fans.

I stepped onto the dark stage next, fingers ready, as Tic settled in behind his drum set.

"My name is Liam, and this is Lexie, Danny, and Tic," Liam introduced us as spotlights illuminated overhead. "And we are—"

Tic hit his sticks together, counting us in, and Liam held his arms out, welcoming our fans' reactions.

"A QUIET PERIL!" the crowd erupted, and I stroked my guitar as the entire stage lit up.

My in-ears could only do so much to drown out the pulsating screams as Liam began the first verse of the night.

Our fans shouted every single word, and I grinned, soaking up their energy.

Our first song bled into the second, and just before the third, Liam did his typical speech, thanking the crowd for spending their hard-earned money to come to see us play for them. If they didn't come, we wouldn't be able to do what we loved doing. We didn't take a single show or a single fan for granted.

"This next one is off our new album and has been one of our most highly requested songs," Liam said, and the fans started shouting song titles. "And we can't deny that this song would be *nothing* without this talented bastard." Liam pointed back at me from his mic stand, and I flashed a smile as I gripped my guitar in preparation. "This one is called 'It All Fades.' Now, let me fucking hear you scream for my boy Danny!"

Hands shot in the air, and deafening screams ensued as I began the song with my solo. My fingers worked intricately up and down the neck of my guitar. I shut my eyes and bobbed my head to Tic's drumming, feeling that sense of euphoria that only ever happened when I was onstage.

Lexie came in next, adding that deep bass to build up the sound. The fans went wild, ready for Liam's lyrics to cut through the speakers as my solo dissolved into the rest of the melody.

But he missed his cue, and my eyes shot open to find out why. I didn't know if he had gotten caught up in the moment or forgotten the lyrics, but he acted quickly and held his microphone out in front of him. The crowd sang the first few lines for him as he leaned forward, resting his foot on a monitor box at the edge of the stage. He finally brought the mic back to his lips and sang the next line, fixed on the fans in front of him. I was about to pull my attention away from him when he nodded back at me.

My gaze fell down to where he'd directed me to look, and I found my sister, jumping and singing every line up at him. I couldn't help the smile that spread across my face.

A second later, the girl standing next to my sister lowered her camera from her face, and I was grateful that my muscle memory kicked in because *holy fuck*.

Logan was here.

Logan was fucking *here*. Standing in the front row at *my* show.

I'd never looked into the crowd for someone that was mine before.

Her wide-eyed gaze and sweet smile made me want to toss my guitar off to the crew backstage and escape somewhere with her, but I played harder instead, never letting my gaze leave hers.

She wore that perfect shade of lipstick, and my eyes fell to her lips when I noticed them moving, but not in sync with the lyrics.

My eyebrows pinched as I smiled back at her, wanting her to say them again because I couldn't make it out.

She repeated the silent words, this time slower.

I. Love. You.

Muscle memory didn't fucking work when your heart stopped. My hands glitched, and I lost my place in the song. It was maybe only a couple of seconds before I found the chords again, but my bandmates all peered over at me, amused.

I moved around my mic stand, walked up to the edge of the stage, and fell to my knees in front of Logan.

Logan's cheeks flushed as she watched my smile grow wider and wider.

I finished the rest of the song, only playing for her.

Logan slowly raised her camera again and took a picture as the song ended. But the fans surrounding her grew excited at how close I was, jostling her around so much that she almost dropped her camera.

Avery was in the middle of it, too, but she was throwing elbows.

A man behind Logan placed his hand on her shoulder and ripped her backward, trying to take her place up front. She stumbled but caught her footing and rubbed her shoulder where he'd touched her.

I shot to my feet and jumped down between the stage and the barricade, handing my guitar off to the nearest security guard.

"Hey, hey, hey!" Liam called into his mic, trying to calm the swarm in front of me. "I know everyone's excited, but you guys gotta be respectful of one another, or we can't play the rest of our set."

I stepped up onto the metal bar of the barricade, and Logan wrapped her hands around my middle while I shouted over her head at the guy behind her.

"Aye, dickhead! Don't ever fucking touch someone like that again! You hear me?" I growled loud enough not to need a mic.

The blond-haired douchebag held his hands up innocently. "I didn't do nothing, man."

"I fucking saw you!"

Logan made soothing circles at my sides. "Hey, I'm okay! It's okay!" I heard her say, feeling her breath hit my chest through my open shirt.

Fans surrounding us still reached for me while some held their phones in the air.

I leaned over Logan, protecting her while pulling Avery into my side.

"You touch people like that, and you're out! End of story!" I told the guy.

He denied it again, which only made me angrier.

The crowd all started chanting, "Kick him out! Kick him out! Kick him out!"

I nodded at one of the security guards beside me. "Get this guy out of here."

They spoke into a walkie, and two security guards waded through the thick crowd from behind to escort him out.

The fans cheered and then booed him as he left. The guy threw up his middle fingers at everyone he passed out of protest.

Somewhere in all of that, I'd forgotten that Logan was still in my embrace, and I certainly couldn't leave her in the crowd after seeing what happened.

"Oh my gosh, Danny!" a fan shouted.

Another let out a high-pitched scream. "I love you, Danny!"

I grinned and waved but looked down at the only girl I wanted to hear those three words from. My hands cupped Logan's face as I brought my mouth to hers and kissed her with painstaking affection. She raised onto the balls of her feet and kissed me back, clinging to my shirt with a firm grasp.

The entire theater erupted in *oohs* and *aahs* while Liam whistled into the mic and Tic thrashed on a cymbal.

"You're coming with me," I said once I pulled away.

Security guards aided me and blocked a few fans who tried to join us as I lifted Logan over the barricade.

I pointed at Avery once Logan was safe at my side and nodded. "Her too, please."

Avery managed to climb over by herself and winked up at Liam before giving me a quick hug. I led them both into the shadows next to the stage and placed them where I thought they'd be out of the crew's way while still having a good view of the rest of the show.

"How the fuck am I supposed to finish my set, knowing you're standing five feet away from me for the next two hours?" I asked, gazing down at Logan.

She smiled. "Hey, this will be hard for me too. The only things keeping me from jumping you onstage are your giant security guards."

"Please jump me. I can fake an injury and leave early," I joked.

She laughed and shook her head.

"I take it, it's just you and my sister? Andre's watching Violet?"

"My parents," she clarified.

My forehead creased. "You mean, your dad knew you were flying across the country to see me, and he was okay with it?"

She teetered her head. "I wouldn't say he was thrilled about it, but I told him he didn't have a say in the matter."

"That's my girl." My mouth tilted up to match hers.

"Is it okay if I take some pictures back here?" she asked.

"As long as you only get my good side." I winked. "Nikko is at the soundboard in the back, but if you need anything, just ask one of the crew members to call him back here."

She peered behind me, and her eyes widened. "Go, go, go," she said, pushing me backward. "Everyone is waiting for you."

I leaned in and pecked her cheek, and then I ran back into the blinding lights.

When I retrieved my guitar and resumed playing, it felt like I wasn't even in my body. I'd checked out. Every song we started after that seemed to last forever. The set list was too long. I thought about asking Liam if he wanted to skip the couple extra surprise tracks we always snuck in toward the end because I knew he was dying to spend time with my sister as well, but I didn't want to take anything away from our fans. They deserved the full experience, so I did my best to put my head back into the music and give them everything I had.

Logan had never heard us all play together live, so I couldn't help but glance backstage between each song to catch a glimpse of her awestruck expression. Sometimes, it was hidden behind her camera, but most of the time, she was just watching me. It was cute as hell, especially when she was wearing my T-shirt.

I couldn't explain what her presence did to me. It was that same feeling of being onstage, where I was, only *better*. The adrenaline rushing through my veins. The lightness in my shoulders. The anticipation of getting to hold her in my arms when I was done. I'd never felt more undeserving of anything.

Two hours later, our last song ended, and our fans were cheering so loud that I could barely think straight. Sweat dripped down the seam of my back as I held my guitar in the air and bowed. I patted a hand over my heart, silently thanking the crowd as Liam bid them all good night. Tic ran his sticks through his drum set like a maniac to show his appreciation while Lexie wiggled her hips up at the front of the stage and blew them a farewell kiss.

With a final wave, I hurried to find Logan backstage. She was still snapping pictures when I all but threw my guitar at one of my crew guys and pulled her away toward the back entrance.

"Wait, Danny," Logan started to protest. "What about everyone else—"

The noise from the venue was muffled when the door shut behind us, and I pushed her back up against it, devouring her lips with a greedy kiss. The hum of Logan's moan met my ears, and it was the best goddamn thing I'd heard all night.

"God, I fucking missed you," I rasped.

Fuck, it felt good to finally have her to myself. Her lips were glistening and swollen when I finally pulled away.

"I missed you too," she breathed. "But I know you didn't plan on me showing up tonight. I don't expect you to drop everything for me. This is your job, and a lot of people count on you."

"I did my job already. I showed up and played some of my music. Very well, I might add. You have proof of it right here on your camera." I pointed with a smirk.

She pursed her lips. "Don't you need to stay and socialize? Or help with anything?"

I raised a brow at her concern. "No. That's what we pay our crew for."

"I just don't want to be rude—"

I held a finger over her mouth to silence her. "Logan, the only thing I need right now is you. I'm not wasting a single second on greenroom drinks or band chitchat when I could be alone with you."

"Okay." Her rounded doe eyes narrowed and slanted into something far less innocent looking.

"Christ, Logan. You can't look at me like that." I groaned. "I'll fuck you right here against this door if you don't leave with me in the next five seconds."

Her giggle sent a bolt of electricity straight to my dick.

"Where are we going?" she asked.

I sent a quick text to set up a ride for us back to the hotel and then flashed my key card in her line of vision. "I have something I want to show you."

27

Danny

Logan sat on the edge of the bed and put my headphones over her ears as I cued up the song on my laptop. I'd started working on it after all of our songs were already submitted to our label for the newest album, so I'd have to wait for the next one to release it. If she'd even let me release it.

I could've played the song through the speakers for the both of us to listen, but I wanted to make sure she could hear every detail of the song—particularly the soft vocals in the background.

She bobbed her head to the beat with a smile, and I knew she hadn't heard it yet.

The anticipation and knowledge of what she was listening to made the blood rush from my head down to my groin.

And then her faint smile fell, and her eyes widened.

My pulse spiked.

She heard it.

She heard *herself.*

Her voice. Her gasps for air. Her moans. All recorded from that night in my basement.

"Danny!" She cupped the headphones and listened closely for another second before she pulled them off. "When did you ... how did you—" she stammered.

"My elbow might've bumped something when we were sitting next to the soundboard." I shrugged.

Her face paled. "You can't use this."

"And why is that?" My grin darkened as I stepped closer to the bed.

"Because that's me. My ... *orgasm.*" Her breath wavered.

When my legs met her knees, I tilted her chin up with a finger and stared down at her lips. "No one will know that but me. Besides"—I leaned down and flicked my tongue against her bottom lip—"those delicious sounds belong to *me*, and I will do whatever the fuck I want with them."

Her face, which was just devoid of color, flushed.

"Did you like it?" I husked.

She fidgeted with the ends of her black hair and then the bottom of her—my—band tee. "I mean, the rest of it was good, but that part ... it's embarrassing."

"What if that song was just for us? What if no one ever heard it? What would your opinion of it be then?" I proposed.

She stiffened slightly before taking a deep inhale and considered it as she exhaled slowly.

I saw the corner of her mouth twitch before she answered, "I'd say it's kind of ... hot."

I wet my lip and nodded. "So fucking hot, Logan."

Her round chin rose as she looked up at me. "Will it stay that way? Just for you and me?"

"That's entirely up to you."

She chewed on her lip.

"You don't have to decide that now," I said, stroking my thumb over her bottom lip as she released it from her teeth. "To be honest, I'm not sure I'd be able to play it live and not have a raging hard-on."

Logan's laugh cut off when her gaze fell down my torso … to my stiffening cock. Her eyes flitted back up to me, and my eyes darkened.

"Well, we wouldn't want that, would we?" she asked, undoing my jeans. "Because this is just for me too."

"Logan, you don't have to—"

"Right?" She raised a brow and grinned, cupping me through my briefs as my jeans fell to the ground.

I sucked in a breath through my teeth. Her confidence was shining through, and I loved it.

"Fuck. Yes. All for you."

The embarrassment that had once peppered her pink cheeks was replaced with a deep, warm flush of desire.

Her fingers hooked beneath the thick waistband of my briefs and pulled them down to my knees, where they continued to the floor on their own. I was relieved to have finally freed my erection from its restraints, but the ache of having it right in line with Logan's mouth had my hands twitching. I wanted nothing more than to grip the back of her head and plunge myself inside, but her rosy lips parted, and she took me in, inch by inch, of her own accord.

"Fucking hell, Logan," I groaned, watching my length disappear into her warm mouth.

She couldn't take the whole thing, but, God, I loved watching her try.

She lifted her eyes up to look at me, groaning around my hard, rigid flesh. It was the best goddamn thing I'd ever seen. I suddenly wished her camera weren't across the suite so I could take a picture to keep with the other one hidden in my bunk back on the tour bus. How she managed to look innocent while my cock hit the back of her throat was beyond me.

I grunted as she bobbed her head a few more times before pulling back to take a breath, catching my soaked length in her hands. Before she could wrap her lips around me again, I tied her hair around my knuckles and pulled her to her feet, kissing her with a hunger I couldn't control.

She moaned at the slight sting on her scalp and the abrupt contact of my lips. Her eagerness soon began to match my own as she tore the remaining flannel from my shoulders, and I stripped her down to her black lace bra and panties.

My free hand roamed from the dip in her back, around the curve of her hips, up to the round swells of her breasts while the other pulled her head to the side to give my mouth better access to her neck. I sucked on her soft skin, feeling goosebumps form beneath my tongue.

"Turn around for me," I ordered next to her ear.

Logan spun and pressed her ass up against me.

My hands fell to her hips, gripping them firmly as I nibbled across her shoulder.

Bending her at the waist, I kept a hand firmly on her hip while the other sprawled between her shoulder blades, guiding her down onto her elbows. "Just like that."

She brought her knees up onto the mattress, arching her back for me. Her thighs trembled as I pushed aside the thin strip of lace and slid my fingers up and down her slick center. Little by little, she eased her knees apart on the bed, writhing with desire.

"I missed your hands. Your touch," she gasped out.

"I missed touching you," I replied, circling her clit. "And the way you say my name when I finger your sweet pussy."

I dipped a finger inside her, and she rocked her hips back.

"Danny," she whispered, giving me what I wanted.

"But mostly, I missed the way you fucking taste," I said, bringing my fingers into my mouth.

She craned her head back and watched me lick them clean. "Oh God."

I grinned and took hold of my cock, lining my hips with hers. When I started to ease the head of my cock inside her, I froze and cursed under my breath. She was so warm, so ready. It took every ounce of strength to refrain from ramming into her.

Logan whimpered, "What's the matter?"

"I don't have a condom on me," I said, readying myself to fall onto my knees and make her come on my tongue instead.

"You don't need one," she said breathlessly, looking over her shoulder at me again.

"What?"

"I got started on the pill a little over a month ago. We're good."

"Are you sure?"

She nodded, swiveling her hips with need.

My hands palmed her ass, and I pushed my hips forward, rubbing my length along her throbbing slit as a reward.

She hummed, throwing her head back. "Don't tease me, Danny."

A dark grin curled my lips as I nudged the tip of my cock at her entrance. "Use your words, Logan."

"Isn't it a little redundant at this point?" she teased, pushing herself back up against me.

It was, but I still enjoyed hearing her ask for what she wanted.

My hand snapped at her ass, spanking her, and a sharp cry escaped her throat.

I rubbed soothing circles over the reddening skin. "Did you like that? Does that turn you on?"

She bit down on her lip and nodded.

I smirked. She didn't just like it—she fucking loved it.

"I didn't hear you," I said, spanking her again.

She yiped, "Yes, *yes!*"

"What do you want?" I rubbed the heated skin beneath my hand again. "Do you want me to spank you until you come? I bet I can."

"N-no." She shook her head, panting. "Please, Danny. I need you. I need *all* of you."

I moaned, letting her know her confirmation turned me on and then thrust my hips forward.

Her hands fisted the sheets on the bed below her as she cried out.

Curling my hands into the soft cleavage of her hips, I pulled her into me in another quick jerk.

"Oh my God," she breathed.

My grip on her tightened, and my movements came faster. My gaze dropped to where our bodies connected, and I felt my pending release build quicker than I wanted. Logan was nearly there too—I could feel her tightening around me every time my hips met her ass.

"Danny." Her breaths were shorter and more ragged. "*Danny*—"

"I know, baby," I said hoarsely. "I know."

But I wasn't ready for this to end yet. Not when I couldn't see the look on her face when she came undone around me.

I bit down on my cheek and pulled out of her before the carnal desire to relieve the ache in my cock became too strong to deny.

"No, wait," she pleaded. "I was—"

I didn't give her a second to finish as I hooked my arm under her knee and swung her over onto her back.

"Jesus, fuck!" She stared, wide-eyed, and then let go of a breathy laugh. "Warn a girl."

I tore her soaked lace thong from her hips, stretched her leg up over my shoulder, and settled my knees on the mattress beneath her. "Where's the fun in that?" I grinned.

She gasped as I quickly filled her again, the sensation too fucking good to ease back into it. I dipped my chin and fucked her harder, finding a faster rhythm and building my release back up again.

Logan's soft moans broke off with every hard thrust. The way she watched my animalistic movements with parted lips was erotic and oh-so motivating.

I turned my head to the side and dragged my mouth down her upper thigh, keeping my pace. "I'm never letting you go, Logan. Never."

The golden hue of her eyes sparked brighter at my words. "Come here," she said, reaching for me. "I want you closer."

I gently dropped her leg and cradled it around my waist, then climbed on top of her and pressed my lips to hers with a scorching kiss.

She clung to me, hands slipping into my hair and tugging tight.

I was so close to the edge that I was seeing stars. Panting, I broke away from her mouth and trailed my tongue down to her chest, stroking one pebbled numb and then the other, before hovering my lips over hers again. I left her walls pulsing around me as her breath hitched, and I knew she was close too. Our hot breaths mixed together as I met the hazy look in her eyes.

"That's it, baby. Come with me."

"I'm—oh God. *Ah.* I'm so close—"

White-hot pleasure shot up my spine as my orgasm crested, so I reached down and gently stroked her clit, and that was enough to tip her over the edge.

"Scream for me, Logan. I know you can do better than that recording."

The way she immediately responded to the challenge overloaded my system. Her name came out with a strangled growl as my orgasm slammed into me a second after hers.

Her hips bucked involuntarily as the spasms washed over her, wave after wave.

"That was music to my fucking ears." I gritted each word out and slowed my thrusts as I finished unraveling.

She wrapped her arms around me and took all my weight as I collapsed onto her and pressed slow kisses along her glistening skin. I settled my head on her chest, and I closed my eyes, listening to the rhythm that gave life to my own heartbeat.

I was falling.

Hard.

Only this time, I was scared of reaching the ground.

The longer I held on to Logan, the more potential she had of destroying me if and when she ever left.

So long as I kept her safe and didn't fuck up, I could keep her. Maybe not forever, but until she deemed me unworthy. Because there was no way I could ever be the one to walk away. Not from her.

"That thing you said to me when you were in the crowd tonight?"

"Yeah?" She held her breath.

"I love you too."

28

Logan

His words knitted between my ribs, and it was like I could breathe again. Like I'd spent my whole life never being able to exhale all the way—until now.

It was lighter.

Freeing.

I'd given myself permission to take control of my life again. To enjoy the things I'd felt guilty about having before, knowing now that I deserved them. Because I did. I deserved to be this happy. I deserved *Danny*.

I sighed, memorizing the way he held me from behind. The way his muscular frame warmed me, protected me, and the scent of his cologne still lingering on his skin. Maybe if we didn't get out of bed, life would just stay on pause for a little while.

As much as I wanted to stay wrapped in his arms forever, I couldn't ignore my stomach grumbling in protest.

Danny chuckled from behind me, hearing my hunger roar through the quiet room.

"You're awake," I said, snuggling against him.

"And you're hungry." His voice was raspy with sleep. "I wish I could make you some breakfast, but I'm afraid you'll have to settle for some five-star room service."

"Ugh. Gross," I teased, swiveling around to face him.

His lips pressed against my forehead. "Sleep well?"

"The little that I got, yes."

His lazy smile gleamed with pride. And then his phone buzzed and stole it away.

Rolling back to grab it from the nightstand, he frowned at the message and threw it back down.

"What's wrong?"

He buried his face in his pillow and groaned. "I forgot I have a radio gig this morning. We just have to go and play a quick cover and then answer a few questions. A couple of hours, tops."

"What's so horrible about that?"

"I'd rather stay in bed with you." He pouted.

"You can't put work on hold just because your girlfriend decided to show up, unannounced." I smiled. "Besides, I don't leave until tomorrow afternoon. We have plenty of time to spend here when you finish."

His brow arched. "You know, I was planning on coming back home today to see you."

"You were?"

"Yeah, you beat me to it." He cocked a grin. "Maybe I can fly back with you tomorrow. Spend some time with you and Violet for a day or two."

My heart tugged at the idea. I twisted my hand around the sheet and raised it to my chest, trying not to get too excited. I knew he was busy. "You have the time?"

He nodded. "I think so. I don't have to be in Santa Fe until Wednesday morning." He saw the excitement in my eyes and chuckled. "I'll have Nikko set it up."

"Okay," I said, watching him climb out of bed.

His sculpted back was vacant of tattoos, making a couple of claw marks on his shoulder blades stand out.

When did I do that?

He stole my digital camera from the sofa and took another picture of me, this time up close and personal.

"Stop." I giggled, pushing the lens away from my face.

"Do you have any idea how beautiful you are?" He pulled the camera away to see how it turned out. "Seriously, you would never have to work again if you sold pictures like this one."

I raised a brow.

"On second thought, I fucking hate that idea. I don't want some pervert owning a picture of you. Forget what I said. They're hideous." He grinned through his lie, continuing to look through my pictures. "Hey, these turned out really good, Logan. The ones you took last night."

I propped myself up on my elbow. "Yeah?"

Danny looked up at me, nodded, and then continued flicking through the shots I had gotten at their show. There were a lot of just Danny, but I had gotten some good ones in of the whole band too.

275

"These are … wow." He stopped on another one and brought the camera closer to his eyes. "You are so fucking talented."

I knew I was pretty good, but to hear him affirm it made a warmth in my chest unfurl. "I'm hoping to show them at the Simonet Gallery in a couple of months."

"Really?"

"As long as Jennifer likes them and I get the go-ahead from you guys."

He chuckled. "I don't even need to ask them. They'll be thrilled. Lexie's kind of a diva. She'll probably want one of herself blown up to take home."

"You sure you won't mind people buying photographs of you?"

"Nah, I'm used to it. Besides, I like being your muse."

"Good, because you've got me feeling all sorts of inspired." I swiped my tongue over my lower lip.

He grinned. "When did you know this was what you wanted to do?"

"Photography? I don't know. I guess I've always liked taking pictures. When I was younger, my mom gave me a Polaroid camera, and I would take pictures of everything. Mainly of the caterpillars and flowers I found in our backyard, but I eventually found other inspiration."

"Yeah, I can relate to that with my music."

"Exactly." I nodded. "I mean, when you're gone from this world, people will remember you for the music you left behind, right?"

"I hope so."

I pushed myself up and knelt in front of him, grabbing my camera. "I want to be remembered for this. Moments like these that I'm lucky enough to witness and capture in time with my camera. The world is constantly moving and changing. It will never be the same again."

He peered down at me softly.

"I can't go back in time and change anything that I've done, but I've learned to hold on to the moments I wouldn't change even if I had the chance. The ones that made me feel something again because they reminded me that it's not all bad." I looked down at the picture he'd stopped on before he handed it to me—the one I had taken of him when I was standing among his fans. "This is the only way I know how to make time stand still forever."

He placed his hands on my hips. "I wish I could make this—right now, here with you—stand still."

I raised my camera up, focused the lens on his deep blue eyes, and snapped a photo. "There. Now, it does."

He dipped his head down and kissed me.

I slid a hand up his chest, and I pulled his mouth back to mine again. But another growl of my stomach reminded us both of the time.

Danny muttered a curse, and he reluctantly backed away. "I have to be across town in a half hour, or Nikko will have my head. I'm going to hop in the shower real quick. Why don't you order some food for yourself and have it sent up?"

"Can I join you?" I called, hearing him turn on the water.

He peeked his head out of the bathroom, groaning, "I will definitely be late if you get in here with me."

I chuckled and dismissed him with a wave before finding the breakfast menu on the table.

"Logan"—Danny's voice echoed from inside the shower—"are you coming in or what?"

"But you said …"

He scoffed. "I'm not scared of Nikko. Get your ass in here."

After I finished devouring my eggs Benedict, I FaceTimed with Violet and my mom for a little while. They were on their way to the grocery store, so I didn't get to chat for long, but Violet had fun making faces at her reflection in the camera on the car ride there.

Once we hung up, I called Avery and fetched my bag from her suite. I screamed when she showed me a very impressive and important piece of jewelry Liam had given her last night. I'd heard of an engagement glow before, but she wore it better than anyone I'd ever seen. It had been hard enough to get Danny out the door for the radio gig they had to go to— especially after our very long shower. I couldn't imagine how hard it must've been for Liam to leave his fiancée the morning after he proposed.

I hung out with Avery for a bit, sharing in her excitement, but left when her friend Nina called. She hadn't heard the news yet, and I wanted to give them their privacy and finish getting ready for the day.

When I got back to Danny's room, I dried and styled my hair, then changed into a pair of leggings and a T-shirt. It was chillier in Colorado than I'd planned for, so I wrapped myself up in Danny's red flannel for some added warmth. Being enveloped in his spicy scent awoke the butterflies in my chest, and I fell back onto the mattress, letting them flutter of their own free will.

A half hour later, I'd nearly drifted back to sleep when Danny called. He was finishing up at the radio station and then heading back. The band was meeting at the restaurant downstairs for some lunch, so he told me to join them in twenty.

After twiddling my thumbs for a few minutes, I decided to head down early and check out the menu to kill some time.

I watched the numbers go up above the elevator as I waited for it to reach my floor. When the doors finally opened, I stepped aside to let the couple that was leaving out.

The brown-haired girl tossed a sideways glance at me as she rolled a small suitcase out behind her. There was something familiar about her, but she turned her back on me before I could get a second look.

Shaking my head at how unaware I was of the man still blocking the doors from closing, I apologized and hurried inside. The lobby button lit up as I touched it, but the man hadn't moved out of the way of the doors yet. I avoided eye contact, hoping he'd leave. But he was still there, watching me.

Out of the corner of my eye, I saw him fold his arms over his broad chest.

"Logan Ellis. As I live and breathe."

My eyes darted up from the floor, and I sucked in a breath at the familiar face.

The corner of the man's mouth curled up as he saw the surprise in my eyes. I hoped that was all he saw because the fear shooting through my veins felt like some type of biohazardous acid that glowed neon green in the dark.

"F-Falcon," I murmured warily. The nickname was fitting, considering I felt like a tiny, trapped mouse beneath his talons.

"You look like you've just seen a ghost," he mused.

I had. Seeing him brought me back to a time when I had been a different person. The girl before Violet.

His brows pulled together in thought. "I guess it's been a while. How long has it been now?"

"Four—maybe five years," I answered coldly.

He looked me up and down, slower than was necessary. "Well, you look great, Lolo."

Another cold, swift kick of memories flooded through me. "It's nice to see you. Can I go?"

"Of course. I just wanted to say hi to an old friend—that's all." He smirked. "You haven't missed me?"

Did he really need an answer to that question?

The doors to the elevator pulsed, wanting to close.

"What are you doing here, Lolo?" He stepped toward me with purpose, letting the doors shut behind him. As soon as they did, he hit the Emergency Stop button.

I stood on shaky knees, my mind strangely empty of all thought. "What are you doing?"

He shrugged, as if this were normal behavior. "Why are you getting so worked up? I'm just trying to have a conversation."

Yeah, in a steel cage I suddenly can't escape from.

I calculated how many steps it would take to get to the control panel, but he was between me and my way out—there was no chance I'd make it.

"I'm visiting my boyfriend. Why does it matter?"

His steady gaze searched mine as he lowered his head. My pulse kicked up double time when he stepped closer and pinched the collar of Danny's flannel.

"Ah, so you're the new neighbor Danny's been hooking up with."

"Danny?" I frowned. "How do you know Danny?"

"Funny thing about the past is, it always catches up with you." He shook his head and laughed. "You always had the worst taste in men, didn't you?"

I clearly had the worst taste in friends too.

"Not anymore," I retorted. "Danny is the best man I've ever met."

"Do you even know Danny?" he asked mockingly. "Out of all my band members, you chose the former addict who used to fuck his dealer."

My stomach sank at the words *my band members.*

Nikko. He's Danny's manager?

Well, I certainly hadn't expected that. I had known Falcon wasn't his legal name, but I never bothered myself with trying to find out what it was.

"You're ..." I trailed off when he placed his giant hand on the wall above my head.

His breath hit my forehead, and I shuddered.

"But I guess you fucked your dealer, too, so maybe your guys' commonalities are a green flag for you."

My wide eyes shot to his. "Excuse me?"

He watched me with cold, calculated eyes, but he didn't reply.

Falcon had dealt to me for years, but I never had sex with him. Ever. He could be really kind some days and then terrifying the next. I did my best to stay as far away from him as possible, but we ran in the same crowd. There had only been so much I could do.

But then, out of the corner of my eye, I saw something peeking out from the sleeve of his shirt—the tips of feathered wings. A tattoo. The one I'd tried to describe to the officers.

A silent tear snuck free as my face blanched with horror. *No.*

"Look, Lolo …"

"No," I whispered.

He heaved out a sigh of annoyance. "Let's keep this between just the two of us, huh? The past stays in the past, am I right?"

I was too stunned to answer him. Too petrified to mutter another syllable.

His hand dropped from the wall and gripped my throat, and I saw that side of him I'd always feared being on the receiving end of.

"Am. I. Right?" The guttural sound of each word dripped with a threat.

I clawed at his hold on me and rose onto my toes, fighting for breath.

"Right," I managed to choke out.

He gave me a look of warning before releasing me.

I slumped over, holding my neck and filling my lungs.

"Good to see you, Lolo." He smiled and punched the Emergency Stop button, making the doors open again. "I'm sure we'll be seeing a lot more of each other now, won't we?"

My whole body shook when he left my sight and the doors closed once more. The elevator dinged as it counted down the floors, and even though I was gaining distance from him by the second, I could still feel his hand constricting my airway.

In a matter of a couple of minutes, my whole world had been flipped upside down. I couldn't think. I couldn't breathe. I couldn't find my balance.

The elevator stilled at the main lobby, and the doors rolled open. Danny was about to walk in when he saw me and paused.

"Hey, I was just about to come up to find you. You weren't answering my texts." He took in the alarmed look on my face and hurried inside. "What's the matter? Is Vi okay?"

The metal doors went to close, and that was all it took for me to find the strength to sprint out.

"Logan!" Danny called, barely escaping in time.

My feet carried me across the maroon-carpeted lobby and came to a halt when I stepped outside the heavy doors. I gulped in the fresh air, but it wasn't without difficulty. Why did Denver have to be so high up in elevation? The mountain air was so fucking thin. Or maybe the air was fine, and rather, I was starting to hyperventilate. I couldn't be sure.

"Hey, talk to me. What happened?" Danny pressed, giving me an arm for stability. "Is Violet—"

"Violet's fine," I answered breathlessly. "I just couldn't be in there any longer. I couldn't go back up to the same floor as *him*."

"Who?" The muscles in his jaw ticked. "Did someone harass you?"

The image of Falcon—er, Nikko's hand returned, and my eyes burned with fear, anger, and betrayal.

Danny held me upright as I heaved two large breaths.

"I'll fucking kill him. Tell me where he is, Logan. You said he was on our floor?"

The invisible vise around my neck squeezed tighter, and I clung to him, begging him to remove it.

"Logan, who is he? What does he look like?" Danny barked.

"Nikko," I managed. "It's Nikko."

29

Danny

I stiffened.

Logan's crippling stance and terrified eyes made my skin burn with anger. I wasn't sure what had made her feel this way, but it wouldn't have been Nikko.

"I'm confused. Nikko?" I gave her a puzzled look. "As in our band manager?"

She nodded.

My eyes flitted back and forth at the ground. "Nikko left the gig early to have lunch with some producers. He won't be back until late tonight."

"Well, he must've gotten done early or lied because it was him, Danny." Her voice was shaky but confident.

Even if that was true, the worst thing I could see him doing was trying to get her number. "Look, I know he's a bit of a man-whore sometimes, but he's not the kind of guy to put that much effort in if a girl isn't interested. I'm sorry if he made you uncomfortable."

Her brow furrowed. "No. He wasn't coming on to me. He was … well, he threatened me in the elevator."

The hairs on the back of my neck stood on end. "Someone threatened you?"

Tears glossed her eyes as she shook her head. "Not someone, Danny. Nikko."

"How do you know for sure it was him? You two haven't met."

She swallowed nervously. "Because I've known him for a long time. I didn't know him as Nikko. We all called him Falcon. He was who I'd buy from … before."

I laughed once. "Logan, no. I've been friends with Nikko for years. That's not him. Hell, he doesn't have the time to be involved with anything like that. He's constantly managing our shit."

Nikko smoked his fair share of weed and had taken some Molly a time or two, but there was no way the person she was talking about was him. I sure as hell wanted to find whoever it was though and wring his fucking neck for making her feel this way.

She sighed, frustrated. "I'm not saying he still sells. I'm telling you who he was. And from the way he squeezed my throat to get me to comply, I'd say he hasn't changed all that much."

Blood drained from my face as I stepped closer, inspecting her neck. It was red—that was for sure—but she'd also been rubbing it since we had left the elevator.

"Where was this person?"

"In the elevator. I told you."

She continued to give me all of the details of what had happened as the muscles in my jaw worked. My molars should've been ground into dust from the way I was clenching.

I took my phone out and growled when I saw it was dead. "Look, let's go inside. I'll call Nikko and see where he is. If he's here, I'll go up to his room and—"

"If he's here?" She paused for a long time, looking up at me, and then shook her head. "You don't believe me."

"I do, baby. But this is one of my best friends you're talking about. Someone I've known since I was ten years old."

"Clearly not very well," she quipped.

I scoffed. "C'mon, Logan."

I knew she was upset, but so was I. My skin still heated at the thought of someone touching her, assaulting her, and I was confused as to why she thought it was my friend. But I hadn't done anything wrong here. I was just trying to sort this out.

"Please," I begged, gesturing back toward the door to the hotel. "Come inside, and we can all talk about this."

Her eyes widened at me. "Danny, I don't want to be anywhere near that guy."

I pulled her into my chest, desperately trying to ease her discomfort. "Hey, I won't let anything happen to you. He'll have to go through me first."

She was silent for a moment, her breaths finally evening out. "Who?"

"What?"

"Who will have to go through you?" she asked softly.

"Whoever did this to you."

She grew rigid in my arms before she slipped out of my grasp. Tears fell down her cheeks, landing on my shirt.

I reached for her again, but she flinched away, as if I were going to strike her.

"Logan?" I pleaded.

She continued to retreat.

"Where are you going?"

"I can't be here right now. I—have to get home to Vi," she said, wiping her face.

"What do you mean? I thought you said she's with your parents?"

"Yeah, I just miss her so much and …" Logan's chin wavered as she held back a sob.

I walked toward her, trying to close the space she had put between us when her hand shot up.

I halted in my steps, feeling a cold shiver radiate up my spine. It wasn't just that she was spooked by what had happened to her in the elevator or that she missed her daughter. She was walking away from *me*.

"Please don't leave me," I muttered.

Her sob broke free. "Danny."

"Let me fix this. I know I can. Just don't—don't give up on me yet." My chest heaved with every word.

"This isn't something you can fix, Danny," she cried.

I ran a hand over my face helplessly. "I fucked up. I know that. I don't always say the right things, but I want to see this through with you. Please. You can't spend your entire life running from vulnerability."

Her expression hardened. "I will spend my life running away from *anything* that puts her in danger!"

Her answer struck me harder than I'd expected.

"I would never put Violet in danger."

She nodded. "But her biological father would."

My heartbeat wavered. "Wh-what?"

"I only just put it all together." She shifted, pulling at the ends of her sleeves.

I clenched my hands into fists at my sides.

"You once said that you'd rip the guy who did that to me apart if you got the chance."

"And I meant it." My nostrils flared.

Logan looked up at me, squinting at the sun. "And yet you're still standing here."

"I will march upstairs and pummel Nikko to death for you if that's what it fucking takes."

She grimaced and shook her head. "I don't want that. Not at all."

"Jesus Christ. Then, what, Logan?" I growled in defeat. "What can I do to fix this?"

Her shoulders fell. "You could've believed me."

I took three long strides toward her and held her face. "I do!"

"You don't," she said evenly. "You can't tell me that if you went up to Nikko's room right now and confronted him, he wouldn't deny everything. Then, it would be his word against mine, and we'd be right back where we are."

My heart sank as she gently closed her hands over mine and removed them.

"I've had people doubting me my whole life. I don't need another one."

"Don't," I pleaded. "I love you, Logan."

Her eyes welled with tears again. "Then, please don't chase after me when I go."

30

Danny

A nd there it was. The other shoe had dropped. Why had I believed this was finally something I wouldn't wreck too?

It killed me to see Logan walk away from me, but that pain fueled my anger, and I was ready to take it out on anyone and anything that got in my way.

First was the door to Nikko's suite. I pounded the back of my fist against the thin wood like a hammer to a nail.

"Nikko, I know you're in there. Open the fucking door!"

Part of me hoped he wouldn't answer. That he was really in downtown Denver, where he was supposed to be, and Logan had been mistaken. It wasn't that I didn't believe her. It was that I didn't want to. After everything we'd been through together, I had to give him the benefit of the doubt.

"Nikko!" I shouted once more.

Don't answer. Don't answer.

I heard a low voice murmur and, a couple of seconds later, the sound of the lock opening.

The door cracked open enough to only see his face, like he was indecent.

"Hey, man." He frowned. "What the fuck is so urgent you felt the need to break my door down?"

"I need to talk to you."

I wasn't sure why my voice was already coated with wrath. I probably should've waited until I cooled down to come to see Nikko, but I needed to know the truth. If he denied it, as Logan had predicted, I hoped I'd be able to see it on his face.

His brows inched up his forehead. "Right now? I'm a little busy."

That reminded me. "Weren't you supposed to be meeting with those producers?"

Nikko's eyes shifted. "Something came up, and they rescheduled."

"Interesting."

"Is that all you needed to ask me?"

Something thumped further behind the door.

"Someone here with you?" I asked.

After a moment, he smirked and raised his brows suggestively. "You know how it is, man. Now, if you don't mind …"

I started to back away, but there was a tingling up the back of my neck that stopped me. Something didn't feel right.

Nikko had almost latched the door shut when I reared back and kicked it open with the heel of my boot.

He landed on the floor as the door ricocheted off of him, and I caught it before it could close.

"What the fuck, Danny?!" Nikko shouted, holding his head where the wood had hit him.

I barely glanced down at him as I marched down the short hallway into his room, finding a familiar brunette.

"Hannah?"

She hurried to block the open suitcase on the bed while wiping the edge of her nose. "Danny, hey."

"What the hell are you doing here in Denver? With Nikko?"

"Um …" She darted her eyes over toward the door. I wasn't sure if she was looking for an escape or if she was waiting for Nikko to get back up, but I didn't need her to answer me.

My head swiveled to the coffee table across the room, and I felt the muscles holding my spine in place petrify.

Coke lines, drawn out with a credit card, sat beside some familiar white prescription pills and half-empty glasses filled with an amber-colored liquor.

I snapped my head back to Hannah, peering behind her tiny frame at the clothes scattered haphazardly over bags of more pills, cash, and white powder. I wasn't sure which one of them was dealing or supplying, but it didn't matter.

Logan was right.

Of course she was right.

That knowledge shot a bolt of violent rage through me because that meant one of my childhood best friends had not only assaulted her in the elevator, but he had also done it years ago.

Nikko stomped back into the room to my right, holding his hands out. "So, what? I can't have some fun with your leftovers?"

Hannah didn't possess a single ounce of self-respect to make a retort, and I didn't give a flying fuck about trying to defend her.

I turned on my heel and rushed him. Nikko's back hit the wall with a loud thud, and I quickly threw two explosive punches to his jaw.

Hannah screamed, hurrying over to pull me off of him, but her efforts were worthless.

"You fucking bastard!" I screamed, putting everything I had into my next swing. It landed on his gut this time, and he released a sharp groan as he toppled over.

"Stop it, Danny!"

Hannah's voice barely registered in my ears as I attacked him again and again.

Nikko cursed as he blocked a few hits, but eventually, he lost his footing and fell to the ground, bleeding and slightly disoriented.

Seeing the crimson-red color drip down his forehead only made my hits come harder. Faster. I wanted him to be covered in it.

He scrambled to reach for something behind him as I moved to kick him. The pistol he pulled from his waistband and pointed up at me stopped me before I could.

Hannah scurried into the bathroom to hide as I righted myself.

"What the fuck, Nikko?" I asked, staring wide-eyed.

A bloody-toothed grin spread across Nikko's face as he peered up at me. "Now, that's no way to treat a brother."

My hands were still in tight fists at my sides as I watched him hobble to his feet. "I'm not your brother anymore."

He grunted, wrapping the hand not holding the weapon around his middle. "I take it, this isn't about Hannah?"

I scowled at the fact that he was finding humor in this.

"So, this is all over one bitch? After everything I've done for you? What happened to bros before pussy?"

I stepped toward him, and his arm stiffened, pointing the gun at my head.

"Tsk-tsk."

I wanted to ask him why—it was right on the tip of my tongue—but I knew hearing his excuses would only upset me more. There was nothing he could say to make this go away. No explanation that would validate what he'd done. The drugs and the years of lying were the least of my concerns. Forgettable at this point. But he deserved far worse than the bruised ribs and bloodied face I had given him after what he did to Logan.

I gazed down the steel barrel and studied the look in his eyes warily. "You're not going to shoot me."

"Oh, no?" He laughed.

I carefully stepped closer, pushing my forehead against the cold end of the gun. "No."

His chin lowered, and his gaze darkened as he turned into someone I no longer recognized. He wasn't conceding. He welcomed the challenge. "Why don't you run on out of here and find your girlfriend?"

I didn't move, but my pulse quickened.

Nikko cocked the gun. "Come on, Danny. Don't make me do this."

The mix of emotions swirling inside me kept me in place for a few more moments, but Logan's laughter suddenly echoed in my ears, and I took a small step around him.

Another step, and I felt Violet's hand tugging me toward the door.

I saw the gun following me like a laser as I stepped again, picturing my sister in her wedding dress.

My back was to the door now, and I backed up, seeing images of Liam, Tic, and Lexie all waiting for me to join them onstage.

I didn't stop until I reached the handle. "You're fucking dead to me, you hear me?"

The notch in Nikko's throat bobbed, but he kept his mouth shut and his aim high.

When the door finally shut, I marched down the long hallway, back to my room, but passed it until I reached Liam's instead.

My knuckles rapped on his door incessantly until he opened it.

"Hey, Danny. What's—"

I shoved past him into the room without thinking and was grateful to find Avery fully clothed, sitting in front of her computer.

"Get out." The words echoed from the pit of my aching chest.

"Excuse me?" Avery asked, taken aback.

"Danny!" Liam scolded me, smacking my arm.

I turned to look at him, on the verge of fucking tears.

Liam slowly nodded over at my sister on the bed. "Can you give us a minute, Av? I'm sorry."

She watched me carefully as she gathered her things and left.

I paced back and forth, faster and faster, but it was all too much. I'd somehow lost the only girl I'd ever loved and learned one of my best friends had betrayed me in one day.

"Fuck!" My fist hit the wall, and I felt the skin on my knuckles break open. Blood smeared onto the cracked drywall as I removed my fist and repeated the motion again. And again. And again.

Liam hurried over to me. "Whoa, what the hell is going on?"

I shoved him off, and he ran to open the door, shouting for Tic. A couple of seconds later, they were both there, trying to come at me to calm me down.

I swung around, ready to tell them to fuck off, but my hands hit a table holding a few empty glasses and a liquor bottle. I sent them tumbling to the floor, glass shattering at my feet. It felt good to break them. Like a sliver of relief had been pulled from my chest. So, I searched for more.

"Danny!" Tic's voice bellowed.

"No. Let him get this out," Liam said, putting a hand over his chest.

Fisting the bottle of whiskey beside the television, I chucked it against the door, watching it explode and fall to the ground. It was satisfying, but it still wasn't enough.

A guttural scream left my throat. No words. Just anger. I wasn't sure if some of the alcohol had splashed onto my cheeks, but my face was wet. It almost felt like … like tears.

"Danny, what's going on?" Tic asked.

I picked up the desk chair and thrashed the legs against the floor until they broke.

"Danny!"

"Get out!" I yelled.

"Dude, you can't kick Liam out of his own room." Tic's eyes scanned the destroyed hotel room. "Well, what's left of it."

"Get the fuck out! Get the fuck out!" I repeated, my hands shaking.

Liam squared his shoulders with me. "No."

I charged him, pointing at the door. "I don't need you! I don't need anyone! Now, get out!"

Liam quickly pulled me into his arms when I turned my back on him.

"Don't fucking touch me!" I roared, fighting against him.

He didn't say anything. He just gripped me harder.

My elbows shot up, struggling to break myself free, but he didn't let go, even when I hit his jaw.

Tic appeared on the other side of me, caging me in. "We've got you, Danny."

"I said, I don't need you!" I tried to scream again, but it came out in a withered cry.

"We know you don't," Tic said.

"But you've got us anyway." Liam's hold on me didn't let up as my fight waned.

I couldn't stop my eyes from welling up with tears as I slid to the ground and dropped my head into my hands. "I lost her. I fucking lost her."

Tic knelt beside me. "You haven't lost anyone, man."

More wetness streaked my face. "She left. She left, and I don't think I can get her back after this."

"What did you two fight about?" Tic asked.

I shook my head, still in disbelief, and then told them everything—from the moment the elevator doors had opened to me backing out of Nikko's room with a gun aimed at my head. I didn't leave any detail out.

Tic had to stop Liam from charging out of the room to find Nikko. There was no point. I was sure he and Hannah were long gone by now.

I started to argue when the room phone rang from the bedside table.

Liam managed to get up and answer it before I could get to my feet. "Hello? Yes, ma'am, that was our room. Ah, we apologize for the noise. Yes, I understand. We'll pay for everything. No, there's no need to send anyone up. Okay, thanks." He hung up and sat on the edge of the bed. "They want us out in the next hour."

Tic clapped his hands together. "Another one bites the dust, I guess."

"I'm sorry, guys."

"Don't worry about it, Danny boy. We've gotten kicked out of plenty of hotels before." Liam smiled slightly. "I'm just surprised we've made it this long in the tour without it happening."

Tic laughed. "Yeah, either the walls in our rooms are thicker, or Lexie packed a gag for her guests this time around."

"Where is Lexie, by the way?" I asked.

"She went to some bar with a girl she had met at the radio station."

"Do either one of you have a card to her room?" Liam asked. "We'll have to get her stuff out."

We shook our heads.

"Nikko had all the extra room keys," I murmured.

Liam's jaw ticked, and he pulled his phone out of his pocket. "Fine. I'll call her then."

Tic sighed. "What the hell are we going to do without a manager?"

The thought of Nikko reignited the burning in my chest. "I can't even think about that right now."

Tic leaned his shoulder into mine. "Hey, I'm glad he's gone. But we've still got a tour to finish. We're going to need someone to take care of things for us on the road. Otherwise, our schedules are going to get a lot more hectic."

Liam dragged his lip through his teeth in thought, and a few seconds later, the corner of his mouth lifted. "What about Avery?"

"Avery?" I snapped my head at him.

Tic bobbed his head. "That's not a bad idea. You think she'd go for it?"

"I'll have to ask her. She'd need to take a break from classes, but her ultimate goal is to find her way into the music industry." Liam shrugged. "This would be a good start."

"Whoa, whoa, whoa, whoa, whoa," I interrupted. "I'm not okay with having my sister ordering us all around nonstop for the next few months."

"Why?" Liam chuckled. "It's not like you're going to listen anyway."

"Yeah, you didn't listen to Nikko half the time," Tic added.

"We just need someone to take care of the logistics. She might not even say yes," Liam said.

Tic looked at me and arched a brow. "She would only do it if you said it was okay. You know she hates stepping on your toes."

I huffed, too exhausted to argue. "Fine, maybe."

Tic pushed some broken glass aside so he could stand. "So, what now? We've got another couple of days before we hit Santa Fe. You flying back to California?"

My shoulders sagged. "She told me not to go after her."

"Man, that's the ultimate time to chase after a girl," Tic told me.

"Nah, give her a few days," Liam said. "We have one more show before a weeklong break. Maybe that will give you both enough time to think things over. Go home and talk to her then."

I looked between the two of them, both giving vastly different advice. "You guys aren't fucking helpful."

"What would you rather do? Miss the gig and possibly fly to her before she's ready and ruin your chances? Or give Logan the opportunity to have some clarity and play for fans who have been waiting months to see us?"

When Liam put it that way, the answer was pretty obvious, but I still fucking hated it.

Tic reached down and assessed my hands. "Are you going to be able to play with these moneymakers all torn up?"

I waved him off dismissively. "Just a few scratches. I'll be fine."

He glanced at Liam and then back at me. "You should probably go get them checked out and make sure you don't need any stitches."

Liam gave a firm nod in agreement.

I was about to argue again when the door slammed shut.

Avery stood at the edge of the room with her mouth agape. "What the hell happened in here?"

Tic smiled awkwardly. "Oh good. The boss is here."

31

Logan

I cupped my warm coffee mug on the porch, wishing my sweatshirt blocked more of the cold air cutting into my bones. Orange and maroon maple leaves drifted in the wind, dusting the ground with warm colors as they fell. Violet would be up soon, and I needed to make her breakfast, but I lingered a little while longer, hoping the calmness and beauty of the fall season could work its magic and bring me the joy it usually did. Even a tiny spark was better than nothing. I was desperate to feel something other than the aching sadness that had followed me home from Denver last Saturday.

I hadn't heard from Danny since I had left him outside his hotel. Even though that was what I needed, not being able to hear his voice somehow made every day a little bit slower and a little darker. Even Avery had dropped off the things I'd left behind at the hotel on my front step without a word. And that made me realize that I'd given up more than just Danny when I walked away.

More wind whistled through the trees above, and I squeezed my arms into my sides, waiting for it to pass. As it did, I noticed a faint melody drifting over toward me from across the street. My eyes immediately looked over the hood of my new car at Danny's white porch. The air stilled, and the familiar sound grew stronger, making my heart sing.

I couldn't see him, but I knew he was there. It was as if he was gently extending an invitation—one I wanted to accept but couldn't.

Go to him, my conscience whispered.

Taking one long sip from my mug, I wiped a small tear away and went back inside.

The next day, I skipped my morning coffee outside and slept in instead. Violet came and cuddled with me, and then Andre visited, bearing pastries. It rained most of the day, so we stayed inside, baking cookies and watching movies. I didn't know why it surprised me when Danny came and knocked on my door later that night—he'd always been persistent with getting my attention—but I made Andre send him away even though he really didn't want to.

On Friday, Violet begged to go to the park to build sand castles. Warm, dry days were becoming harder to come by with the cold and rainy weather we'd been having, and I hadn't seen any movement at the band's house, so I figured the coast was clear.

Wrong. The coast was very much *not* clear.

I had just sat on the bench between the giant sandbox and swing set when I heard footsteps approaching from the sidewalk behind me. I wasn't sure how, but I knew it was him. There was a certain spark in the air that ignited when we were around each other, and I could feel it now.

"You don't have to talk to me if you don't want to." The huskiness of Danny's voice still startled me.

I glanced over my shoulder enough to see his form and then turned back around. "What are you doing here?"

"Oh, uh, the monkey bars are a hidden talent of mine. I've gotta practice so I don't lose my edge."

I rolled my eyes, annoyed with myself for smiling.

"Nikko's gone."

My face fell as I stiffened.

"I went and confronted him after you left," he continued. "It wasn't that I didn't believe you. It was that I desperately wanted you to be wrong. But everything you said was true. Everything."

Danny came around the bench, and I immediately dropped my eyes to the angry, bruised red skin covering the tops of his hands. He quickly shoved them into his front pockets.

"I just wanted you to know that we're done with him. For good. He won't be around me or the band ever again."

I swallowed the lump in my throat and found his blue stare. He looked like hell. Sunken eyes and unwashed hair. A shadow of stubble framed his jawline. It looked like he hadn't slept in days.

"I'm so sorry, Logan." He continued to approach me carefully, as if he was one wrong move away from making me flee. "I'm sorry I didn't put more faith in you when you were scared and hurt. And I understand if you hate me for it."

305

I slowly stood and frowned. "I could never hate you, Danny."

A flicker of hope made his solemn expression soften.

"But it still hurts," I whispered.

"I know it does. If there is anything I can do to make you—"

"Danny!" Violet screamed. She ran over from her place in the sand at full speed, her baby-blue tutu bouncing in the wind.

"Hey, sweetheart," Danny said, bending down to give her a hug. "I've missed you."

"I missed yew too!" she told him, twirling her skirt back and forth. "Awe yew hewe to make Mommy feew bettow?"

"Feel better?" Danny frowned, stealing a look up at me.

Violet's brow furrowed as she pouted. "Yeah, she's so sad aww the time."

I ran my hand over my eyes. *It's a good thing she's cute.*

"I think she misses yew too," Violet added.

I pressed a kiss to the top of her head and pointed at the sandbox. "Baby, look. I think that boy likes your sand castle. You should go show him how you made it."

"Okay!" She smiled and skipped away, always excited to show off her talents.

Danny turned back toward me. "Take me back."

"What?" I snapped my head up at him.

His eyes were deep and pleading.

"Danny …"

"Take me back and let me do better. Please," he begged.

"I can't," I sighed.

"Can't or shouldn't?"

I shook my head because I didn't want to answer.

He removed the space left between us, taking my hands and folding them into his chest.

I looked down at his hold on me, contemplating whether or not I wanted to pull away. If there was a moment that would make me want to flee, it was this one. But my feet were firmly planted where I was, with him.

"Fine. Then, tell me you don't love me."

I blinked up at him.

His smile made my insides melt.

"Words, Logan. I know you know how to use them. Now, tell me you're not madly in love with me."

"I …" My voice broke. "I can't."

He leaned in a fraction. I could see the look in his eyes, the need to kiss me. But I dropped my chin.

"But I can't love you and lose her," I whispered.

"Why do the two have to coincide with one another?" He shook his head, forcing me to look back up at him. "You don't have to lose anybody. Violet isn't going anywhere. I will never do anything to change that. I promise you. I love you, and I know you love me, and that's enough."

His words wrapped around my heart, strong and steady.

"I'm just scared." Scared of falling even more in love with him, just to lose him again.

"I'm scared too! I'm going to fuck up—I know I will. But I will do everything I can to make you feel safe and loved every minute of every day so that you'll forgive me again and find me deserving of you. We don't have to have it all figured out, but we owe it to ourselves to try and make this work."

Tears fell down my face, and his fingers wiped every single one. I could feel myself caving, and as scary as it seemed to give in, the idea of it also brought relief.

"Why couldn't you just let me be miserable on my own?" I whined.

His eyes lit up. "Wait, are you—does that mean you forgive me?"

"Yes, you big idiot."

Danny grabbed my face with a grin and brought his mouth down on mine. It was a gentle kiss, but I could feel the carnal side of him struggling to refrain from devouring me right in the middle of the park.

"Gwoss." Violet's tiny voice beside us made Danny and me quickly part.

Danny chuckled as she scrunched her nose up in disgust.

"Do yew guys wove each othew?" She glanced between the two of us.

Danny smirked at me, waiting for me to answer her.

I sighed and gave him a look. "Yes, baby. We do." I quickly wiped away whatever tears were left on my face and knelt to Violet's level.

"Wike you wove me and give me hugs and kisses?"

"Exactly." I poked her nose. "How do you feel about Mommy loving Danny?"

She fidgeted a little until she smiled. "I think it's gwate because I wove Danny too."

"You do?" My eyes welled with tears.

She nodded up at Danny shyly.

"I love you too, sweetheart," he said weakly. He leaned down and kissed her on the cheek. And then another, making little monster noises as she giggled.

The squeal Violet let out when Danny started chasing her around the playground sent a jolt of light through my heart.

I should've been cursing at myself for forgetting my camera back at home, but I didn't need one.

This was one of those memories that would stay with me forever.

32

Logan

Danny woke me up the next morning, playing his guitar on my front porch. I had to admit, it was much better getting to hear it right outside my front door than from across the street—even if it woke up Violet an hour early.

I brought out an extra coffee for him, and he handed me his jacket, arguing that it was far too cold out for only a sweatshirt.

Violet came outside in her pajamas not long after, groggy but smiling. I wrapped her up in my arms, folding the extra bit of jacket around her as we listened to Danny's songs change from one to the next. Violet watched his fingers work across the strings and tried to mimic them on her own.

Danny noticed and waved her over. The guitar was far too big for her, but she stretched her fingers as far as she could and stroked her hand through the chords.

"I'll have to get you your own so we can play together. Does that sound fun?"

Her eyes widened. "Yes! Can I have a powpow one?"

"Sweetheart, I'll get you one in every color if you want." Danny smiled and then glanced at me.

My mouth curved up, and I shook my head. "One is plenty."

He chuckled and went back to his lesson with Violet. Eventually, he ended up holding the neck of the guitar while she strummed.

I only had another day and a half with Danny before he had to be back on the road, but I couldn't wait until this became the norm for us.

Liam's truck pulled into their driveway across the street as the sun began to rise higher in the sky. Avery and her friend Nina climbed out and waved at us before heading inside. With their extra time, the rest of the band had decided to fly home with Danny for a quick visit, which prompted Avery's friend to catch a last-minute flight to throw an engagement party for her and Liam. I had asked Andre to watch Violet so we could attend, but he was busy. Luckily, my parents were free and more than willing to spend extra time with Violet, so they were stopping by just before dinner.

We ended up taking Violet back to the park again before lunch, but the wind picked up, so we weren't there for long.

As we were headed up the driveway, Danny slowed to a stop in front of me and Violet.

"What are you doing?" I asked, peering at the side of his face.

"You locked the door when we left, didn't you?"

I frowned. "No. Not when we were just down the street. Why?" I asked, following his gaze.

The front door was cracked open, gently weaving in the wind.

"You two wait here," Danny said.

I laughed, but he turned and gave me a look that said he was serious.

"The wind probably blew it open. I'm sure it's fine."

He blocked me from passing. "Just wait here. Please."

I pulled Violet in front of me to shield her from the wind as Danny ascended the front steps and snuck inside. Three minutes passed before he came back out, unscathed.

"I didn't see anything." He shook his head. "Everything's still there. Your TV, your watch beside the bed, my guitar."

I wiped my brow with exaggeration.

Danny quirked a brow at my lack of concern.

"Hey, if this band thing doesn't work out, you should ask my dad for a job. You'd make one hell of a cop," I teased.

"You'd rather have me shot at than play guitar?"

"I don't know. Your fans can be very aggressive. I feel like your odds of survival are pretty even."

He rolled his eyes, and then we all darted into the house for some warmth. I couldn't help but glance around the house once we were inside, but it was just like Danny had said. There wasn't anything out of place.

Danny and Violet were out in the living room, playing a board game, while I got changed and ready for the party. I'd warned him that she wasn't a fair player in any game and that she made up her own rules just so she could win, but he still seemed shocked at her negotiation tactics when she quickly went from losing to winning within a couple of turns.

I laughed as I swiped some gloss across my lips, hearing them argue back and forth until Danny ultimately caved.

Since our reconnection in the park yesterday, I'd questioned my decision to let Danny back in so quickly and not give myself more time. But I was also scared of what would've happened if we had finished out the rest of his tour apart without seeing or talking to one another. Four months could've changed so much. Moments—like when he offered protection to Violet and me, like giving me his jacket to ward off the wind, or when he was teaching Violet how to play guitar, just like his father had taught him—had made those doubts quickly fade.

I'd made plenty of mistakes in my past and only ever wanted to be given a chance to make up for them. To earn back my loved ones' trust. Danny deserved that chance too.

I tossed my curls over my shoulders to get a final look at my emerald-green dress. Danny had said the event was at a winery just outside the city, so I wanted to dress nice. Danny hadn't bothered to change, but he still looked delicious in his black jeans, white shirt, and leather jacket.

I was just finishing clasping the back of my necklace when I heard my mom's voice ring through the house. Grabbing my camera and purse, I hurried out to greet them so Danny and I could get going.

"Oh, honey. You look gorgeous." My mother beamed at me.

I hugged her and kissed her on the cheek. "Thanks, Mom. I really appreciate you guys coming over at the last minute."

"Yeah, thank you, Mrs. Ellis," Danny said, walking around the couch.

"Our pleasure. And please, call me Charlene, honey," Mom said.

Violet ran over and hugged her. "Hi, Gwandma. Wayew is Papa?"

"He's here. Just letting Moose go potty real quick."

"You look stunning," Danny whispered, placing his hand on my lower back.

I smiled up at him. "It's not too much?"

He shook his head. "Perfect."

The front door swung open as my dad and Moose came through.

"I like the new car, Lo," he said, leaning back to take another look at it before he shut the door behind him. "That one has top safety ratings, I hear."

I chuckled. "Uh, yeah. I think so."

Violet offered my dad a hug, then waited patiently for Moose to finish his perimeter check so she could give him pets.

"Who did you say is getting married? Your sister?" Dad asked Danny.

"Yes, sir. She and my best friend just got engaged."

A smile tugged at his lips. "Good for her."

"You ready to get going?" I asked Danny, looping my arm through his.

Moose whimpered from behind the couch, getting the attention of the whole room. He looked up at my dad and barked twice, sitting anxiously.

"What is it, boy?" Dad frowned, striding over to him.

He barked again, sniffing Danny's guitar.

"What's wrong?" Mom asked.

"I'm not sure, but he's giving me an alert," Dad said. He grabbed the neck of the guitar and lifted it, giving it a little shake.

Something rattled inside, and Danny dropped his hand from my back and stepped closer to see. "What the—"

Dad squeezed his fingers behind the strings and pulled a bag of white powder out through the center. His eyes darkened with malice as he slowly raised them to look at Danny.

A shiver ran up the back of my neck as I peered between him and Danny.

"Where the hell did that come from?" Danny shook his head.

"You tell me," Dad snapped.

"That's not mine." Danny pointed, already halfway across the room.

"This is your guitar, is it not?"

"Well, yeah. But I've never touched that stuff."

"What is it?" Violet asked.

Mom pulled her against her side. "It's nothing, sweetie. Just … sugar."

Oh God, how I wished it were merely that. But Moose barked again, signaling that it was something far worse.

Dad slid the bag back into his guitar and shoved it into Danny's arms.

Danny grunted and worked his jaw. "Sir …"

"Charlene, go and grab a bag full of Violet's things from her room," Dad said slowly, fixing his eyes on me. He stepped away from Danny, leaving Moose between them.

I shook my head, just as shocked as the rest of the room. "There has to be an explanation for this."

My mom ran her hand through her hair. "John, I really think we should just take a second to process—"

"Now, Charlene!" he barked.

Violet jumped at the anger and volume of his voice and began crying.

"Dad, you're scaring her. Stop it," I cried, reaching for her.

Violet's little arms stretched out for me, and my dad quickly snatched her from the ground and shielded me from her.

"Daddy," I whimpered.

"Sir, this isn't mine," Danny repeated, trying to calm the situation. "I think I might know who put it here, and I'd like a chance to find out and prove it to you."

"Absolutely not! I know exactly what kind of person you are, young man. I warned my daughter to stay away from you. She didn't listen. And now, look." His eyes darted back to me. "Look at where your choices led you to. Again. You're never going to change, are you, Logan?"

Tears formed and quickly fell down my face. "Dad, please. There has to be some mistake. I know that isn't Danny's. I just know it."

"She's right, sir." Danny tried to move closer to my dad, but Moose growled at him, and he stilled again. "Mr. Ellis, please …"

"The only mistake is me thinking you could be trusted to make decisions on your own!"

A sob broke loose from my throat. "I'm not that girl anymore! You know that!"

"There are drugs in your boyfriend's instrument! In your house! Where my granddaughter sleeps!" Dad erupted, each word louder than the last.

Danny's face twisted as he looked at Violet. "Can you lower your voice, sir? She's terrified."

My heart ached for Violet, and I wished I could soothe her tears away and take away this traumatic moment from her. Watching her face crumple in fear with tears streaming down her cheeks nearly killed me.

"Please, let me hold her," I pleaded, raising my arms out for her again. "She doesn't understand."

"No!" The vein in his forehead popped. "I will keep her safe! I will stop her from making your mistakes!"

Mom returned then with a small pink duffel, full of Violet's clothes and her favorite stuffed animal, Quilliam. She swung her arm through the strap and opened her arms. "Shame on you, John. You're scaring the girl half to death. Let me hold her."

Violet wailed as he handed her off to my mom.

"Take her out to the car," he told her.

"No. No, you can't take her," I begged.

Mom hesitated when Dad ushered her toward the front door.

"Mom, please don't take her away from me." My vision blurred with more and more tears.

Her shoulders fell. "John, maybe we should—"

"Now, Char!" Dad ordered her.

That sliver of hope—of having my mother on my side— vanished with a curt jut of my father's chin.

I fell to my knees as my daughter left through the front door, my darkest nightmare coming to life right before my eyes. "No!" I cried, feeling tremors shake my whole body.

I was losing her. I was losing my daughter, and I wasn't going to ever get her back again. Not after this.

"Sir, if you would just listen!" Danny's voice grew angrier.

"Don't make me give that command to Moose—because I *really* want to," Dad threatened. "One word, and your arm will be shredded, son."

"I'm not your son," Danny snarled coldly.

"Dad," I choked out, bracing myself on the cold, wooden floor. "Please don't do this."

It was like he couldn't hear me.

He wouldn't even look at me before he addressed Danny with another darkened scowl. "No. You're not my son. And thank the Lord for that," he quipped. "You know, I'm not even sure I can say he'd be disappointed with you over this. Not after what he did."

"What the hell did you just say to me?" Danny growled.

"I thought there could be nothing worse than what your father did, but you somehow managed to top him. But I guess you two are one and the same. You both tried to take a daughter away from their mother. Only he failed. You didn't."

"What the fuck are you talking about, old man?" Danny glanced at me, searching for an explanation, but I was of no use.

My dad pointed a finger in Danny's face. "Your father and your sister didn't crash off that bridge on accident. Every cop at the scene knew it. Including me."

No, no, no. Everything was imploding.

319

Danny curled his fingers into a fist at his side.

"Don't," I begged Danny, seeing his wrist twitch with the need to hit something.

Dad lifted his chin. "You want to hit me, tough guy? Go ahead. It'll be the last thing you ever do."

Danny stared him down with a murderous, terrifying expression. But after a few heated breaths, he slowly uncurled his fingers and stepped back. He kept on retreating until he was at the doorway, pausing to look down at the mess of me on the floor. The pain etched into his features matched my own.

"I'm so sorry, Logan," he said, his voice shaky.

I blinked up at him with sore eyes, wanting to reach for him and beg him to stay, but he was gone before I could utter the words.

Silence fell between my father and me. Moose came to comfort me, but my dad recalled him before he could.

"This isn't fair," I eventually whispered. "I can't lose her."

"It's too late for that, Logan." His words were lower, quieter, but just as scary. "And you have no one but yourself to blame."

And then he was gone, too, and I was alone. Stripped of everything and everyone who had ever mattered to me.

I curled my arms around myself tightly, trying to keep as much of the pain sealed in. Too afraid that if I let it slip out, I'd split in two. But my father was right. It was too late.

I'd failed her.

I'd failed Violet for the last time.

33

Danny

I threw my guitar into the backseat, wishing it'd break, and then tore out of Logan's driveway.

"Your father and your sister didn't crash off that bridge on accident."

I tightened my grip on the steering wheel as I took a sharp turn and then another, trying to stop my hands from shaking.

"Every cop at the scene knew it. Including me."

My foot hitting the floor of my car, I sped through Stop signs and red lights, and I tore down the on-ramp of the freeway. My vision was laser-focused as I switched lanes and weaved between traffic until I was out of the city.

I shook my head back and forth in disbelief. Logan's dad had found my weak spot and pushed. That was all. He wanted to get a rise out of me. What he had said was absurd. A lie. My father had always been laughing and cracking jokes. He had loved us three more than life itself. Especially Avery. She was their trophy kid. The perfect child parents dreamed of having. Why the hell would he try to harm her?

But Mr. Ellis had been a police officer, which meant he very well could've been there after it all happened. Maybe he had seen something that didn't add up.

"Fuck!" I screamed out, feeling bile rise in my throat.

I needed answers, and I only knew one person who could give me real ones.

Seeing my exit, I took a hard right, crossing two lanes to make it. I heard disgruntled horns fading out behind me as I turned down the suburban street leading me to a dirt road.

My headlights illuminated the dark countryside, vacant of any city lights or signs of overpopulation, until the dainty lights of the vineyard came into view.

Screeching to a stop in front of the valet drop-off, I didn't even bother closing my door as I hurried toward the vineyard entrance.

"Excuse me, sir. Sir! We need your keys!" a boy called after me, but I was already through the doors, following the signs to the Lockwood party.

I climbed a set of stairs, passed through a narrow hallway painted with vinery, and pushed through a set of cedar doors.

Avery was easy to find, being the only one wearing a white dress in the room. She was laughing with an old Stanford classmate of hers while pinching the stem of a wineglass.

Seeing the innocence and pureness of her smile only confused me more. If something like *that* had happened to a person like Avery, they wouldn't be able to mask their scars so easily. Would they?

My chest rose and fell with heavy breaths as I stalked across the room to find out.

Tic called my name from my left, but I didn't acknowledge him.

"Logan couldn't make it?" Lexie asked, standing from her chair.

I ignored her, too, but the image of Logan destroyed on the floor sliced through my heart.

I had been completely distracted by Mr. Ellis's statement about my dad when I left that I'd forgotten about the mystery drugs planted in my guitar. Something told me I already knew who was behind it, but that was a problem I would solve tomorrow.

Avery's eyes lit up when she saw me, but her smile quickly fell. "Danny? Is everything okay?"

It took everything in me not to blurt out my question when I stepped in front of her, but I grabbed her arm and pulled her aside.

"What are you doing?" She stumbled over to the corner with me and shrugged out of my grasp.

"Avery, I'm going to ask you something, and you need to be honest with me." I didn't realize how thin the thread holding me together was until I heard the shakiness in my voice.

"Okay …"

My heart was hammering against my chest. "Was. It. An accident?" The words were hard to get out, so I said them slowly.

Her face switched from confusion to hesitation. "Wh-what?"

Liam jogged up next to her. "What's going on?" he asked, concerned.

I didn't take my eyes off my sister. "When Dad died ... were you—" I stopped to swallow back the emotion. "Were you supposed to die with him?"

The color in Avery's face drained as she and Liam exchanged glances.

"I mean, you know it could've been a lot worse had it not been for the seat belt," Liam said.

Avery put a hand on his arm. "I don't think that's what he's asking, Liam."

Waiting for her next words was torturous.

"Don't lie to me, Avery."

She took a shaky breath and muttered, "No."

At first, I wasn't sure which of my questions she had answered. But the tears in her eyes answered any doubts I had left.

"So, all this time ..." I shook my head.

"I'm so sorry." Avery's face twisted in discomfort.

Liam leaned in. "Danny boy, can we talk about this outside?"

"Did you know about this?" I asked, looking up the solid few inches he had on me.

He sighed heavily. "Avery showed me his journals just before she moved out of our place. It wasn't my story to tell."

"What fucking journals?" I snapped.

"Oh God." Avery dropped her head in her hands and then ran them up through her hair.

"Tell me," I urged.

Liam put a hand on her back for support.

"After Dad passed, Mom couldn't go in his office, so she asked me to go and search for anything of his that was worth keeping before she hired someone to clear it out. I found a few journals he'd stashed away in the back of his desk drawer."

"And you kept them to yourself?" I shouted.

Avery's lip trembled. "It wasn't good things, Danny. It didn't even sound like him."

I laughed once. "I can't believe you. Where are they? I want to see them."

"I threw them over the bridge. The only thing left of them is … 'Hollow Again.' "

"You mean to tell me that our song … the one that we recorded for our last album … that played on radio stations across the country … that was something *Dad* had written?"

Mascara darkened under her eyes. "Yes."

"What the actual fuck, Avery? Do you know how many times I've played that one onstage? How could you not tell me that?"

She sniffed. "I know. It was a mistake at first. Lexie found them and gave one of the pages to Liam. And then you fell in love with the lyrics, so …"

"She just wanted to help," Liam said.

I shot him a glare. "You stay out of this."

"Hey, blame me." Liam patted his chest. "I saw what was inside those pages, and it wasn't pretty. His whole elaborate plan was written down. I'm the one who suggested she get rid of them."

Avery heaved out a sob. "I only wanted to protect you."

"What, do I have *fragile* written across my fucking forehead? You could've told me! I could've handled it!"

"Well, I couldn't!" she cried out.

I sucked in a breath.

"I hated the thought of ruining him for you. I wanted to keep your image of him alive. Because he was still all of those things you believed him to be, Danny. Kind, proud, loving. There were just other parts he kept hidden away. Ones we were never meant to see."

The fact that she could still see good in him after he had driven her off the side of a bridge made my soul ache for her.

"You should've told me," I murmured.

She shook her head. "Would you have believed me if I had?"

Her response hit me harder than it should've. "I ... would've tried."

Avery reached out for me, but I jerked away. My body began to shake, and my breaths came harder. As weak and angry as it made me feel to find out she'd kept so much from me, I couldn't help but pity her as well. She shouldn't have carried the weight of that on her own all these years.

But she was right. I couldn't stand her before the accident—blame it on jealousy or sibling rivalry—but I'd wanted nothing to do with her afterward. In my head, she was the reason our dad was gone. I wouldn't have entertained the idea had she told me that it was really some elaborate, fucked-up plan he'd made.

"I'm so sorry," she whispered.

My eyes burned as I looked at her. "All these years, you let me blame you for it."

"It's okay, Danny."

"No. It's not. If the roles were reversed, I don't know if I could've been as strong as you. I wouldn't have been able to keep it all in to save everyone else."

She dropped her head against Liam's chest, and he kissed her hair.

Nina came up and tapped Liam on the shoulder. "Hey, do you guys want me to bring everyone downstairs for a wine tasting so you can have more privacy?"

Liam finally tore his eyes away from Avery long enough to look around the room. The background music had hopefully muffled most of our conversation, but everyone was staring silently at the bride-to-be.

"Shit, I wrecked your party." I winced, adding it to the list of my latest fuckups. "I should go."

"I don't want you to leave like this," Avery said.

"I'll be fine." I nodded and turned.

"Danny!" Liam called after me, but I kept on going, desperate for air.

The valet wasn't happy with me when I returned for my car, but I slammed my door in his face, incapable of another confrontation. It felt like someone had just pulled the pin on me, and I was moments away from destroying everything and everyone around me. Or maybe this bomb was for me because I'd successfully done that already.

In a last-ditch effort to gain some clarity, I decided to take the south exit when I reached the freeway again instead of heading back home.

Between Nikko, Logan's parents taking Violet, and now this, I was beginning to question if karma was paying a visit to me for believing I could have a happy ending. I'd finally gotten

Logan back, only to lose her again, and I wasn't sure I could survive it this time.

I grabbed my phone from my pocket to call her, selfishly needing to hear her voice, but she didn't answer.

Throwing my cell onto the passenger floor, I kicked up speed. I didn't slow until I reached the middle of the bridge twenty minutes later. There wasn't a place to really pull over, but I didn't care. I parked as close as I could to the guardrail, got out, and walked around the front of my car. And I finally exploded.

I let out a guttural scream into the empty, open space above the river. The cold night air filled my lungs, and I screamed again, down at the water flowing beneath me.

How could you, Dad? How could you leave? How dare you try and take her with you!

I knew what it was like to feel utterly alone in the world. To feel hopeless and empty. There had been a time when I couldn't believe it would ever get better because it only ever got worse. It took several fuckups to finally lean on the family I had, but I did, and it got easier. It took time. Not every day was better than the next, but I found my purpose through my music and my friends. And then I had met Logan, and it'd all started to make sense—why I'd had to go through all that. It was to find her and to heal with her. So, we could fall back in love with life together.

My dad had been the strongest person I knew. If I could find a reason worth fighting the darkness for, why couldn't he?

I couldn't take it. My chest felt like it was being torn apart. I couldn't breathe. I couldn't think about anything other than the pain coursing through my veins and wreaking havoc on my heart.

Marching around to the driver's side, I climbed back inside and slammed the door shut. A strange hiccup broke free from my throat. A sob. And it wouldn't fucking stop.

I begged into the silence for someone to come and take it all away. To take away the sharp ache in my gut and the unfriendly voice growing louder in my head. But no one answered, and the pain remained.

I needed to escape.

An out.

And there was only one way I knew how to get it.

Reaching into my backseat, I grabbed my guitar and set it beside me in the passenger seat, stretching my fingers through the sound hole for Nikko's bag of friendly white powder. The sheer adrenaline of making this choice, of going back to my old vices, numbed me enough to stop the cries. But it still wasn't enough.

I was sick of people thinking I was too weak. Too vulnerable. Sick of being lied to and betrayed. Yet somehow, I'd managed to be the villain in everyone else's story. And somehow ... I was alone again.

To hell with it. I'd been here before, and I could go back again.

I could be the villain.

34

Danny

The constant, steady beeping was the first thing I heard in the darkness. Like an alarm starting out soft and slow, gently easing you into consciousness, and then it grew louder and more obnoxious.

I wanted to end it. Smash it against the wall. Take a hammer to it. Drown it in the pool. Anything to go back to sleep. I couldn't remember what I'd even set an alarm for in the first place. Whatever it was, it wasn't a good enough reason not to hit snooze at the very least.

I reached out for it, but my muscles felt like they were being torn from bone when I tried to lift it off the bed. Maybe the pulsating pressure in my temples was really what was making that noise and not an alarm—because, *fuck*, it hurt.

Thump, thump. Thump, thump. My pulse and the beeping matched in tempo.

A gentle hum of conversation grew closer as the clouded haziness began to clear. Pain blanketed my body from head to toe. I could've screamed if my throat wasn't filled with gravel.

What the hell is going on? I thought to myself as my lids creaked open.

Bright lights burned my retinas, so I closed them for another moment and then braved another try.

My vision went in and out of focus a few times before the blobs of color in the stark white room became human-shaped.

I released a sandy groan at the dull throbbing in my head.

"Look, look. He's awake," a deep voice called.

"I'll tell the nurse," another voice said.

An arm stretched out, holding a water cup and a straw by my lips. I desperately sipped and felt immediate relief.

"Take it slow, Danny."

I looked up at the hero holding the water and frowned. "Who—do I know you?"

The room all sucked in a silent breath and held it as I watched Liam's face twist with fear.

I let them suffer for another second and then gave a small smile. "I'm just fucking with you guys."

Liam heaved out a sigh.

"Dammit, Danny. That's not funny," Avery whined from the end of my bed, wiping tears away.

I had to look over a raised leg, set in a cast, to see her. *My leg.*

Well, fuck. That's going to suck.

Lexie rolled her eyes and shook her head at me, fighting the urge to throw punches.

"You guys look like hell," I told them, shifting my gaze from Liam to Avery and then Lexie.

"Us?" Lexie laughed. "Want us to get you a mirror so you can see the damage?"

My smug little grin fell, and I painfully reached a hand up to my face, discovering gauze around my forehead.

"Your face is fine," Avery said, giving Lexie a disapproving look.

Lexie smirked. "Gotcha."

I chuckled, but the movement sent a sharp pain through my abdomen. "Ah shit."

Liam cursed, setting the water down. "Where the hell is the nurse?"

Another moment later, Tic hurried into the room, followed by a nurse.

"Hey, Danny. Glad to see you awake. How are you feeling?" the man in blue scrubs asked.

I grunted once. "Never better."

Tic patted the edge of the bed. "Good to see your eyes open, man."

The nurse smiled, stepping beside me to check the monitor and then my vitals. "Okay, tough guy. I'm going to fix up your IV bag just in case you start to feel any sort of discomfort."

I laughed again, wishing discomfort was all I felt.

"You've had a lot of *family* here, looking out for you, Danny." Scrubs nodded around the room.

My eyes flicked over the four of them, concern gripping their expressions tightly. The hovering was unnecessary, but was likely responsible for how calm I was. I turned my head to the empty doorway, wishing for one—no, two—more people to come walking around the corner. Knowing that wasn't going to happen caused a new pain in my chest to ache. One no amount of medication could dull.

"How long was I out?"

"You've been in and out for about three days." My nurse patted my shoulder.

Surprisingly enough, that part of my body didn't hurt.

In fact, the pain was quickly subsiding and becoming more tolerable.

"Do you remember what happened?" Tic asked.

I thought back to when I had left the engagement party, angry and speeding. Instead of going home, I ...

"You were on the bridge," Avery prompted, her voice sounding strained.

I remembered parking, getting out, and screaming. And then holding my guitar.

Liam's shoulders sank like he already knew what had happened next.

They all did.

I blinked, suddenly remembering the next few seconds.

No, I'd changed my mind.

I'd leaned back to put my guitar behind my seat, and when I'd turned back around, I hadn't had time to react.

"There was another car. Its headlights were coming right at me." The beeping on the monitor sped up. "It all goes blank after that."

Avery gave Liam a nod, looking like she was ready to cry.

"You and a drunk driver got into a head-on collision. They swerved across the road to where you were parked and hit you," Liam told me.

"Fuck. That's … inconvenient," I growled.

"You were lucky not to go over." A nervous sound escaped Avery's lips.

I processed what she had said and pulled my brows up as I looked at her. "Hey, I'm right here. I'm okay."

She nodded and smiled through her unease.

"I take it I won't be walking on this for a while?" I asked, pointing down at the hard cast wrapped around my left leg, up to my mid-thigh.

My nurse shook his head. "You've got a long road to recovery ahead of you. Just focus on resting now. Your doctor will be in soon to talk to you, okay? Let me know if you need anything." He turned and left.

I arched my brow. "I guess I've just made this tour a whole lot more interesting."

"Don't worry about it." Tic found two pens to tap on my patient chart. "We're canceling our shows until further notice."

"What?" I snapped, flinching at the pain erupting in my head.

Lexie pushed her pink hair over her shoulder and sighed. "It will be fine. We can reschedule."

"It's not like my arms are broken!" I exclaimed.

"Thank God for that." Tic's eyes widened.

Avery sympathized. "Your fans will understand, Danny."

"No! I can play with a broken leg!" I argued. "Just put me in a chair or something!"

"You could've died, you fucking idiot!" Liam's voice cracked with emotion. "You have a shattered leg and bruised ribs! Not to mention, a concussion! Can you just—look, can you …"

My shoulders fell at the sight of my best friend crumbling. Avery came to his side and held him as he regained his composure.

"I'm sorry, man." My throat worked. "I didn't mean to scare you again."

"We'll figure it out," Avery reassured me. "Just do what the nurse said and focus on resting."

Another set of scrubs wandered through the doorway, only this one wore a white coat and a familiar, cold face.

My mother.

I'd always hoped that if I ever found myself in need of a hospital, it wouldn't be the one she performed open heart surgery at on a daily, but here I was.

"If she's my doctor, just pull the plug now," I mumbled to my bandmates as I stared at the doorway.

She stood there, all stoic-like. A fucking statue, devoid of any emotion, other than her typical discontent.

And then the unfathomable happened. Her face scrunched into an ugly, pained expression, and she … cried.

"What the—"

Liam and Avery jumped aside as she hobbled over to my bedside and collapsed on top of me. All I could do was stiffen as her bony arms wrapped around me and held me tightly.

I glanced over at Avery for an explanation, but she looked just as dumbfounded as me.

"I'm so glad you're okay," my mother eventually said through muffled cries.

I frowned. "You are?"

She pulled back, sniffling. "Yes, of course."

"I was expecting something more along the lines of *I told you so*."

Her expression turned wounded. "Oh."

I laughed once, gesturing down to my broken body on the hospital bed. "Don't pout and pretend like this isn't exactly where you said I'd end up one day."

"No, you're right. I was horrible." She shook her head. "But I never wanted to get the call, saying that my son was in the ICU. I was so scared ..." Her voice wavered. "What were you doing on that bridge, Daniel?"

My heart pounded as I shot Avery another glance.

Her eyes pleaded with me.

"I, uh ... I'm not sure," I said, bringing my attention back to my mother. I waved a slow hand in front of my forehead. "My head is still a little foggy."

Out of the corner of my eye, I saw Avery's shoulders visibly relax.

No matter how my mother treated me, I couldn't destroy her husband just to get even with her. We'd all lost enough. That decision made me empathize with Avery even more.

"Oh, right. The concussion." My mom nodded. "Things will clear up after a few days."

A familiar, small voice echoed from the hall and warmed my heart. I quickly turned my head to make sure it was her.

Violet bounced through the doorway after looking back at someone for directions and immediately spotted me. "Danny!" She ran across the room, giving me a flashback to the first day we'd met when she ran to check out my guitar. "Mommy said yew wew sweeping."

"I was, but I woke up just for you," I told her.

My mother pretended to check my monitor as she watched the two of us.

Footsteps padded through the doorway, and Logan froze when she saw everyone surrounding me.

"Hey, beautiful." I lifted my mouth at the sight of her.

"Oh my God," she gasped through mirthful tears. "You're okay?"

I nodded, unsure of how this was possible. "And you're here?"

Violet stretched her arms up over the bed as high as she could, hugging my arm.

I smiled down at her, covering her hands with mine, and then looked back up at Logan.

"She hasn't left, Daniel," my mother whispered to me.

My brow furrowed, and my heart tugged.

"Let's give them a minute," Tic told the group.

My mother brushed off her emotions, gave me a warm nod, and left first. Followed by Tic and Liam.

Avery tilted her head down to Violet and offered her hand. "You want to come to the gift shop with me and find something that will make Danny feel better?"

She nodded with excitement and followed her out.

Lexie leaned in next to me before she left. "I know you don't like your mom, but she really seems frazzled about this. She was ordering your nurse around like a madwoman, trying to make sure things were done right."

I stared blankly. "That's just a normal afternoon for her."

Lexie pursed her lips. "Other than Avery, we're not supposed to be in here outside of visiting hours. Your mom pulled some strings and made it happen so you could have

everyone here when you finally came to." She sighed. "Just …
go easy on her."

Several seconds ticked by after Lexie left, and Logan hadn't
moved from her spot.

Having her just out of reach was killing me. "Will you come
over here before I climb out of this thing?" I begged.

Breaking free from whatever spell she had been in, she
hurried to my side. She hesitated for a moment, unsure of
where she could touch me that wasn't injured, then finally
lifted her hand to stroke my cheek.

I closed my eyes at the embrace, then grabbed her soft
fingers and brushed them over my lips. "How are you here?
How are you *both* here?"

Logan took a long, exhausted breath. "It's a long story, but
I found a video from my porch camera of Fal—er, Nikko
sneaking into my house."

"What?" I gritted through my teeth, unintentionally
squeezing her hand.

She stroked my arm as my muscles tensed. "It wasn't the
wind that day, Danny. It was him."

I wasn't surprised that it had been his drugs in my guitar—
no one else I knew had a newfound hatred for either one of
us—but I'd never thought he'd go as low as to break into her
fucking house. What if we hadn't been gone? What if Violet
had been coloring in the living room and we were out of sight
for a few moments? What if I hadn't been there?

My head spun. "What was the point?"

She shrugged. "I can only guess that he went in to plant it
on me, saw your guitar sitting there, and took a shot at
destroying us both. I mean, he hung around my old friends, so

he knew that my dad was a cop and that I had gotten clean. And of course, whatever else he learned about me through you and possibly Avery."

"Fuck, Logan. I'm so sorry."

"You didn't know, Danny. This isn't your fault. Besides, it backfired. He's sitting in a holding cell right now, waiting to be processed."

"What?" I choked out. "Did you show your dad the video?"

"It wasn't easy to get him to listen to me, but my mom helped break him down." She nodded. "Because I could identify Nikko, he called it in and was able to get someone to search his house."

"And?" I waited.

"Between the breaking and entering and the substances in his possession … well, let's just say, he's going away for a long time." She smiled at the little victory, but it quickly faded.

I traced my thumb in circles over the back of her hand. "What is it?"

"I just can't believe that he's Violet's …" Logan shook her head in anger. "I can't even say it."

"Listen to me, Logan," I told her. "Nikko doesn't need to be anything to you other than some guy you once knew who ended up in prison. I know you can't erase what he did to you, but you can't let him hold any more power over you just because your daughter and he share DNA. Violet has everything she needs and more, having you as her mom."

"Thank you," she whispered, moisture pooling in her eyes.

I weakly reached for her chin, wanting to pull her down to me, but she stilled and shook her head.

"I don't want to hurt you."

"Having you in my arms will never be painful. Come here."

She hesitated again and scanned down my body. My sterile white blanket and dotted nightgown covered most of the parts that hurt, but the giant cast encasing my leg and the complicated machine I was hooked up to brought fear into her eyes.

"Logan …"

"The doctors kept reassuring me that you'd wake up," she whispered and sucked in some air. "But three days of walking in here and seeing what that car had done to you, waiting for your eyes to finally open … it felt like weeks. You really scared me, Danny."

I nodded. "I shouldn't have driven out there. I should've just gone home, and then none of us would be here."

"Why did you? What were you doing?" she asked.

"Looking for clarity," I said. "Or maybe closure."

She squeezed my hand. "Did you find it?"

I was quiet for a minute. "Not in the way I'd expected."

Logan cocked her head. "What do you mean?"

"I had a moment of weakness." My throat tightened. "I just wanted to stop the hurting. I wanted to give up and lose control. And my guitar was right there in the backseat."

She lifted the back of my hand to her cheek, understanding all too well. "Oh, Danny."

A tear escaped, angling down my jaw and leaping onto my pillow. I clenched my teeth, angry with myself that I'd gotten as close as I did. "I had it in my fucking hands."

Logan glanced up at the monitor, and I tried to steady my breathing to ease her nerves.

341

With glossy red eyes, I took her in. "Your face."

Her eyes rounded.

"It was like you were there in the car with me the way you flashed in front of me. You brought me back. I rolled down the window and tossed it over the edge. I didn't do it, Logan. I didn't break." I shook my head, as if I was still trying to convince myself.

"You didn't break," she repeated back softly. The creases of her smile were wet as her mouth lifted.

Tentatively, she leaned down and touched her lips to mine, and the beeping of the monitor slowly kicked up.

She pulled away and giggled.

And thank God for it because the tension and sadness were becoming too much.

"Don't laugh at me. I'm injured."

The light sound of another laugh echoed through the room.

"Hey, I'd like to hook one of these things up to you the next time I go down on you in your little red room."

"*Dark*room." She grinned and rolled her eyes at me.

"Why limit ourselves?" My brow ticked up suggestively.

"You're so bad."

The laugh that left me hurt and felt good at the same time.

"I know, but you love me."

"I do," she agreed. "Unfathomably."

I hadn't lost her this time, and I was keeping the promise I'd made to her and never letting go again.

She nuzzled the cute tip of her nose into my neck and clung to me.

I released a rocky breath into her hair and then breathed in her lavender and vanilla scent, the tension in my shoulders ebbing away.

Violet's bright laughter sounded from the hall a good fifteen seconds before she returned to the room. She stood with her hands behind her back, trying to hide some white fabric.

I briefly looked over her short frame into the hall, seeing my mother and Avery talking. Liam stepped up next to her as Avery lifted her left hand up and showed her the ring. Avery relaxed and smiled at whatever our mother's reaction was before I dropped my gaze down to Violet again.

"What do you have there?" Logan asked.

"A pwesant." She twisted her torso giddily.

I hooked a thumb into my chest. "For me?"

"Avwy said to get somefing fow yew that I wiked."

Tic walked in with Lexie and flicked one of Violet's braids. "Go ahead. Show him your gift."

My sister and Liam came back, and the whole room watched as Violet swung a white T-shirt up onto my bed.

Logan chortled down at it and then lifted it up so I could see.

"How in the heck did you find something with a porcupine on it at the gift shop?" I laughed in amazement, spinning it around so it could lay across my shoulders. "Oh, I'm definitely wearing this our first night back onstage."

Violet let out a high-pitched noise, beaming from ear to ear. "Does it make yew feew bettow?"

Sighs erupted at her cuteness.

"Yes, sweetheart. So much better."

35

Logan

Faint music played through some hidden speakers as I looked around the gallery. Lights hanging on the white walls were angled down, highlighting my photographs on display. Everywhere I turned, there was another familiar moment, another memory staring back at me.

There wasn't a picture that could ever capture what it felt like to reach a dream like this, so I took my time, soaking it in.

The doors hadn't opened for the viewing quite yet, but I was able to get the band in to see it first. It was their faces blown up, covering the walls, after all.

I could hear my parents' laughter tangle in the air with Violet's from across the gallery. I had asked them to preview it early as well so they could take her home before it got too late. I hadn't expected them to love my collection as much as they did, but it was the closest I'd ever seen my dad come to crying. Oddly enough, my dad hadn't tried to sneak Moose in, though

I doubted something like that would've gotten past Jennifer anyway.

Moose had started to attend fewer dinners after Danny got out of the hospital. I thought the only reason he still came at all was because Violet missed him. It was a huge step toward my dad trusting me again.

Tic and Lexie hovered at Danny's side as they walked around the gallery together. He insisted on wearing a suit tonight despite the cast still on his leg. He'd tried to convince his doctor to take it off early, but the guy wouldn't allow it. I thought his mother might've had some sway in that. If she had, I was glad someone had strings that Danny couldn't pull.

Danny hadn't been too thrilled about the constant babysitting he was getting between me and the band since he had gotten out of the hospital, but as the weeks went by, he had started to argue less and let us help when it was necessary.

The band had put off the sale of the house until Danny was healed. I couldn't help but wonder where they'd all live once the cast came off and he could walk properly again. Danny and I had already talked about moving in together, but I also knew he would need to stay close to Liam, Tic, and Lexie.

I shoved that thought into the back of my head as Jennifer stepped up beside me. Her green-and-blue dress looked like a painting stripped from a canvas.

"You look fantastic," I told her, giving her a one-armed hug.

"Me? Look at you, my dear." She leaned back and admired my long red button-down dress and strappy heels.

I spun around once, allowing myself to take the compliment.

"Stunning."

I smiled back, grateful.

"Tell me, did you finally decide on a name for your collection?" She surveyed the room in front of us. "When I open these doors, I'm going to need to tell the crowd what it is."

I'd waited until the last minute to finalize the title. Being my first gallery showing, I wanted to make sure it was perfect. When Danny had hobbled through the doors earlier on his crutches, dressed in a killer black suit with a swoony and proud grin, it had come to me instantly.

"Unconditional," I said, staring ahead at my favorite picture of the collection—if not *ever*.

It was of Danny staring directly at the camera right after I'd told him I loved him. His sharp, dark brows rose up slightly. His jaw almost slack, if it wasn't for that sexy, crooked smile. And his eyes … they screamed, *I love you*, back at me with an intensity I could feel through the print every time I saw it.

Loving someone the way Danny loved me was loving an imperfect person perfectly. They saw the sides of you that were dark and ugly, the parts of you that you didn't think were worth loving and they did it anyway. And you hadn't had to do anything to earn it. They simply took your broken parts and put them back together again. It was real and pure. A rarity to find in any lifetime. It was unconditional.

Jennifer pulled her brows together as she watched me admire my work. "I'm not sure I get it."

"I do," Avery muttered, glancing at me with a knowing smile.

I hadn't realized she'd walked up next to me. She quickly introduced herself to Jennifer and then continued strolling around the gallery with Liam.

"Well, congratulations, Logan. You should do something to celebrate afterward." Jennifer turned to me and handed me a bottle of champagne with a smile. "You've earned it."

I let those three words sink in for a moment. *"You've earned it."*

"She's right, you know," Danny said, his breath hitting my shoulder from behind.

I spun around, my racing heart already slowing back to a normal speed. "Were you trying to scare me?" I gaped, setting the bottle down on a nearby table.

Putting almost too much faith in his coordination and the stability of his crutches, he leaned forward and cupped my face with both hands. "I wanted to come and get as many kisses as I could before your fans steal you away from me the rest of the night."

I glanced over my shoulder to where Jennifer was opening the gallery to the waiting viewers. People filtered in, one after the next, and my eyes bulged.

"Oh my God. I wasn't expecting that many—"

Danny captured my lips the moment I turned back to him, silencing me. And he hadn't been joking; he poured every ounce of effort into that kiss. His warm, heady tongue slid across my lips and pushed inside, tasting me with motions I vividly remembered between my legs the night before. Sex with a one-legged Danny was an obstacle we had quickly conquered. In order to keep him from straining himself, I found myself in charge more often than not. Danny no longer had to ask me what I wanted because I took whatever it was with a confidence I'd never had before.

I smoothed my hands up his black dress jacket and tugged on the lapels. He swayed, and I quickly broke away to steady him.

He shook his head and reached for me again with a dark grin. "I wasn't finished."

"Not here. Later," I said.

He dabbed his thumb on the corner of his mouth. "Yes. You *were* told to celebrate."

The ideas that came to my mind left me aching, and I tugged on his jacket again. "Can you keep this on tonight?" I whispered my request.

He reached up and pulled on the knot of his tie. "As long as you wear this."

"Deal."

Epilogue

Danny
Eight Months Later

The curtains shielding me and Avery from the long, flower-covered aisle parted open, and her hand tensed on my arm. She'd set her wedding date far enough out to make sure my leg would be healed in time for me to walk her down the aisle. That had given her time to settle into her new role as band manager and to help us finish out our delayed tour. It was funny how I'd tried so hard to keep Avery away from me and my career, and now, I couldn't imagine her not being a part of it. She belonged in this industry just as much as I did, and I enjoyed having her around.

The guests all stood on their feet, staring at my sister in awe and admiration and weepy eyes.

I looked over at her to make sure she wasn't scared. There were tears welling in her eyes as she looked straight ahead at her husband-to-be and my best friend.

Her white satin dress was simple and elegant and contrasted with her bouquet of black roses. Her short, curled hair was pulled back out of her face with a veil draping down her back, all the way to the ground.

I wished our dad were here to see her. To see how happy she was. To see the life she had made for herself in spite of what she'd been through.

Avery took a giant step forward, like she was ready to sprint down the aisle toward Liam. But that wasn't how we had rehearsed this thing yesterday, and I didn't stray from perfection. I had one job, and it was to get the bride down the aisle safely. As much as I'd love to hurry this along, I wasn't going to fuck it up by letting Avery face-plant in front of everyone because she lacked all coordination and basic athletic ability.

I stiffened the elbow she was holding and squeezed her once for reassurance. "Deep breath, Avery."

She tore her eyes away from the aisle to look at me. Tears glistened in her gray eyes as she smiled. "Don't let me fall. Okay?"

"Never."

"I love you," she whispered.

I struggled to swallow the lump in my throat. "I love you too."

After another deep breath, I walked Avery down the aisle and handed her off to Liam, then took my place at his side as the best man.

Nina fixed Avery's train into place while Lexie held her flowers. The two wore sapphire-blue dresses that matched our bowties.

Tic stood on the other side of me and gave me a well-done pat on the shoulder, struggling to hold his shit together.

What a softie.

But then I looked at Liam and discovered I was no better. Liam's wobbly smile and tear-streaked face made my eyes burn with emotion. I'd never seen him that way. I mean, I'd seen him cry. Once after he'd called the cops on his dad and the other when he had found me on the bathroom floor. Those were tears I'd be grateful to never see him shed again. But the ones falling down his face now, as he looked at my sister, his forever … *fuck.* I craved that kind of eternal bliss for me and Logan.

I darted my eyes around the room, searching for my girl. It didn't take long to find the one pointing a large camera at the bride and groom. Logan was stunning in her lavender dress, hair pulled back in a gold clip, and a camera in her hands. My mind started to picture what she'd look like, standing up here with me in a white gown and those golden eyes staring up at me, and my eyes started to well with tears all over again.

Logan's smile lit up as she brought the camera away from her eye like she'd caught the perfect shot, and she quickly peeked over at me from the sidelines.

I winked at her and then found my other girl, sitting next to Andre a couple of rows back, behind my mother and her date.

Violet swung her feet over the edge of her chair, ruffling the soft pink layers of her sparkly dress while Andre held on to Quilliam for her.

I chuckled and turned back to the task at hand, supporting Liam all the way through until "I do."

When the ceremony ended, pictures were taken, food was served, and toasts were made. The small number of friends and family in attendance celebrated the new Mr. and Mrs. Lockwood with cheers and smiles, and then it was time for Liam and Avery's first dance.

I'd wanted to surprise Avery by playing a live song for them, so I asked Liam for song suggestions, expecting him to want the one he'd written for her a couple of years ago, but he had asked for "Vienna" instead. Since it had been one of my dad's favorite songs, I figured there was no better time to finally break out his old guitar.

The lights dimmed, and the DJ welcomed the newlyweds out onto the floor as I settled in front of the mic.

My heart sprang the moment Avery saw me, a shocking but happy smile stretching up her already-glowing face. I hadn't sung a full song alone in a long time, and I didn't want to mess it up.

I began strumming the intro, feeling my father's instrument hum to life beneath my hands. It was heavy in both weight and importance, and I couldn't help but think he was here, playing alongside me.

Avery clamped a hand over her mouth when the melody registered in her ears. Liam wrapped her up in his arms, swaying her gently across the floor.

It wasn't your typical wedding song, but it fit the two of them. It was a song about being who you were and slowing down enough to enjoy the ride before the destination. It was about finding joy in the smaller moments and knowing that it was okay to fail.

It was the promise of future happiness.

Logan was standing beside the dance floor, taking pictures and smiling from ear to ear. I watched her as I sang the next verse, realizing that the song was fitting for her as well. For the girl I'd met last summer. There needed to be a song for what happened after you found Vienna. After the girl learned to accept her mistakes and took everything day by day. A girl who found strength in what she had overcome and a life worth living.

Logan shifted her focus to me and took my picture. She clicked it a few times and then dropped it low enough so that I could see her lips as she mouthed the words *I love you*.

I didn't hesitate as I skipped over a few lyrics to say it back into the mic as loudly as I could.

Avery and Liam peered over at the two of us and chuckled.

Logan blushed and quickly covered her face back up with the front of her camera.

When the song ended and Liam dipped his bride, Avery came over to give me a long hug and thanked me.

Violet was on the dance floor before the DJ could cue the next song. That was where she spent most of the night— dancing hand in hand with Avery and Liam.

They swung her forward into the air, and she squealed with a giggle that made my stomach flip on itself. When she wasn't with the newlyweds, she was spinning around with Lexie, slow dancing with Andre, or being hauled around on top of Tic's massive shoulders.

Logan caught it all on her little time capsule of a camera until it came time for her to pack it up and enjoy the rest of the wedding as a guest.

Her satin black curls enveloped my shoulders when she hugged me from behind my seated position, trailing kisses up the side of my neck.

I craned my head and stole her mouth, sinking my tongue between her soft lips to taste her. She hummed when she broke the kiss and sank down into the seat next to mine.

I threaded my fingers through hers, bringing her left ring finger to my lips. "I'm going to put a ring on this finger someday and give Violet a little brother or sister."

Her eyes lit up. "Wh-what?"

"I promise you." I grinned, pressing my lips to her hand again.

Her other hand slowly dropped down her abdomen, and she looked at me warily. "Would it matter what order that happens in?"

"Of course not. But I …" I raised an eyebrow, letting her words and the placement of her hand sink in. "Wait … are you?" My eyes flicked down to her stomach and then back up at her, and I waited for her to answer the question I couldn't quite form.

Tears sprang to her eyes as she nodded, and my heart burst open in my chest.

"I know it wasn't planned, but—"

I captured her mouth in a kiss. The music, the laughter, the people around us—it all seeped into my veins, filling me with a sense of peace. The kind that obliterated any loneliness that had dared to linger and found a home in my very full chest.

When I finally pulled away, I covered her hand with mine and smiled so hard that my cheeks hurt. "You're serious? I'm going to be a dad?"

THE PIECE THAT BREAKS

She dragged her liquid-gold gaze across the room to where Violet was dancing and smiled. "What made you think you weren't one already?"

Author's Note

Our past has a way of marking our bodies in different ways, and sometimes, that leaves behind wounds that no amount of time can heal. Wear these scars like armor. Wear them with pride. Because no one understands what you went through and the strength it took to get you to be standing where you are today. I'm so glad you're here, and I'm so happy you are who you are because of the pain you overcame. Your past does not define what you're capable of or what you deserve. Never doubt that. Xx

Acknowledgments

First and foremost, I want to thank all of you. My lovely readers. The ones who read Liam and Avery's story and wanted a second book. I am blown away by the love you have shown for this series thus far. It made writing the sequel that much more exciting, knowing I had all of you supporting me along the way and anxiously waiting to see what happened next. I apologize for the long wait, but hopefully, it was worth it.

To my husband and fur babies—thank you for giving me the at-home support I needed. I know it's not always easy when I'm up late at night writing, but I appreciate the patience, cuddles, and faith. I love you.

To Sarah. You never think I have a bad idea, and as dangerous as that is for my ego—I really love you for it. Thank you.

To Amy. You helped me feel sane again. I don't think you realize how much you've impacted my writing journey and helped bring this book to where is it now. Thank you for all that you do. Truly.

To Pru. Thank you for hyping up all my ideas and telling me I'm brilliant. Even after I decide they are terrible ideas, and I am an awful writer. I couldn't do this without you battling my demons alongside me.

To my mother. Thank you for being my biggest fan. I always know how proud of me you are and that pushes me on days I don't have pride in myself. I love you more.

To my editor, Jovana. Thank you for helping me turn my burning dumpster of a manuscript into this beauty. I love learning from you every time we work together. I don't know what I'd do without you.

To Helena. You really are a *Boss Bish*. Thank you for helping make this book happen, and for supporting me as an author from the beginning. You're the best.

To Amelia, Brian, Amanda, Matt, Khristi, Lisa, and everyone back in Minnesota cheering me on. Thank you for your constant support and love from afar. I miss you all.

Many thanks to the authors and readers in the book community that have connected with me. Your messages and kind words keep me going and always seem to find me when I need them most. I am thrilled to be part of something so uplifting and motivating. You all mean so so much to me.

About the Author

N.J. Gray was born and raised in Minnesota, but she is currently exploring the Rocky Mountains with her husband and two rescue dogs, Jango and Korra. She loves to indulge herself in hard-fought romance novels and swoon over tattooed fictional men. She writes from her home in Colorado Springs, Colorado.

Please visit her on Instagram at www.instagram.com/thenjgray or check out www.authornjgray.com for a complete list of her books and upcoming projects.

Printed in Great Britain
by Amazon

40860574R00209